Asgaard

By

D. Alan Johnson

Copyright ©2009

All rights reserved.

This is a work of fiction. Any similarities to persons living or dead is coincidence. Any mention of actual political figures, corporations, or countries is used in a fictitious manner.

IBSN: 978-0-9843752-0-2
Published by SigInt Press.
Georgetown, Texas

www.dalanjohnson.com

Chapter One

Captain Ashunta Rodriguez shivered. The early morning mist coated the brush and soaked his clothes, yet he knew it was not the wetness, but his terror that gave him the shakes. He remembered his last battle in Angola. Visions of tanks roaring out of the jungle played in his head. Fire and smoke sprouted from their guns as they shredded bodies in their tracks. Again he was about to go to battle against those visions from hell. He wanted to vomit. What am I doing here?

He peered over the edge of the bluff and reviewed the mission: harass the northern edge of the RCD territory, ambush and destroy several armored fighting vehicles, and then fade back into the jungle. Snipers sat high in the trees to his left and right, and his tank-killer teams were in position overlooking the road from the tantalum mine. His American "advisor" commanded the next squad to his left, the one that would protect his flank and their escape. He looked right and motioned his squad to move up into position. The river bank here towered above the water, over sixty meters tall, steep, rocky and heavily forested. Behind and below them the mighty Congo River flowed past, brown and dangerous like an enormous snake. It was the rainy season in the mountains, and the waters swept down everything: trees, lumber, trash, bodies.

The long wooden canoes that had brought their team across before dawn were now hidden under the overhanging arms of the jungle. Ashunta looked back, and longed to be in his ponga, safely moving down the river away from the mining area. But their job was to kill some of the guards and draw out some of N'dalu's armor so that the tank-killer teams could use their rocket propelled grenades to destroy the fire-breathing steel monsters. Ashunta's heart pounded and he could not breathe.

"These aren't really tanks! I've told you over and over, these are only lightly armored fighting vehicles. Old Soviet BTR-70's and BMP-2's. They are not heavy battle tanks. Your rockets will go right through them." The hairless white monster from the CIA had lectured the team about anti-armor tactics over the last five days.

"Keep your teams together. Support each other and you can pop those tanks like balloons," Mick Cooper kept repeating. He was very confident, but everyone knew that whites were crazy.

As a deserter from the Angolan army, Ashunta could never go home, so his pay now came from the Americans trying to force N'dalu to give up the tantulum mines. He wondered why he ever let Beka talk him into leaving the Army to mine diamonds. He never found his fortune, only starvation. The Rwandans hunted him and eventually killed old Beka. Ashunta joined a roving band of soldiers for food and protection. After serving in a series these of militias, Ashunta got sucked into this new group started by the Americans.

Because of his experience and Angolan training, the Americans made him an officer. The food and pay were the best he'd ever had, but there was no pillaging. Even worse, his new masters wanted him to actually train and fight like the Angolans. Unlike the raiding and raping parties of the other militias, this unit's operations were planned, but much more dangerous. I need to find a new group. I am going to get killed fighting for these white devils, he thought.

Low clouds spit rain on the fighters, but that was better for their purposes. It would limit the off road mobility of the tanks. The gloom made it seem closer to sunset than morning. The jungle dripped, and rivulets gurgled across the rocky ground, combining with the low roar of the river so that Ashunta needed to raise his voice to be heard by his nearest companion, his radio operator. The boy was on his first mission, but he spoke good French and English, and like many educated young people took to electronics much better than his older soldiers. Besides, the lad was big and strong, and the extra weight of the radio and spare batteries seemed as nothing to him.

A rifle cracked to his left, making Ashunta jump. He checked his watch. 0630. A sniper was starting the attack. Like every battle before, the first shot calmed Ashunta. His breathing slowed and his legs relaxed. He eagerly looked through his binoculars to gauge
the enemy response.

Another shot, then another. Soon, the RCD quick reaction force would sally out to beat back the attackers. This rocky bluff was the least defended area of the mining complex, because N'dalu depended on the river to thwart any large scale attack. A mortar round landed a hundred meters past the RCD guardpost. Another came in forty-five seconds later, much closer.

"Lima squad! Move out!" Ashunta screamed in his accented French. Their objective was to take the guard shack and secure the perimeter road, funneling the tanks onto the main road and into the sights of the hunter-killer teams.

As the reinforced squad scrambled up the last six feet of embankment, the mortar fire lifted and moved five hundred meters east to pound the perimeter road and keep trucks from bringing up reinforcements. The RCD guards had deserted their post at the first sniper fire, and Ashunta walked in after his men had cleared the one room brick building.

From the elevated site Ashunta used his binoculars to monitor the access road running south to the main highway. The Belgians had cleared the rainforest eighty years ago for farming; the timber floated down the river was probably furniture in some hotel in Brussels. But two years of neglect showed in the thick short bush that had grown up. Six minutes later, three tanks and a five ton truck rolled off of the highway and onto the muddy track toward Ashunta's position. Everything was going according to plan.

But instead of continuing down the road to recapture the guard shack, the tanks stopped out of range of the tank-killer teams, pulling up three abreast, blocking the road. Their turret-mounted 14.5mm heavy machineguns belched fire, and the tank commanders sprayed every likely position that a tank-killer team might be hiding. While the tank's machine guns had a range of over 1,500 meters, the anti-armor rockets used by his teams could only reach out four hundred meters. Infantry poured out of the truck behind the tanks, and they fanned out in good battle formation seeking out any threats to the armor. Ashunta nodded in reluctant admiration. Perfect armor tactics.

The bum-bum-bum-bum-bum, bum-bum-bum-bum from the turret guns filled the clearing with heavy vibrations that bounced off Ashunta's chest. In the dim light of the morning, the muzzle flashes blinded, and the bright green tracers recorded the flight and impact of every fifth round.

"Call in the mortars. Give them the road intersection, and I'll call in adjustments." Captain Rodriguez waited for a reply from his radio operator. When none came, he lowered his glasses, turned and saw the boy frozen in horror, holding down the transmit button on the handset blocking all communications on their command net. Rodriguez moved toward the boy, but he ran out the back of the guard shack.

To distract the tank gunners, Ashunta ordered his machine gunners to open fire on the tanks. His men looked at him and hesitated, not wanting to bring down fire on their position.

"Fire on the tanks," he yelled, waving his right arm toward the battle. The light machineguns spewed out a few short bursts. Rodriguez again put his binoculars up to see how his tank-killer teams were doing.

"Stay put, boys. They can't see you, and you'll be protected in those ditches," Ashunta said aloud to his tank-killer teams, as if they could hear him. Last night the men complained about using the drainage ditches as cover, standing waist deep in water until the tanks rolled into range. They were more worried about snakes than the enemy. Now those ditches could not only hide them, but protect them from the machinegun fire.

"No!" Captain Rodriquez yelled as he watched his best tank-killer team break and run for the jungle as the machinegun fire swept closer. The light 7.62mm machineguns rigged on top of the tanks cut down the boys as they tried to get to the river embankment. Swiveling his binoculars, he saw the second team break toward his position. They were also killed.

"This is not good," he muttered. The RCD had destroyed the tank-killer teams, and he recognized that his position was now untenable. Out of the corner of his eye, he saw that his radio operator had returned, and was staring out the front window.

"Fall back to the boats," Ashunta said, saddened by yet another defeat. He looked over at his radio operator. The terrified boy was already screaming retreat instructions into the handset. One last look through his field glasses, and Ashunta saw the turret on the center tank swing toward him. The heavy gun belched fire, and he could see the tracers arcing in slow motion. The concussion of the rounds splitting the bricks knocked Ashunta down, and when he looked over at the boy, the right side of his head was missing.

*****

A light snow fell across the whole earth, or so it seemed to Bixby Wilson. He trudged across the gloomy lawn muttering curses under his breath, ignoring the unwritten rule about walking on the grass. This little disobedience made him smile. He was wearing his only suit and his right hand grasped his honey colored leather satchel. One couldn't really call it a briefcase: it was too big, too ugly, and too worn for an important presentation like this. But it expanded nicely on these pop-up trips to not only carry his laptop, but a change of clothes and some shaving gear.

As the Chief of Corporate Information and Strategy, the fancy name for their internal intelligence department, he had been tasked by Rudy, the CEO and founder of Ramuda Corporation, to find out why the cost of tantalum had tripled over the last year.

Now after two months of grueling work, much of it unpaid overtime, he received his just reward. He was about to give a briefing on a Sunday evening in freezing cold Boston. Oh well, no good deed goes unpunished, he thought. His audience consisted of company brass, some folks from Samsung, Nokia, Intel, LG, and a few government types. But it sure seemed like a lot of cars parked all over.

"Why couldn't we have had this shindig in Palo Alto at our company headquarters?" he mumbled.

The bag was getting heavy, and the cold penetrated his light weight suit. He didn't own an overcoat. Looking at his watch, he cursed under his breath; he hated being late. Looks like I won't even get to go piss before my speech.

The huge front door, opened by an unseen butler, led him into warmth and light. He shook the snow off of his shoulders and out of his unruly hair. The butler appeared from behind the door and tried to take the leather bag from Bixby.

"Nope. I need this here bag for my presentation."

Remaining silent, the butler held out a white gloved hand indicating the direction in which Bixby should proceed. As he passed a large dining and living room on his left, Bixby could see the makings of a big party. Large round tables were scattered about, each one surrounded by fancy chairs and decorated with brilliant white tablecloths, fine china and fresh flowers for center pieces. A long table on the side wall was covered with food, and a barkeeper stood behind his bar at the back of the deep dining room, ready to lubricate the event with Scotch whisky, bourbon, and vodka.

He pushed open the door of the meeting room, and stopped. The size, the hardwood floor, the arching ceiling, all suggested that this room had once served a robber baron as his private dance floor. Rudy told him there would be up to twenty people here, but the room was packed with over seventy-five executive types. Mostly men, mostly white, but with a few Asians thrown in. The animated conversation stopped. Striding up to meet Wilson was a friendly face: his boss.

"Bixby, so good to see you," said Rudy Munoz, shaking Wilson's hand vigorously. "We are all looking forward to your presentation." Mr. Munoz started a small company twenty-one years ago supplying raw materials to chip makers, circuit board fabricators, and cell phone manufacturers. That company grew into a multibillion dollar behemoth by being an indispensable supplier to these manufacturers. He was also the undisputed leader of this industry and the one who had called this meeting. Rudy escorted Bixby to the podium, and started the introductions.

"Ladies and gentlemen, I'd like to introduce my best intelligence analyst. I was able to steal him away from the Office of Naval Intelligence a few years ago, and since then he has been a driving force for the growth of my company." Pause. "Bixby Wilson."

Bixby took just a minute to open his laptop, hook up the cable, and get acquainted with the remote control for the Power Point presentation, the mini screen set into the podium so that he could tell what was being projected behind him, and the microphone. He hated public speaking. Several times in his life, he had been in tough spots. He'd even been shot at. I think I'd rather be getting shot at right now than be here, he thought. He clicked the remote, and his first slide hit the screen in back of his head.

"You are all here because of one thing. Tantalum. I recognize some of you as our customers." He nodded to the security chief of Nokia, the head of Competitive Intelligence for SONY, and then the CEO of Samsung. "Some of you look like you are from the government, and I'm sure that you're here to help." He smiled and got a polite laugh from the crowd.

"I've been tasked with finding out why the price of tantalum is going to the moon. There are several factors at work here. First tantalum is used in nearly every modern electronic device. This remote, you son's Game Boy, your wide screen HDTV, and for you NSA types, your CRAY computers.

"As we've become more addicted to electronics, the price of tantalum has continued to rise. No mystery there. What has us baffled is the quadrupling of the price over the last four months from four hundred dollars a kilo to sixteen hundred dollars a kilo. As a supplier of miniature components to most of the industry, my company, Ramuda Corporation, has been hard hit by these increases. As we have passed along our costs to you, you've been hurt, too."

He changed the Power Point Slide to a world map.

"Most of the tantalum comes from three places: Australia, Eastern Europe, and Central Africa. Small amounts can be found in Egypt, Thailand, and Malaysia."

Now a map of Congo came up on the screen.

"However, eighty percent of the tantalum, or coltan as the Africans call it, in the world is located in Eastern Congo. This is where the treasure is, make no mistake. This region's been at war since 1998. The First African War, as some have called it, has killed over four million people. This is the bloodiest war since Hitler rolled his panzers across Eastern Europe and Russia.

"This war has been about the natural resources of the Congo. Rwanda invaded first, claiming that they were chasing the Hutus guilty of genocide against the Tutsis. But instead to chasing the butchers, the army went right for the mines." Here Bixby used his laser pointer to show the mining areas.

"And then they started carting off diamonds, gold, and especially the coltan. Can you imagine that?" No laughs. Tough crowd.

"Seeing all the riches to be had, Angola, Zimbabwe, Namibia, and Uganda also invaded. All got into the mining business. They used the Congolese as slave labor, and millions died under their whips. They failed to get EPA approval or set up OSHA required working conditions. Disease, pollution, and deforestation plagued the region.

"But during this time, the coltan continued to flow, and Westerners couldn't have cared less that the Africans were killing each other. We were building cell phones, laptops, and game consoles. Computers became standard in our cars and trucks. The internet required massive new servers taking up whole square blocks. All of these things, not to mention even our microwaves and toaster ovens, required coltan."

Bixby could see that a few of the execs were nervous. They knew these facts. They knew that the trail of blood led from Africa right up to their door. The government people on the other hand seemed angry that he was going over all of this again. Bixby had dealt with their type too often when he was still in the Navy.

"The world is an ugly place," one State Department official had told him a few years back. "We've got to have tantalum. They are willing to sell it, and we are willing to buy it." Bixby picked up his water glass, took a drink, and then continued.

"In 2005, the UN put pressure on Congo's invading neighbors to withdraw. All of those countries removed some of their soldiers from the Congo, and the UN put in 17,000 peace keepers. Seventeen thousand soldiers for a place the size of Europe. But the income to Congo's neighbors never wavered. Instead of standing armies, these countries just used militia groups and terror instead. While the major groups were relatively disorganized, the UN peace keepers were too busy getting drunk and raping the local girls to keep the peace."

The Power Point flickered and a handsome black face came up on the screen.

"That is until 2007, when this man, Francois N'dalu, united the militias by force. From out of nowhere, this guy emerged with tanks, mechanized infantry, earth-moving equipment, and a natural ability as a general. He pushed out the militias, one by one, absorbing the best soldiers, and killing the rest. He expanded his operation such that he now controls an area the size of Belgium.

"Satellite imagery shows that he has used bulldozers, power shovels, and trucks to cut a wide swath in the jungles of Eastern Congo, causing massive deforestation and pollution of the Congo River system. The Rwandans and Zims even allied for a few weeks to push him out, but he destroyed their armies in the field.

"Now the mysteries. Where did this guy come from? Where did he get his arms? These photos show a huge investment in infrastructure, and massive mining and shipping activity. Estimates are that he has quadrupled the production. That means that the price of tantalum should have dropped, but as we all know, it has increased.

"There are a few diamond buyers who've been to Matai, the city that he has made his headquarters. They've told us that the equipment is Caterpillar, but imported from Russia, and that there are Russian advisors on scene. One theory is that the Russian mob has taken over the diamond, gold, and coltan mining in Eastern Congo, hoarding the coltan to manipulate the price."

A hand went up in the back, and Bixby paused. A slight, balding man in a two thousand dollar suit pushed up through the crowd. He seemed familiar, but Bixby couldn't quite pin him down. Then Wilson recognized him and grinned.

"Hi, Jeff," Bixby said. The man was surprised and looked at the ground for a second. He then stood up straight, turned around and looked at the crowd. Jeff Slayton was the bag man for the State Department. Whenever there was a nasty job to do and the US didn't want any money trail leading back to Congress, Slayton was the guy dispatched to get collections for clandestine operations. Sometimes it was rich sultans who contributed, other times bankers and financiers. Even churches and veterans groups had been touched. Now, since this was a business problem, Slayton would be talking to the multinationals.

"I just wanted to let you all know that the Administration is already working to rectify this situation. We have assets, um, you know, ahh, contractors, moving in right now to displace N'dalu. I'll be talking with the head representative of each major group here to answer your questions."

Yeah, right. Answer questions. More like shake them down for money, Bixby thought. As long as the big corporations pony up for these paramilitary ops and keep the campaign contributions coming in, the USG will overlook moving jobs overseas to avoid pesky regulations and taxes.

"Why hasn't the US military gone in there to protect our interests?" a middle aged woman called out.

"Jeff, can you answer this nice woman's question?"

"Er, ah, yes. Or course I can." Slayton turned and looked at Bixby with death in his eye. Bixby laughed, but turned from the mic, put his fist over his mouth and pretended to cough.

"The military is trying to recover from our wars in the Middle East, ma'am, and the Administration doesn't think that it would look right to use the Army to protect the interests of big business," Slayton said.

"You mean the president doesn't want to look like she likes corporations. Not politically acceptable," the CEO of Motorola said.

"But the Administration can sure take our taxes, campaign contributions, and funds for these "security operations, can't they?" shouted an unidentified voice.

Sensing a mob atmosphere, Rudy Munoz rushed to the microphone. "I am sure that if you have any more questions, Mr. Wilson will be around to talk with you privately. Our host has set a fine dinner for us in the dining room."

Hearing the dismissal in Rudy's voice, the crowd began to break up and head for the bar or the bathrooms.

"Good job, my friend."

"Thanks, Boss. But I didn't even get one third through."

"You got the job done. These guys all have a copy of your Power Point and White Paper. I'm sure that some of them will want to talk more in depth with you. In the meantime, enjoy the party."

****

Camilo Quartalino searched the morning traffic for a taxi. I can't miss this flight. I've got to find a taxi. Even at four in the morning, a taxi should be cruising around to pick up the hookers going home, if nothing else. The light freezing rain bit into his face, and the cold soaked through his leather jacket. A small spear of panic tried to rise up out of his stomach. A couple of deep breaths, and he calmed himself. He had overslept and his flight left for Kinshasa in less than an hour. The freezing rain gave way to a soaker as the yellow clouds, lit up by the sodium streetlights, hovered halfway up the Baroque buildings.

Why did I drink all that rum? I knew better than that.

The dense fog seemed to mirror his psychological state. He shook his head trying to clear out some of the mental mist. He worried that his ex-wife might be right. He just might be an alcoholic.

A black Mercedes taxi glided around the corner, and Camilo jumped out into the street, waving his right hand. The gloom of the winter fog in Brussels might have caused another driver to fail to see the black man in a black jacket and blue jeans standing in the street, but Camilo knew that Belgian drivers understood this type of weather and he took the chance. He really needed to catch this flight.

The heavy black car slid a long way on the smooth cobblestones, the Anti-skid Braking System chattering, before stopping right in front of Camilo. I wonder why all the taxis here are Mercedes, he thought as he ran around the right side and clambered in.

"Airport. Trans Afrique gate. Please hurry," Quartalino said in his African accented French.

"It will be difficult in this rain, sir."

"There'll be a big tip for you if you help me make my flight. It's in fifty-five minutes."

Quartalino saw the driver nod with confidence and pull out into the traffic, cutting off a delivery truck, and speeding toward the freeway. The yellow Sofitel Hotel shown prominently on the right as they sped up the on ramp.

"Goodbye, I had a great fifteen hours," he said.

When the travel agent had first told Camilo that there would be a fifteen hour layover during the trip from Atlanta to Kinshasa, he was furious. But then she told him that a hotel room and dinner were provided as part of the first class fare.

Quartalino intended to sleep the fifteen hours, but it was early afternoon and the sun was shining when he arrived. Since the Sofitel Hotel was on the old square in downtown Brussels, he decided to walk around looking at the mimes, cathedrals, and statues.

A wide, short wooden door set in an ancient wall caught his eye as he walked past the National Museum. A small brass plate on the door said "The Rummery". He pushed the door open, and felt the warmth of the Irish style pub. The room was small with a low ceiling, and it was filled with smoke, older men, and a few scattered middle aged women, all speaking English.

"Rums from around the world," a round Scots bartender proclaimed in English as Camilo closed the door behind him.

"Try out our sampler platter." He pointed to an elliptical wooden tray displayed prominently on the end of the old bar. The light oak platter was about an inch thick with eighteen evenly spaced holes drilled around the edge. Each hole was just the right size to hold a miniature shot glass, and they were labeled with the brand and nationality of the rum that each glass held.

Intrigued and always wanting to try something different, Camilo purchased one of the platters, and sat at a table. Soon, others in the pub were coming around and explaining why their favorite rum was the world's finest.

"Here, try this one." An old English gentleman in a tweed jacket pointed to a glass.

"No, you old fart, this rum from the Bahamas is the best," a tall, well preserved woman in her late forties said as she came over, sat down next to Camilo, and pulled out a shot glass for him to sample. Her white blouse strained to contain two large English breasts.

"Thank you, my dear," Quartalino said in a flawless British accent. Almost like a verbal chameleon, he could hear an accent and mimic it instantly. He downed the shot, and looked at her, nodding and savoring the burning liquor flowing down to warm his whole body.

She put her arm around his muscular shoulders, flicked back her long blonde hair, and leaned close to his right ear.

"What is such a handsome man doing here in gloomy Brussels?"

"I'm an aircraft electronics technician here to survey a local company bidding on a cockpit refurbishment for some of our airliners." The lie came easily, and flowed out with a convincing normality.

"Which airline?" she asked as she pressed her breast against him, reaching for another full shot glass.

"Oh, now that would be company confidential, my lady."

I don't remember how I got back to my room, but if the staff hadn't called me to be sure that I was awake, I'd have missed this flight for sure. He felt a small bit of guilt that he could not remember the name of that handsome English woman he left sleeping in his bed.

Quartalino checked his carry-on bag for his passport, cash, and boarding pass for the third time. The Mercedes swayed as the driver changed lanes, hurtling past slower cars. Camilo Reinaldo Quartalino listened to the rain hit the windshield and the tires whine as they parted the water on the divided highway. He let his mind go into neutral, knowing that worry could not help the driver make the airport any faster, and would only use up energy.

The big Mercedes slowed enough to get behind a lorry, changed lanes and sped down the exit ramp marked "Airport" in four languages. Quartalino got out on the right and pulled his backpack after him. The long single wiper blade threw water into his face as he paid the fare along with the promised tip.

He ran to the curb-side check-in kiosk and gave them his boarding pass, asking them to hold the 747 until he could get past security. With his first class pass, he went around the long line of colorful Africans going home and the dark suited business men seeking their treasure and into the empty portal marked "First Class Only". He was whisked through the metal detector, and picked up on a golf cart usually reserved for eighty-four year-old women who couldn't walk the half mile to the gates, even using the moving sidewalks.

As Camilo ran aboard, the smiling flight attendant led him to his seat, 2A, where he plopped down, shrugging off his wet jacket and letting her stow his bag overhead. He felt the plane lurch as they pushed back. Before the fourth engine was started, he was asleep.

*****

The cutter ant picked up a piece of leaf three times its size and fell in line with his company of thousands carrying their food down the finger sized hole and into the rock hard ground. Dolph Zimmerhanzel stood on his bed and looked out the barred windows of his cell enjoying the antics of the ants as they systematically cut down the rain tree in back of the jail. There was a balance to nature. It seemed that the old tree grew just enough to make up for the leaf loss each day.

The early morning sun just peeked over the tin roof next door. Soon the heat would be pounding him, but he had grown used to it. How many days, or was it months, had he watched these ants? It saddened him that he didn't know how long he had been imprisoned. *I think it's been over two years.* It was hard to know the seasons here close to the equator, since there was no winter, and no summer, only rain and sun.

What's my family doing? He missed his home in Central Texas, his church family in the village of Beta, and even his parents. Most of all, he got depressed thinking of the missed opportunities. His life was dripping away, day after day. First he lost his lovely wife to a bout with malaria, now he was imprisoned. Only prayer kept him sane.

Being in jail instead of out winning souls to the Lord had one good effect. He had lost fifty pounds, and his clothes didn't even fit him anymore. *How could I ever have been so fat? I didn't see myself as fat, but these clothes, or what's left of them, prove that I was a glutton in the eyes of these good people.*

Dolph was proud of his new body. With all the time in the world, he had pledged to himself that he would finally get in shape. In addition to his daily prayers and meditations, he did push-ups, sit-ups, deep knee bends, and as many stretching exercises as he could think of. Months ago he traded his now too-big belt to a guard for a cold Coca Cola, so a piece of rope tied around his waist kept his pants from falling to his ankles. He was barefoot, and a ragged white tee shirt hung on his shoulders. His dark blonde hair was long, but clean, and tied into a ponytail that hung down his back. The guards allowed him a shower every third evening.

A tall black soldier brought a blue plastic tray, opened the door, and placed it on the rough heavy wooden table against the side wall. There was a generous slice of bread with butter, a fried egg on a wooden platter, and most importantly, a large mug of sweet French coffee. The aroma lifted Dolph's spirit.

"*Merci*, Seko. It's good to see you. How is your family this morning?" Dolph asked in French.

Captain Seko Seki M'Bai stood over six feet tall, muscular, handsome, and immaculately dressed in his RCD Army uniform, boots shined and medals hung in perfect rows high on his left breast. He had been promoted to the chief of the prison almost four months ago, and Dolph had been helping Seko's son learn English for an oral examination. Even as chief he still delivered Dolph's breakfast, just as he had when he was but a guard.

"Much better, sir. My son has entered the third level now thanks to you and your teaching."

"Your son is a credit to his father, bright, handsome, and hard working."

Seko smiled, bowed, and stepped backward out of the cell, closing the door, and locking it.

The Lord has been mindful of me. Perhaps He has put me in a place to influence a leader. Not a great leader such as Paul the apostle when he was imprisoned by Felix, but a leader none the less. Dolph looked around his cell as he sipped his coffee.

It was part of a prison built by the Belgians in the 1920's. Round iron bars set into foot and a half thick masonry walls, flagstone floors and heavy iron doors with precision hinges that worked as smoothly today as they did eighty years ago, all spoke of the riches and workmanship of the Europeans. The size of the prison and its torture rooms told of their inhumanity to the Congolese. Dolph lived in the best part of the jail. He knew from the screams that there were other older sections where pain greased the tongues of N'dalu's enemies.

Dolph could also hear the noises of the city as it came awake. Matai had been an important city to the Belgians, as they had used it as a headquarters for the gold and diamond mining here in the southeastern section of the country. Today, the RCD made it their capital during this "war of liberation", although the only thing that was being liberated was the coltan, diamonds, and gold from the surrounding mines. The Congo River ran along the northern side of the city and provided drinking water, food, transportation, and a place to dump garbage and sewage.

At least Francois N'dalu stopped the slavery and moved in heavy equipment to mine the coltan. The gold and diamonds were extras, merely bit players in the economic drama being played out in the Lake District of Eastern Congo. But N'dalu brought in the machinery not to alleviate suffering; he made the decision based on greed. The slaves were slower diggers than the Caterpillar 385 shovels and D-10R dozers. People with wheelbarrows could not compete with 771D heavy dump trucks. And even with the meager food that Francois provided his slaves, humans were still more expensive per ton mined than his new equipment.

The slaves had been "freed". Yeah, free to starve, thought Dolph. The remnants of Congolese black families wandered the Lake District trying to steal enough food to survive. Anyone who farmed had their crops stolen and their women raped by the roving bands of young men. The city teemed with white mining engineers, parts and pump salesmen, arms dealers, accountants, drug runners, prostitutes, and security specialists detailed with overseeing the safe delivery of the bounty.

But for the black Congolese, there was nothing. No jobs, no churches handing out food, no opportunity. They were exiled to the bush. If caught sneaking into the city, they were summarily shot by security. If they didn't starve, they could look forward to dying from AIDs, malaria, or parasites.

Ever since the first interviews with N'dalu, Dolph had set out to influence him to be kind, to rule wisely and perhaps even someday to become a believer. Later, Dolph found out that N'dalu, a staunch atheist, interviewed each preacher, imam, and witchdoctor before condemning them to death. But N'dalu spared Randolph Zimmerhanzel. He still didn't really understand why he had been granted life instead of death.

Then Seko Seki received a command to move Dolph to a better cell. That first month of sharing a large cell with many men, was a distant memory. Still he felt sorrow for the ones left living in squalor with no baths, poor food, and only a bucket for a toilet. Now he had his own bed with a mosquito net, a toilet, a table, and a regular shower.

At first, it puzzled Dolph that he was called in every few days to have long talks with N'dalu. These talks touched on current events, history, the personalities of great leaders, philosophy, the role of religion, and being a father and husband. N'dalu's grasp of history and economics impressed Dolph, as did his devotion to philosophy. After Zimmerhanzel focused less on his own discomfort and possible release, he was able to see Francois as a lonely man seeking someone for some rational conversation, even justification.

After he finished eating his breakfast, Dolph went to his bed, got on his knees, faced the wall and prayed silently in English:

Oh Father, I thank you for the beautiful morning that you have given me. For my health, for the food. Give me more love for my enemies, even these that have imprisoned me.

Strengthen me, Oh God, that I might be an influence for good on all those around me. I know that I am a sinner, weak and helpless. But through your power, let me move N'dalu toward you. Open his eyes, Lord. Make him see the light.

Each day, my God, I come to you with the same request. Allow me to escape this hole. I want to see my family again.

I have served you faithfully. Grant me this, Most Holy God, as I know that it is in your power. I have been patient, Lord. I have trusted in You. As your child, I beg your blessing of freedom.

As he repeated his desires over and over, his concentration increased until his body shook with the intensity of his pleas, yet to the guards, he was silent. They had witnessed this prayer ritual daily for several months. Sixteen minutes passed with Dolph staring at the ceiling, raising and lowering his hands, then grasping his shirt front and stretching it forward. Spent, he slumped and his head was almost between his knees.

"Forgive my weaknesses, Lord. I need your strength. As always, I invoke the name of your Holy Son as I pray. AMEN."

He turned toward his door, smiled at his guards, and changed to the lotus position. Sitting up straight, and looking refreshed instead of exhausted, Randolph Milton Zim-

merhanzel started his morning meditations. For the last year, he had focused his mind and his thoughts upon only one thing:
    Escape.

Chapter Two

Francois N'dalu stepped out of the shower and a black woman handed him his thick white towel.

"Thank you, Desiree," he said, and scanned down her perfect body. She shivered a little, and he felt a rush of power, pleased that she feared him.

N'dalu preferred women as his valets and body guards, hoping that they were not as stupid as male body guards: not as susceptible to large bribes inducing them to murder their charge. Francois was well aware of how that tactic worked. Three years before he had suborned General Illunga's body guards to shoot him as he sat on the toilet early one morning. Of course, N'dalu was then forced to kill those same body guards. No one could trust a body guard who shot his own master.

He glanced at the clock, seeing the digital readout of 0813, and felt at peace. He was on schedule. N'dalu was, above all, a man who lived an ordered life. He arose each day at 0600, stretched and worked out with his sensei for forty-five minutes. At 0650, he sat down to a breakfast of fruit, eggs, juice, and half of a Belgian waffle. While eating he read the reports of his commanders, his intelligence officer, his mine supervisor, and a copy of the London Financial Times.

From 0730 to 0800, he talked in English on his encrypted sat phone to his benefactor. In this way, his body guards did not know his business. These discussions went through a normal progression of the report on coltan output, security considerations, and any support that was needed from the home country.

At 0800 each morning Francois started to get ready for his meetings. Exiting the shower at 0813 meant that he was two minutes ahead of schedule. The fact that he had no appointments scheduled this morning did not deter him from the fact that he needed to be completely dressed and in his main office by 0830.

Francois Orgumba N'dalu, the first born of a South African mining executive working in Matai and his black mistress, grew up more privileged than his black peers, but sneered at by the white elites of Matai. He worshipped his father, Andrew Vanderholden, even after he was old enough to understand why his mother did not live with his father, that he was a bastard, and that his father had a large family in Johannesburg. Vanderholden loved his Congolese family and paid for Francois to attend the best private schools where he excelled in history, political science, and sports.

Francois was physically perfect; handsome, muscular, and graceful to the extent that women, both black and white, from fifteen to fifty propositioned him. His mixed race heritage showed in his face, with smooth milk chocolate skin and chiseled features.

At twenty years old, when the country was still called Zaire, Francois won the national championship in Kung Fu. The first prize was the opportunity to study martial arts in China for two years. In an ancient temple in Wuhan, Francois studied the subtleties of oriental thought and tradition, the disciplining of his body and mind, and English. Since his instructors could not speak French, and Mandarin was exceedingly difficult, the teachers decided that English would be an easier language to use to teach the youngster. This was not an unusual tactic, as English was used with students from South America, Eastern Europe, and the United States.

Upon his return, Francois found that his father had fled the war torn region and gone back to his family in South Africa. Matai was occupied by the Zimbabweans who were stealing the gold, diamonds, and coltan as fast as they could haul it away. The Zim soldiers had raped and murdered his mother when they ransacked her apartment, stealing everything they could carry off.

Francois found himself cast adrift from his family, impoverished, and wanted by the Zims. Since N'dalu's education included two years in a military school, he enlisted in the RCD, the **Rassemblement Congolais pour la Démocratie,** or the Rally for Congolese Democracy, as an officer.

Eleven years later I am the commander, N'dalu thought. My private fortune is spread among several banks in Europe and Hong Kong. My army numbers two thousand five hundred and is the combination of General Illunga's Christian Militia, the Mai Mai Militia, and the best of the Tutsi, Angolan, and Zim mercenaries. I have powerful friends who can give me support and international recognition. What can hold me back from the Presidency of the Congo?

But N'dalu did not deceive himself. Without the help from his benefactors, he could have never climbed to this position. He had accepted their goals, plans, money, influence, intelligence, and counseling. His gratitude welled up daily, but he knew that he was still a puppet. But it is good to be the King!

*****

Bixby Wilson felt the heat and humidity flood into the plane when the extra copilot opened the cabin door of the Gulfstream 550. For this trip, the company jet carried a double crew, so that they could rotate sleeping during the long flight. After cruising fourteen hours from Miami, Kinshasa was nothing like Bixby had imagined. The terminal looked at least forty years old, the international ramp was small and full of potholes, and jungle threatened to engulf the south side of the ramp with a tall umbrella tree overhanging the parking area. Ferns and palm fronds grew around the base creating a wall of vegetation. But the biggest impression, and the one he knew would stay with him for years, was the smell.

An undercurrent of rotting garbage, punctuated by the occasional waft of human excrement caused Bixby to hesitate at the top of the airstair. He hitched up his pants, adjusting his belly, and tucked in his shirt. Taking a deep breath through his nose, he took his first step down toward the reality of his new assignment. At least the afternoon sun is on the other side of the plane, Bixby thought. Even in the shade, Bixby's shirt was soaked through with sweat in less than two minutes.

The pilot headed to the tower to close his flight plan and activate the new one for his return flight to the Canary Islands where they would spend the night. No one in the company wanted a fifty-four million dollar jet to sit out in the open in Kinshasa overnight.

Once on the ramp, Ron, the male flight attendant, who doubled as a security officer, helped him unload his bags from the rear baggage compartment.

"You take care, here, sir. This is not a good place," Ron said. Bixby smiled, remembering the first time the retired Special Forces soldier came to interview for the job. Bixby was part of the majority who voted to hire Ron for this sensitive position.

"Don't worry, Ron. I'll be careful." He shook Ron's hand and turned for the terminal.

A battered white Ford van pulled up alongside the jet and a happy, skinny young black man jumped out of the driver's seat, opened the back doors, and without permission started loading Bixby's two bags. He lifted the heavy bags like they were nothing, and threw them onto the greasy metal floor of the van. He turned to Bixby and held out his oversized hand. Bixby felt uncomfortable as his small pudgy hand was engulfed during the handshake.

"Zacheus is my name. You must be Mr. Wilson. They told me that you speak English. Is this all of your bags?"

"Yeah. I travel light. I'm glad they got me a driver that I can talk to."

"Get in, and I'll get the AC going."

"Where did you learn to speak American?" Bixby asked as he slid up into the right front seat.

"Studied for two years at Stanford. I was going to be an electronics engineer. But the country started this big war, and I lost my scholarship. Besides, I needed to come back and check on my family. Grand Hotel, right?"

"Yeah. Then I'm going on up country tomorrow."

"Right. I'll pick you up at five thirty. Then we'll go to the cargo side of the airport and I'll get you hooked up with the charter that's taking us to Tondo Kivu. You don't want to ever ride the airlines around here. Too many of them crash."

"Did you say 'us'?"

"Yeah, didn't Whitehorse tell you? I'm your body guard. My job is to keep you out of trouble."

"No, Whitehorse didn't tell me. Who is Whitehorse?"

"Oh. They told me that you were read in. You'll find out."

Bixby was a little nonplussed that this kid knew his schedule. This was supposed to be a confidential operation. And who decided that he needed a body guard? And if they were going to provide him with a body guard, he'd like an ex-Navy SEAL with a big assault rifle, not some skinny youngster who looked like he was just out of high school.

This must be Thursday, Bixby thought as they rode through a rough neighborhood near the airport. Was it just four nights ago that he had given that speech? At the dinner afterwards, Rudy and Jeff Slayton had come up to him arm in arm. Wilson smiled without mirth as he remembered his sinking feeling watching them approach.

"Bixby, you are our resident expert on this operation, now," Rudy said. "Jeff here suggested that I send you to the Congo to keep an eye on our interests there, if you know what I mean."

Yeah, I know what you mean, Bixby thought. You and your friends are spending a lot of money over there, and you want someone to be on scene and watch so that your "donations" aren't wasted.

"I don't know who this N'dalu is, but we've been talking with President Kabila, and we have an arrangement." Rudy looked around to make sure that no one else was creeping in to eavesdrop.

"If we can drive out N'dalu, Ramuda Corporation will have the exclusive mining concession for Matai."

"Do the others who're contributing to this project know that you are out to get all the marbles?" Bixby asked.

"They won't care as long as they can get the coltan they need." Bixby looked at his boss and then at Jeff with some disbelief.

"Ride back to Palo Alto tonight with me in the G-V. Get your affairs in order and your bags packed, and then the jet will take you on to Kinshasa."

"Great. How long will I stay," Bixby asked, not doing a very good job of sounding enthusiastic.

"Just a couple of weeks. This op will be over before you know it," Jeff said. Bixby stared hard at Slayton, despising him.

"Sounds like I should pack for three months then," Bixby said.

"Don't be so gloomy," Rudy laughed. "You'll have a great time, and you'll do a great job."

Bixby knew from past experience that this was Rudy's little code that translated, "There will be a big bonus in this if you get it right."

"Hey, watch out!" Bixby yelled as Zacheus swerved to miss some kids playing in the street. "Slow down, will ya?"

"Don't worry, man. This is Africa. This is the way we live and die. The Grand Hotel just ahead. Oh, yeah. You have dinner plans with some of your compadres at 1900 in the restaurant on the top floor. They are the pilots for this little party."

"I don't have any compadres here."

"Oh yes, you do. You'll be able to pick them out of the crowd. One is black and bald. The other is white with short hair. Both mid-forties, both unusually fit."

"Great," Bixby said, the sarcasm lost on his new body guard.

The bell boys unloaded the luggage. Zacheus crushed his hand again.

"It's 1630. You've got plenty of time for a shower and a rest. See you at dinner."

******

Elmo Struthers called Quartalino's room and woke him.

"Mr. Quartalino? Mo Struthers here. I just got in from Tondo Kivu on the charter. I understand that you're the new pilot."

Quartalino held the phone away from his head and squeezed his eyes closed, trying to return to the land of the living. Who is on the phone, why does my head hurt so bad, and oh, yes, where the hell am I? Staring at his watch,

Camilo realized that he had been sleeping for over ten hours.

"Camilo? Mr. Quartalino?"

"Yeah....I'm up. Whada ya want?"

"I'm Mo Struthers. I'm the other Paladin instructor pilot here. I'm to take you down to Tondo Kivu in the morning. We're meeting upstairs for dinner in half an hour. I thought I'd pop by your room and I could brief you on the job we're trying down range."

"Sorry. I just woke up, and this jet lag is killing me. Why don't I just meet you for dinner?" He didn't wait for the reply, but slowly put the room phone back on the hook.

A score of evil little men poked the center of his brain with sharpened screwdrivers. His tongue was dry and swollen, and his mouth tasted like the inside of an old garbage can.

Memory came flooding back as he jumped out of bed and headed for the shower. I'm in Kinshasa. Came in on the 747. Too many cocktails. Note in my room saying we are having dinner upstairs at 7 o'clock.

Camilo turned on the cold water full force, knowing that a cold shower was the best thing for waking up. He hated cold showers. The cool water hit him in the face, and as the shower ran it became even colder. When he turned and let the water hit his back, a muffled scream escaped even though his lips were closed. The icy needles made him forget his hangover for a minute as he raced through soaping and rinsing so that he could escape the cold water. The warm, thick towel felt good as he quickly and roughly dried himself, his heart beating nicely.

Walking across the room in the nude, the tile cold on his bare feet, he reached into the mini-bar and opened a bottle of water. He stretched his neck from side to side before downing the whole thing in one breath.

Wow, that was good. I'm dehydrated so I'll have another. The cold shower and the two bottles of water helped Camilo focus. He dressed in blue jeans, tennis shoes and a black tee shirt. Looking in the mirror, he saw that he needed to shave his head again. There was already some stubble. If he didn't shave soon, everyone would see that he was bald on top with a gray halo growing around the sides.

He waited for the elevator, and noticed that the little men in his head had at least slowed down their pounding. At some deep level of his conscience Camilo realized that he had developed a "problem" with alcohol. He used to drink in the Navy, of course, but it seemed like for the last four weeks he was getting drunk on a very regular basis. Every other day or so, maybe even every day. His mind recoiled at the word 'alcoholic', but there it was in the front of his brain like a billboard.

Ellen. His lovely wife. This is all her fault. She took my kids, my beautiful daughters. These thoughts bowed his shoulders, and Camilo had to put his hand up to the wall to steady himself.

Ran off with that sorry lawyer from church. Then they sued me for child support. Is it any wonder that I'm drinking? All my so-called friends believed her lies about me psychologically abusing her, drinking too much, sleeping around. Well, yeah, I drink some, and there was that one flight attendant, and Sheila…

The door to the elevator opened, and Camilo straightened up and got in, pressing the button for the twelfth floor restaurant. Anyway, those things were nothing compared to ruining our marriage and taking my babies.

He glanced at his Breitling Aviator's Chronometer as he walked into the Le Carnet Restaurant. Six fifty-five. Right on time for Camilo. If he was not five minutes early for an appointment, he was shaving it too close. A cool, light evening breeze filtered across the rooftop. There were no walls around this restaurant, only panes of reinforced safety glass four feet high that formed a transparent railing, giving the diners a great view of the city. The clay tile roof above was held up by thick wooden pillars, and African masks and weapons completed the décor.

Camilo noticed a muscular white man standing at the bar. That's got to be him, he thought. He had short white hair and dressed like a pilot in a white uniform shirt with epaulets and twin front pockets, dark blue pants with cargo pockets on the side, and polished black leather tennis shoes. Striding over, Camilo grasped hands with the man, having to look up to his six foot plus height.

"You must be Elmo Struthers. Camilo Quartalino."

"Good to see you, mate. I've reserved us a table in the back with a little more privacy. Our two mechanics are already there. The other two should be along in a minute." Mo moved toward the back, bringing his glass of beer with him.

"What accent is that, British?"

"No, South African. I flew in the South African Air Force for twenty-five years before getting on with Paladin."

"Worked with Paladin for long?"

"About four years. I've been working a little border surveillance contract. Watching the Angolan border with the Congo. You know the Angolans are a little paranoid that the Congolese are going to try to take the oil fields in the northwest of Angola."

"Yeah, but it didn't seem to worry the Angolans too much about invading southeast Congo for diamonds and coltan," Camilo said. They both laughed.

"You know, I've never met a black man with an Italian last name before," Mo said.

"I have asked my dad about that. No answer. Must mean that there was some hanky-panky in my past somewhere."

A short, balding, overweight American approached their table. He was dressed in dark suit pants and a long sleeved white dress shirt. Camilo recognized him from his photo shown at the departure briefing.

"Excuse me. I am Bixby Wilson. I'm supposed to be meeting some pilots here. Is that you guys?"

"You got it straight, my good fellow," Mo said. "Have a seat here. Can I get you a beer?"

"Yeah, that'll be great. Sorry, but I don't know y'all's names."

"Camilo Quartalino. New pilot for Paladin."

"I'm Elmo Struthers. Just call me Mo. I understand that you are like the auditor for this op."

Bixby felt a little ill at ease with the mechanics and especially these two pilots. Both were obviously in great shape, no doubt because that was required in their job. Bixby, on the other hand, had let himself go his last few years in the Navy when he had gotten a job as an analyst for ONI. The corporate world was no better. Long office hours, lots of corporate travel and tradeshows, and weekends with his wife in their house in the foothills left no time for exercise. He was very self-conscious about his large belly, narrow shoulders, and skinny arms.

And being accused of being the watchdog, which he guessed he was, didn't help the relationship either.

"Not exactly. I have been sent along to watch over things, but I'm not an accountant. I'm an intel guy, actually."

"For being an intel guy, you're sort of out of the loop," Camilo said. He laughed and the whole table lit up.

Bixby saw that Camilo could use his laugh as a weapon, both defensive and offensive. He had just insulted Wilson, but the use and timing of his chuckle disarmed everyone, while still getting his point across.

"All of this happened pretty fast, actually." Bixby smiled big as the waiter brought his beer. "I give this speech, you see, to a bunch of corporate and government brass on Sunday about this problem. Next thing I know, I'm on a jet over here to 'watch over things.' I was surprised to hear that we are out of here in the morning."

"That's right, the charter leaves at 6 o'clock African time. To you, that means anywhere between 6:30 and 9 o'clock. It takes about an hour and a half to get to Tondo Kivu," Mo said with a huge smile on his face. Bixby decided that he was going to get along just fine with the big South African.

"Don't we have to check in with the government, get work visas, or something?" Bixby asked.

"No, no, no. No one is supposed to know that we're here," Camilo said. "Did they stamp your passport?"

"No, some fellow picked me up at our corporate jet, and things happened so fast, I completely forgot to go through immigration."

"Hey, Bixby. Who's the skinny black guy hanging in the corner? I noticed him follow you in. I see him looking our way, then checking the restaurant. Looks like a pro to me," said Camilo.

"He's my body guard. He's the one who picked me up at the airport. Somebody named Whitehorse sent him." The pilots exchanged knowing looks.

"Who's this Whitehorse, and does everybody know him except me?"

"Look, if Whitehorse sent him, he's good. I take it he's going with us tomorrow?" Camilo asked.

"Yeah."

"Good."

Friday

It was still dark when Camilo and Mo Struthers rode out to the cargo side of the airport in the hotel shuttle. Zacheus picked up Bixby Wilson in the same beat up white Ford van, and Bixby got even more grease on his luggage. They met at the ramp of an especially dirty and worn Ilusyan IL-76.

The Soviets copied many American inventions and aircraft types, sometimes improving them, sometimes falling short. In the aircraft department, they copied the DC-3, the B-29, the Space Shuttle, and the C-141 Starlifter, among others. Their version of the Starlifter is called the Ilusyan IL-76. They improved this design of the American four engine jet transport by increasing the overall size almost to that of a 747, by adding more wheels so that the aircraft could use dirt runways, and the designers included a crane in the top of the cargo compartment allowing the aircraft to self load without a forklift.

These IL-76's, remnants of the Soviet fleet abandoned in Africa after the fall of the USSR, ply the skies of Africa delivering food to the starving, fuel to miners, and most importantly, arms to youthful armies all over the continent. Too loud to operate in Europe, and kept out of America by regulation, Africa loved these giants, and greeted them enthusiastically whenever they arrived at their airports.

"Are you sure that this thing will make it to Tondo Kivu?" Bixby asked.

"Oh, this is one of the better cargo airplanes on the field," Zacheus said, trying to distract Bixby from studying a hydraulic leak in the tail. Bixby stepped up onto the giant ramp and struggled to drag his bag after him.

"What's that in the crate?"

A shipping container built of thin plywood reinforced with boards on the corners and across the sides, painted olive green, squatted in the middle of the cargo compartment of the big jet. It was about the same size as an ocean container, forty feet long, and eight feet wide, but a bit higher. There was no printing on the box, and even the normal "THIS SIDE UP/USE NO HOOKS' stencils were missing. Several chains held the crate in place. Smaller crates, each a different color, were stacked and tied down toward the front of the cargo compartment. Bixby recognized a Pratt and Whitney logo on some of them.

"Come on, we're sitting up front in the nice chairs, where there's some heat. It gets real cold at thirty thousand feet," Zacheus said as he scrambled up the side of the compartment toward the front.

"Just put your bags in that bin with the others."

Bixby noticed several bags in a heavy wire bin. Inside, he saw a name tag that read "Camilo Quartalino" on a big black bag, and felt comforted. With difficulty he threw his two bags over the side, and clambered up front.

Surprisingly large and comfortable passenger seats perched up in the front of the airplane so that the passengers had a great view through the glassed-in nose. The red upholstery showed some wear, but no holes. Camilo and Mo sat in the first row with the best view and chatted like little boys about how great this airplane was and how they wanted to fly one someday.

All pilots must stop their mental maturation at fourteen, Bixby thought. As he sat down, everyone stopped talking and looked surprised when they heard the APU start. Soon the number one engine spooled up. All the doors closed with a sequence of bangs and thuds, and the air conditioning flowed out of the big ceiling vents causing cascades of fog where the cool air hit the moist. After takeoff, the big aircraft turned east, giving the passengers a fabulous view of the sunrise.

"Where's the coffee?" Bixby turned to his right and asked Zacheus.

"No coffee, no tea, and no breakfast on this flight, sir," Zacheus said. "We're just happy to be going on time, and not on fire."

In order to change the subject, and take his mind off of the mechanical condition of the transport, Bixby turned left to talk with Camilo sitting across the narrow aisle.

"How'd you get into this business, Mr. Quartalino?"

"Well, sir, I'm still trying to figure that one out. By the way, all my friends call me 'Q'. A nickname I picked up in high school."

"Q. I like it. You were in the military?"

"Yes sir. Twelve years in SEAL Team Ten. Enlisted in the Navy right out of high school to get away from working in Dad's shop in Brooklyn. After being a gunner's mate on a destroyer in the North Atlantic, I asked to do something else. Anything else. The old chief of the boat told me that there was no other job open for an uneducated screw-up like me except to volunteer for the SEALs. So, I did."

"Took a big risk there, didn't you?" Bixby asked, fascinated by Q's story.

"Yeah, I had to sign up for another hitch to qualify for training. Then they told me if I busted out of SEAL school, I was subject to a transfer and duty 'at the convenience of the Navy.' I'm sure that would have been a cook in Antarctica."

"How then did you get from being a SEAL to being a pilot? SEALs are shooters, right?" Bixby asked.

"SEAL Team Six decided that they needed their own aviation assets piloted by SEAL team members. They opened the gate, so to speak. All the other teams wanted the same capability. Me, with only a high school education, ended up going to pilot training to fly the civilian aircraft that the SEALs purchased for the Teams. Pretty lucky." Q smiled at Bixby.

"So you're just out of the Navy, then?"

"Oh, no," said Q, waving his hand. "I got a job with a little commuter airline out of Atlanta, and I was working my way up. Been with ASA for almost seven years, but my wife decided to divorce me."

Bixby could hear the catch in his voice, and was embarrassed that he had pried into his personal life.

"She won a big settlement and child support. Paladin's been after me to go to work for them, and they offered me more than double what I made as captain on a regional jet. So, here I am."

"So, tell me about this Whitehorse fellow," Bixby said, hoping to change the subject.

"Ahhh. Victor Jackson," Q said, with relish. "Mr. Jackson is the CIA boss of this op. He was station chief in Colombia during the Arauca uprising a couple of years ago."

"Yeah, I remember that. But I never heard of him."

******

Whitehorse Jackson looked over the camp as he unfolded himself out of the Cessna Citation V that had been like his personal aircraft for the last three months. The seven passenger twin jet was a little small for the trips back home to Malabo, Equatorial Guinea, where he was Commercial Attaché, but with its slow landing speeds, it could get into places like this clay strip just south of Kamina.

Brett Descoteaux watched his boss stride across the ramp, taking in everything with those grey eyes. Brett could see that Whitehorse was happy to be out of the office and back as a field agent again. Meeting him halfway, they shook hands warmly, looking like father and son.

Whitehorse's two year stint as Station Chief in Colombia had ended in disaster, except for his marriage to Ann. Over those two years he slowly fell in love with his Counter Intelligence Officer, and after they barely defeated a guerrilla thrust into Northern Colombia, he proposed marriage. But because the FARC had killed all of their CIA informants, destroyed the Colombian military air capability, and almost taken control of the biggest oil producing area in Colombia, he and Ann had been demoted and reassigned to Equatorial Guinea: Ann as a Cultural Attaché and Whitehorse as the Commercial Attaché. Their real job was West African Operations for the CIA. As a team, they recruited agents in terrorist cells in Nigeria, in President Obiang's cabinet, in Oil Ministries in the Congo, and interfaced with other intelligence services both national and corporate.

Only a month ago, Jackson had been tasked to set up a "Direct Action Operation" to take back the mining operations at Matai. Tantalum, a strategic metal, was being choked off by a young rebel leader named Francois N'dalu, and American and European industry was suffering.

Just an hour after dawn, and the sounds of the awakening camp were already wafting over the adjoining airfield. The force that the CIA paramilitary had gathered together was the leftovers and stragglers from at least six different armies. There were Zims, Rwandans, Angolans, Congolese, black South Africans, and even some Muslim warriors from Somalia. This army was held together by food, better living conditions than they had ever known and regular pay, although some bridled at the "no pillaging and no raping" rules.

"Whitehorse, glad you could come back to our little party," Brett Descoteaux said.

"You've done a good job on this runway. So much smoother than last time. And a nice crown. That water will run right off." The north-south strip measured about fifty meters wide and nearly two thousand meters long. During their occupation of southern Congo the Zims had used this landing strip to support the coltan pit nearby. Boeing 727's used to land here to pick up ore during the biggest demand back in 2000. When the pit played out, the strip was abandoned. Brett Descoteaux and Mick Cooper had been sent in as an advance party to patch it up.

"Amazing what one can do once they provided us a roller and a backhoe. We got some gravel from the river, spread it with the back hoe blade, and rolled it into the clay right after a rain. We've got our first IL-76 coming in at 0730. That should be a good test."

"What are they bringing in?" Whitehorse asked as he accepted a steaming cup of coffee from a black maid.

"Let's see, they've got the second airplane, spare parts, and two instructor pilots. Oh, and we've got a corporate guy here to watch the money."

"Yeah, I heard. Just what I need. At least they didn't send a whole team of auditors this time. Brett, I'm going to need a list of current expenditures to show this guy, to convince him that we know what we're doing. We wouldn't want our funding to slow up in the middle of this thing. It sure was easier when we were internally funded."

"Yeah, but that isn't going to happen with this president or this congress. Having seen that they can pick the businessman's pocket, they can boast to the American people how much they've cut CIA funding, how much they love peace, yet still field armies to influence world events." Brett turned toward the conex that served as his office and his bedroom.

"I'll get that financial info printed out, and make up a little Power Point real quick. It'll be ready when they get here," he said over his shoulder as he walked away.

"Good man," Whitehorse said.

A hint of a jet engine noise, like distant thunder, caused Whitehorse to look up. Just over the clearing to the west he could make out the IL-76 coming in. He couldn't see the speck well enough to make out the aircraft type, but the cloud of black smoke trailing behind was a well-known signature of the type.

Between flights the runway served as a road, a meeting place, a playground, and a bazaar. This all changed with an aircraft arrival. The children, the soldiers, their sisters and mothers, and the assorted food sellers and fortune tellers scattered towards the edges of the runway. They knew the drill.

Almost instantly, it seemed, the big jet passed overhead west to east, turned north to enter a left downwind approach, and lowered the rest of the flaps and the landing gear. A sharp left bank brought the hulking monster down short final.

Full flaps, nose high, Whitehorse just knew that the plane was impossibly slow. But it continued drifting down, with occasional black puffs and growls from its engines, to settle heavily onto the clay just a few meters from the end. Reverse thrust threw up clouds of dust, trash, and sticks, and bowled over a couple of small children who stayed too close to the edge to get a better view.

Each end the strip flared out like a dog's bone to give the jets room to turn around. It was just big enough, with the big right wing passing over several shanties on the end. The IL-76 taxied at a high speed back to the ramp set off to the side midway down the strip. They turned in, and then locked the left brake and pivoted so that the tail faced the scores of metal shipping containers that served as offices, barracks, kitchens, and secure weapons storage. The soldiers just got the black shade netting taken down before the jet turned tail and pelted each container with dust and stones.

The pax filed out the back. The front door was opened to let a breeze into the cockpit, but there was no ladder for the crew to use. Whitehorse stood there in his spotless white polo shirt, blue jeans and cowboy boots.

"Hi Whitehorse! Imagine seeing you here," Q said from the top of the ramp.

"They had to pick me back up off the floor when I heard that Paladin finally got to you. I thought you were bound for that airline career."

"I was, but a divorce got in the way, and that sorry rascal Richard Murski just offered me too much money. I succumbed in a moment of weakness."

"Well we're happy and honored to have you here with us, Mister Q. I guess we haven't seen each other since Angola in '95."

"Yeah, I think that's right."

"Do they still call you "Mister Q"?

"No one has for years. Just Q now."

"Well, you're Mister Q again in this operation," Whitehorse said as he grabbed Camilo around the shoulders and gave him a big hug. Q disentangled himself and looked around.

"Whitehorse, this is Bixby Wilson," Q said, reaching around and pushing Bixby to the front. Whitehorse could not help but notice the differences between himself and Bixby. Where Bixby was short and fat, Whitehorse was tall, fit, and had broad shoulders. Bixby had shaggy brown hair and his skin was sallow from working too much inside, while Jackson had a close cut mass of bushy white hair and a dark tan on his face and arms. We've got to do something about him. He looks like a walking heart attack. We'll get him in shape. I'll get one of the SAR guys on it, Jackson decided.

"Glad to meet you, sir. I've heard a lot about you from Lyle Rosenthal," Whitehorse said. Lyle was the head of intelligence for Exxon-Mobil Oil.

"Yeah, Lyle and I do a lot of work together," Bixby said. Whitehorse watched the play of emotions across Bixby's features. Obviously no one briefed him.

"We'll have to get together and compare notes. Right now, you guys need to find bunks. I see Zacheus already has your bags loaded onto the Gator. He knows where y'all can find an empty rack." Bixby responded to the dismissal in Whitehorse's voice, and got into the Gator with Zack as it pulled up.

Turning to Q and Mo, "You guys get settled and then we'll all go to breakfast, and talk about a few things.

I'll come by and get you in about half an hour. Tell the newbie."

After breakfast, Whitehorse strode across the grass that passed as a parade ground and/or soccer field to the double conex that served as the command post. The office had started out as two forty foot by eight foot steel ocean shipping containers. They had been welded together, side by side, and the inner walls removed with a cutting torch. Torches also cut holes in the sides for air conditioning units and windows. Normal doors were welded in instead of using the cargo doors on the ends. The tropical sun could get these metal boxes so hot that no one could touch them, but a double covering of shade cloth both camouflaged them from satellites, and protected them from Old Sol.

The cold, conditioned air was a wave of refreshment for Whitehorse as he came inside. He took in the new tactical map posted on the north wall, the computers that had been installed since his last visit, and Brett now sat at one of three desks instead of a plastic table "liberated" from a little restaurant nearby. He was pleased. The new funding was making a difference.

"How is the 802 doing?" Whitehorse asked.

Brett was still engrossed in producing the accounting presentation for Bixby, but Whitehorse knew that he could multi-task.

"Took it on a mission day before yesterday. Yeah, on Wednesday. Complete success. The RCD has about fifty armored fighting vehicles. Those tanks and APCs have been tearing through our lines intimidating our troops, and I've been pulling my hair out trying to get our boys to stand and fight. If they just believed in the tank-killer team concept, we could wipe out all that old Soviet armor.

"Anyway, the mission Wednesday was just a test. We took a company out to probe the perimeter of Mine Number One. The RCD sent out two BTR-70 wheeled fighting vehicles. Our 802 circled just out of sight waiting for a radio call. When we heard the tanks coming up the road, we called in Mo, flying backseat with Colonel Neguma. The fifty cal took care of both tanks. They didn't even have to launch any rockets."

"Good job. We'll get the second airplane together, and then we'll plan some offensives to see if we can't make N'dalu give up on Asgaard," Whitehorse said.

Bixby walked into the air conditioning of the ops center, chilly after being caught in the rain between the thatched hut that was called the restaurant and the office. Breakfast had been horrid. Black beans with a small piece of crusty bread. At least the coffee was good, and they had given him a Styrofoam cup to take with him.

Whitehorse and Mick Cooper were already in the room. The only new face was Colonel Neguma, who, Bixby had learned at breakfast, was a Congolese fighter pilot due to be trained in close air support. He was the only one in uniform, and Bixby wondered where he had gotten his flight suit pressed and his boots shined.

"Mr. Wilson, my name is Brett Descoteaux, and I will be briefing you today on our mission here and how your network of companies has contributed to this work. As you are well aware, this is a very sensitive mission, and nothing that we say or that you see here can be revealed to the press or anyone outside of your CEO level contacts. I am happy to see that you didn't bring a digital camera, video recorder, or cell phone. OK, since we've gotten through the preliminaries, let's start, shall we?" He turned his back and started a projector.

Brett Descoteaux stood exactly six feet tall and had not one ounce of fat on his frame. Bixby estimated that he weighed one hundred eighty pounds, and the grace of his movements reminded him of a dancer or a professional killer. The definition of his chest muscles stood out through his tight desert tan tee shirt.

"I've been told that you are read in on N'dalu and his adventures over here as virtual dictator of this side of the Congo, stripping it of the gold, diamonds, and especially the coltan. Our operation was first proposed as a way to bring more stability to this region by helping President Kabila rid his country of the militias that control most of the countryside. But as our electronics manufacturers got squeezed out of the market for coltan, we've sort of entered into an alliance with you guys. This briefing is to let you know what we're planning and how we're spending your money."

The picture on the screen was an excellent satellite photo of Matai showing the city built in the central valley, and the five giant mining areas surrounding it. The open pits looked like white scabs on the photo.

"This is Matai and its mining areas. We've code named this area Asgaard after the home of the Norse gods. Like the mythological Asgaard, we have a central flat area, but instead of five mountains surrounding it, we have five mines.

"Our goal is to force open these mines. We know from satellite imagery and from water pollution levels, N'dalu has increased coltan production by a factor of four. Yet there is less being sold to Europe, America, and Japan than before he took the city from the Zims. Whether he's hoarding the extra production, or selling to someone else doesn't matter. Our electronics industries need that coltan."

The screen changed again showing two types of armored fighting vehicles. Bixby recognized them immediately. The first one looked like a boat hull with four large tires on each side. This Soviet amphibious design could carry 12 troops inside, had a heavy machinegun mounted in the turret, and was called the BTR-70. The picture under that one showed a low-profile tracked vehicle, also with a small turret sporting a machinegun. It carried 8 infantrymen and the Soviet designation was BMP-2. It was also amphibious.

"These two vehicles have been the scourge of our troops. Not being trained anti-armor soldiers, they are intimidated by these vehicles, and run each time one comes to battle. At least they are not truly amphibious, or they would have already overrun this camp. The banks of the Congo River are too steep, and the current is too swift for these vehicles to cross. When the rainy season ends in four months, we could be in trouble, since the low water crossings will then become usable. To combat this threat, we have purchased a new, low cost counter insurgency aircraft called the AT802M."

The new image on the screen was of a large turbine-engine crop duster outfitted with a three barreled Gatling gun under each wing, rocket pods, and a hanger for a bomb between the non-retractable landing gear. The grey monster had a tandem cockpit and armor plating around the engine and cockpit and thick, bullet proof glass around the pilot seat.

"We think that the key to defeating N'dalu is to defeat his armor. So, we're training the Congolese Air Force to fly these aircraft in combat against the tanks, giving our troops the support they need to push N'dalu back into Angola." The screen changed again to a simple spread sheet.

"As you can see, Mr. Wilson, we've spent your money on two aircraft, two spare engines, soldier and pilot salaries, travel, and ammunition. So far, we've only spent about 8.5 million of the 12 million pledged. Actually, a very cheap operation, don't you think?" Brett smiled as only a government man spending someone else's money could.

Bixby was blown away with the audacity of this plan. He had heard of a small force making life miserable for a foe like N'dalu, and seeking a negotiated settlement.

But to completely force out a strong, established player who obviously has major outside support—the Russians, Bixby believed—was surely doomed from the start.

"Do you really think you can actually make N'dalu leave?" Bixby asked.

"Oh yes. We're helping our ally President Kabila enforce the UN Security Resolution to rid the Congo of all foreign militias, especially those that are here to exploit the natural resources of the Congo," said Brett with a false smile. But they all knew that they were there to support the American economic juggernaut.

Chapter Three

Saturday

Angelica N'dalu floated in a huge garden tub surrounded by candles and potted plants. The water jets massaged her flawless skin, and the scented oils soothed her restlessness. She tried to relax, to empty her mind. Her husband was out checking on the troops, and she had the day to herself. Her servant, Maura, stood just around the pillar waiting for her to express her slightest desire.

I am richer than the fabled Queen of Sheba, she thought. I have gold and diamonds as did she, but I have more. That queen never had air conditioning, a powerful car, or even a television. She smiled as she let her body float up to the top of the hot frothy water until the cool air hit her nipples, then she retreated, shivering, back into the warmth.

Without the responsibilities of the normal political wife, she had few things to keep her busy. Her broadband internet connection was one of the few in the city, and she used it to order items for herself and her husband from stores in France and Belgium. Their freight forwarder bundled her designer gowns, jewelry, and perfume together with the machine parts, cutter teeth, and cases of gear oil for the mining machinery.

But soon the familiar darkness settled over her empty mind. She could not rid herself of the images of the starving people of Matai. Even with every luxury, her dissatisfaction grew more potent every time that she went out among the "subjects", as Francois called them.

"Don't do that, you will only encourage them," he would rebuke her when she threw coins to the children that ran beside their car. She longed to be useful and helpful, not just a bauble on the arm of a petty dictator. Her Catholic upbringing taught her to give to beggars, to help the fallen, to comfort the dying. Her liberal education taught her that government could help people by providing the basics of life: education, healthcare, and food for the starving. Her husband, the devout atheist, looked at his subjects as stupid and deserving of their fate.

When they first married, Angelica would bring ideas to him of helping out the poor. At first he said, "We'll see, my love."

As N'dalu became more powerful, more secure in his position, the response had changed to:

"If they had any ambition, they'd get up and make something of themselves. They're just lazy. Satisfied to steal enough to eat something and then get drunk at night. It is all because of the witch doctors. I wish that I could kill them all!"

Her memory raced back to her African politics class when she studied in Paris. The images played like a movie on the backs of her eyelids.

"A great leader must care for his people," Dr. Le Blanc repeated once again. Was it only two years before that she had studied abroad? She could still see the old white scholar standing before the class, swinging his arms to emphasize his points.

"Africa has no national identities. There are no national personalities. Each man coming to power is only interested in the wealth that he can steal from the land. There is no social contract; no feeling of responsibility in the leadership to improve the lot of their subjects."

Then she remembered how Francois swept her off of her feet when they met at a formal dinner a year ago. She was twenty-three, had just graduated from the University of Paris with a degree in Political Science. Her goal to come home and help the Congo grow into a politically stable member of the community of nations was pushed back by the Great African War.

Francois, invited to Goma to discuss ways to end the war, had seen Angelica, then an aide to President Kabila, and single-mindedly pursued her to be his bride. He spoke of justice, land reform, healthcare, and education for the villagers. They were married, against her family's wishes, within a month.

At first, Francois promised to start one of the programs that they had discussed. "As soon as I get things a little more consolidated. The Hutus are giving me a hard time right now."

After two months, she realized that he would never make good on any of his promises. The riches flowed into her hands as Francois sought to make her forget her people. And it worked for a few months. She was distracted with the baubles and gadgets available to a wife of a rich rebel leader. Somehow the luster of each new shipment from Europe faded, and she saw in herself the very characteristics that she had hated about the rich wives of the corrupt leaders she had studied while in university: Greed, materialism, and lack of pity.

She saw her husband become harsher and more vicious with his subjects. No, not worse than before, it is just that Francois is no longer trying to hide his real self from me, she thought.

Worse, when she had asked to go back to Kinshasa to visit her parents, he refused. They argued bitterly. He threatened her, and now there were guards around her quarters, and she could no longer drive herself anywhere. One of N'dalu's men always drove and another vehicle followed. She was a prisoner in a golden cage. But she would escape.

She cried as she climbed out of the warm water. Maura appeared with a huge warmed towel, wrapping her perfect body and guiding her to the dressing room.

*****

Seko came to his door, unlocked it and swung it open.

"Sir, it is time for your shower. After you bathe, General N'dalu has requested your presence in his command post."

"Wonderful!" Dolph rubbed his hands together. Usually he got to wash every third day, but since N'dalu wanted to talk, he would get to shower two days in a row. A rare luxury. It has been over two months since N'dalu has called me for a chat, Dolph thought. I wonder what he wants to talk about today.

After the lukewarm shower, Dolph got into his good clothes for the audience with N'dalu. All of the prisoner's clothes came from used clothing bought from churches and Good Will Stores in the United States at two cents a pound and sold in the Congo at fifty cents a pound by the Jewish rag merchants. First time visitors often wondered how the Africans in even the remotest villages came to wear blue Kansas City Royal tee shirts and yellow button down shirts with "Rockingham Concrete" embroidered on the left breast.

As he exited the shower, still drying his long hair with the thin towel, Dolph saw a nice pair of khaki pants and a white short-sleeve dress shirt laid out for him. Beside them was a pair of white New Balance running shoes. No underwear and no socks. Dolph had gotten used to that lack of civility after the first month.

Now that Dolph was properly dressed, Seko unlocked the front door and took him outside to the waiting black Toyota Land Cruiser for the short ride to Francois N'dalu's "palace".

When he first conquered the city, N'dalu took up residence in the largest house in town. Built by the Belgians for the manager of the government mining company, it was even larger than the magistrate's house. With the passing months, N'dalu grew more imperious, and coveted the grandest building in the city: the Intercontinental Hotel.

Early on the morning of the first anniversary of his victory, seven of his armored fighting vehicles rumbled down the main street and arrayed themselves around the ten-story Intercontinental Hotel and Convention Center. N'dalu strode inside followed by forty armed soldiers. They fanned out and posted themselves at every major entrance and on every floor. N'dalu woke the manager.

"This hotel is now mine. You have twenty minutes to clear out. All of the guests will stay. Cooks, maids, drivers, and staff will work for me. All of the furniture and equipment belong to me now."

"This hotel does not belong to you. I must call the owners. You will leave right now," the manager was almost screaming. Calmly, N'dalu pulled his pistol and shot the manager in the forehead.

"You now have nineteen minutes to clear out. And take this," he kicked the body, "with you."

I was still a free man when he took this hotel. My wife had just died, and I had moved to the city to preach, Dolph thought as he walked up the wide limestone steps to the grand entrance. I should have run that day, but I thought that I could still do some good here in the city. Who would have thought that he would imprison me for no reason?

N'dalu became worse and worse. Soon, he was taking active Christian and Muslim clerics and witchdoctors and imprisoning them. He had no trouble finding them because Congolese law required them to register every year. One by one the clerics and preachers would disappear. N'dalu spoke of trials, but no one saw any trial. The people only read about them in the RCD Good News, N'dalu's propaganda sheet printed every Friday for his people.

Dolph walked into the large marble floored lobby, and saw that Francois had commissioned a large painting on the twenty foot tall east wall depicting N'dalu triumphantly entering Matai at the head of a column of troops.

The front desk was now gone, and the room had been redone to mimic a throne room. Guests still came and went as this was the only decent hotel in the mining district. The rates were exorbitant, but here one could sell arms and equipment to N'dalu, luxuries to the officers, and buy gold and rough diamonds. But there was little or no coltan for sale.

Dolph walked around the back wall of the lobby and into the dedicated penthouse elevator wondering how he could influence General Francois N'dalu for the good of his people. Dolph breathed a short prayer. The cool dry air, the tall airy lobby, and the modern elevator were all such a contrast to his cell. But his heart was thankful that he could escape to the real world for a few minutes, to wear real clothes, and to suck up some of N'dalu's air conditioning.

The guard inserted his plastic key so that the elevator could go all the way to the eleventh floor. Dolph ached to know the date, but he waited in silence as the elevator hummed toward the penthouse, having learned that any questions posed to the guard would earn him at least a rebuke, and possibly a rifle butt to the head.

As he walked out of the elevator into what was once the Presidential Suite, N'dalu got up from his massive desk and shook Dolph's hand. The clock above the desk started chiming.

"So glad to see you again, my friend," Francois said in his British accented English. With a sideways movement of his head, he dismissed the guard.

Dolph knew that that Francois had no fear of him. Even though Dolph had often enjoyed the fantasy of overcoming N'dalu during one of these meetings, taking him hostage and escaping in his Land Cruiser, the reality was that N'dalu was a deadly opponent with or without weapons. Besides, Dolph was distracted by one of the gorgeous sentinels lurking on the far side of the leather couch.

N'dalu motioned that they should sit at a small table in front of a picture window. Dolph lingered at the window forcing himself to remember every detail of the city for that day when he might escape. The sun was rising on the left, so he was looking toward the north. The mighty Congo River ran from right to left.

"Why so silent, Reverend Zimmerhanzel?"

"Please don't call me Reverend, sir. I'm just a preacher." Dolph turned and sat in the expensive antique chair.

"Oh yes, I remember. In your flavor of religion, the leaders do not take on the titles of holiness like some others. A very nice touch, what? Do you find that makes it easier to recruit believers?"

"It's funny that you would use a military word, 'recruit', for conversion, General. We don't use titles because of something Jesus said,

> Call no man your father upon the earth: for one is your Father, which is in heaven. Neither be ye called masters: for one is your Master, even Christ.
> But he that is greatest among you shall be your servant.
> And whosoever shall exalt himself shall be abased; and he that shall humble himself shall be exalted."

N'dalu was silent for a moment.

"Very good. But I thought I had your Bible taken away from you. Would you like some fruit?" N'dalu motioned and the beauty floated over with a large wooden bowl filled with apples, oranges, and grapes. She placed blue plates in front of each man along with a knife and napkin.

Dolph was torn between staring at the black female beside him and the fruit bowl set in front of him. The angel retreated back to her post, and so he took some fruit. His hand trembled, and he tried to be slow and look as if he was not a starving prisoner. He didn't want to give N'dalu the pleasure of seeing him devour this blessing.

"Yes, you took my Bible from me, but I still have some of it in my head." He smiled as he used the expensive, sharp knife to slice an apple in half. *What arrogance to provide me a knife. But I must assume that N'dalu could disarm me with his martial arts skills. Is he really that good?*

"I saw you look at Desiree. Do holy men still have carnal desires?"

"Of course, you know the answer to that, sir. We're just men, and right now I have a huge desire for a woman. After all, it's been over a year since you imprisoned me. In all that time I've scarcely even heard a female voice."

"Perhaps we can do something about that. Would you like that?"

Dolph tried to concentrate on eating his apple, knowing that N'dalu would like nothing better than to have him begging for a woman. *No, the contest would go on, and Dolph would continue to play along.*

"Why haven't you killed me like the others, General?"

N'dalu laughed for a long time, then looked out the window, unwilling to hold Dolph's eyes.

"I find you different than the others," he said, still looking outside. "You do not grovel, you do not curse me, or tell me that God will punish me." He turned and held Dolph's eyes.

"It is not often that one finds a real man, especially in the field of professional shaman. I enjoy talking with you and find that although your life is misguided, there are chunks of wisdom to be mined from you and your experiences." N'dalu reached out and plucked grape from the bowl and placed it in his mouth.

Dolph cut off a bunch of grapes from the main group and placed it in his plate, then plucked one and placed it in his mouth, imitating N'dalu. The juice squirting into his mouth as he bit down caused a burst of gratitude to fly through his brain. Now if he could just keep the conversation going until he could finish the bowl.

"Why would a rational man like yourself waste his life preaching a foolish concept like religion?"

"General, when I was a teen, I was a baseball star. I became very popular in my high school. My life was full of parties, women, and whiskey." N'dalu perked up and leaned forward.

"I did not know that you were an athlete. Yes, that sounds very normal. Go on."

"As I tried everything that life had to offer, I could tell that each experience gave me less pleasure and more pain. Especially for my parents. Looking for something more, I got into heavy drug use. First thing that happened, I was kicked off of the baseball team. Soon, I was expelled from high school. A little while later, I was arrested for dealing cocaine."

"That is very hard to believe, looking at you now," N'dalu said, completely engrossed in the story.

"While I was in juvenile detention, an old preacher came by every Tuesday and Thursday night. A World War II veteran. He spoke harshly to me, but he really made me take a hard look at myself. When I came out a year later, I had dedicated my life to serve the Lord of Heaven. I found the woman of my dreams in seminary. After I worked at a couple of churches, God put it in my heart to be a missionary. I raised support to come to the Congo to preach the gospel."

"Now that was foolish," N'dalu said and laughed at his own joke. "See what it has gotten you. What has service to your God gotten for you, except another jail cell?"

"That is where you are wrong, General. I am but a tool to tell a world leader, you, about the great truths of the universe."

N'dalu leaned back and looked at Dolph. The silence lengthened, and Dolph took another bunch of grapes and placed them on his plate.

"I believe that the truth of the universe can be found in the teachings of philosophers Ayn Rand," N'dalu said. "Have you read *Atlas Shrugged* or *The Fountainhead*?"

"Ah, Objectivism. Yes, General. I've read them both."

"Don't you think that the main duty of man is to seek his own good? A society is better off without the altruistic fallacies of self sacrifice and the 'good of the community'." N'dalu smiled, and Dolph realized that the general thought that he had outmaneuvered the preacher.

"In those novels, the community had taken over the individuals by force of government. You are right, that altruism which is forced upon a group or individual by government is bad for the group." Dolph stared at N'dalu.

"The individual is ennobled by serving his fellow when he does so of his own volition. However, sir, you are making the same mistake as the governments portrayed in her books. Except you are on the other side. You use government force to push your philosophy on your subjects just as the liberal governments did in the novels.

"Life is a balance, sir. A ditch runs along each side of the road. Too much one way, and one falls in the ditch. Too much the other and one still ends up with mud on one's knees."

N'dalu laughed.

"Your imagery is good, Randolph. But I think that your reasoning is poor." They ate again in silence. N'dalu just looked out the window, and a great sadness crept over his face. The silence deepened, and Dolph grew apprehensive. What is he thinking? He has the power to kill me. Does that hesitation mean that he is about to sentence me?

"Randolph, I have called you here because I need some advice." Dolph nearly choked on his grape. "You have told me that you were happily married for several years. Is that right?"

"Yes sir. I was very much in love with my wife."

"I want the secret. I want my wife to be happy."

Dolph looked away to hide his surprise. Every other time that he was brought here to talk, N'dalu projected the image of the confident dictator of Matai and someday President of Congo. But in a flash of insight, Dolph knew that N'dalu could not talk of this with anyone else without damaging his image of a perfect leader. Here, speaking in English, he could keep his problem a secret.

"Sir, I am not competent to give that type of advice," Dolph said. N'dalu jerked forward and slapped the tabletop with his palm.

"Randolph, that humility is exactly what qualifies you to advise me." Dolph looked deep into the eyes of N'dalu, and N'dalu stared back across the table with equal intensity. Contradictory thoughts bounced around Dolph's brain. If I give him advice and it doesn't work, he could have me killed. So, what is different than now? I am a servant. I must serve even one that I hate. After a long minute, he decided to risk advising the general.

"What is troubling your wife?" Dolph finished the last grape and reached for an orange. This might work out really well; the fruit was over half gone. N'dalu looked back outside.

"Sir, she is unhappy. When I try to draw her out, she is, how do you say it, evasive. I have given her money, fine things from Europe, servants—everything. Why can she still be unhappy?"

As N'dalu's accent faltered and his grammar worsened, Dolph could hear the emotion pour out of N'dalu. For a second he pitied him.

"You must love your wife."

"I do, and I long for her to be my queen. But she seems to go farther and farther from me in her emotions."

"We have never talked of your wife before, and I haven't met her."

"Then you shall." Life came back into N'dalu, and Dolph could see his hopes rise. "I will have her come to the prison and talk with you. You find out why my wife is unhappy, then you shall instruct her, and we shall be happy again."

If only it were that easy, Dolph thought. The general is the one I probably should be counseling. Most of the marriage problems that I have seen come from a failure of the man to love his wife and care for her. But every relationship has its own dynamics, and Dolph needed to hear from each side before he really could help. He also knew from past experience that marriage counseling humbled many who thought they knew it all.

N'dalu barked at his bodyguard in a dialect that Dolph didn't understand. She walked to the elevator and pushed the button. A surge of lust coursed through Dolph as he watched her body ripple under the red silk dress. The elevator door slid open. The big male guard had been waiting inside the whole time. Dolph filed this away also as a detail he might need for escape.

N'dalu stood, forcing Dolph to mirror him. Dolph looked at the last apple and two oranges left in the bowl, longing to ask N'dalu if he could take them. But he would not give this tormentor and murderer the pleasure of seeing him ask. It took all of his fortitude to turn his back on the fruit bowl and walk with N'dalu to the elevator.

Shaking his hand, N'dalu looked into Dolph's eyes and nodded.

"I shall send my Angelica to get teaching from you on how to be happy. I know that you will not disappoint me."

After the elevator door closed, N'dalu looked at his watch. 1031. He was one minute late. He took out his cell phone and checked with his Chief of Staff to see if his next appointment was ready.

At 1033 Colonel Noel Bunuri came in and sat down at N'dalu's desk. Bunuri was an excellent field commander, but N'dalu despised him. He was corpulent and Christian. Two fatal flaws for anyone in his senior officer corps. Soon, some of N'dalu's chosen younger men would have the experience to take command.

"My dear Noel, how are you today?" N'dalu was pleased to see the older soldier quaking in the chair in front of his desk.

"My General, I am well," Bunuri answered in his best formal French.

"Tell me the good news about my anti-aircraft gun."

"Well sir, after the air attack last week, we ordered a ZPU-4, as you requested. It came in on yesterday's cargo flight along with a gunnery instructor."

"Excellent. I want the gunnery instructor to live close to that gun. Did we get the radar guidance system?"

"No sir, the end user certificate for the radar was much more difficult to get. But remember our spies say that this new airplane is very slow. I have talked to the gunner, and he guarantees a kill on the first engagement."

"I hope that gunner is right, because if he is not, both you and he will pay dearly. And the other electronics?"

"All here. We are setting up right now."

*****

Q pushed hard on the right rudder as the tail came up on the take off roll. The torque and gyroscopic precession pushed the nose to the left, and that tendency had to be offset with large rudder inputs. The big tail-wheeled aircraft handled just like a giant grocery cart being pushed backwards: unstable and always trying to spin around. At least it was early morning and there was no wind.

"Keep 'er straight, there, buddy boy," Mo said calmly from the backseat. Normally a single seat aircraft, each of these two aircraft had been modified with an instructor seat positioned straight behind the pilot seat.

Man, this is harder than the simulator, Q thought. At eighty knots he pulled back on the stick and the 802 leaped into the air, all 1,600 horsepower pulling for altitude. This was Q's first time in a heavy tail dragger, and it showed in the sloppy take off.

"You're doin' just fine. Hold steady while we learn how to make this beast dance," Q said, talking aloud to himself, trying to relax his grip and steady his control inputs.

Two months ago, when this operation had gotten into trouble after the first series of failed assaults, Jeff Slayton remembered the two experimental light attack aircraft purchased by the Army for secret trials. Air Tractor had converted two AT802's, the largest crop duster they made, into cheap counterinsurgency aircraft by removing the spray gear and fitting them with fifty caliber machineguns and anti-tank rockets. They were just hulking in a hangar gathering dust at Dugway Proving Grounds, Utah.

The Army was only too happy to sell them to the CIA for almost nothing. The Department of Defense had only bought the clunkers to mollify a Texas senator needed for an important appropriations vote.

Paladin, a private military contracting company, was tasked with finding two pilots who could speak enough French to teach the Congolese to fly combat missions, and who already possessed a US secret clearance or better. Q and Mo Struthers were the answer. Even though they had never fired a weapon from an aircraft, they were the only pilots available who met the other parameters. Mo met the first airplane in Kamina and was checked out by a factory instructor while Camilo was sent to Orlando, Florida and given six hours of simulator time, then put on a jet for Kinshasa.

"In no instance shall you fly actual combat missions," their employment contracts read. "It is your duty to train the Congolese to fly. United States citizens will not engage in armed combat."

You've got an hour to take this toy out and figure out how to play with it. So, let's put it through its paces, shall we? Q thought.

"Notice that the airplane is unstable. That makes it more maneuverable for the duster pilots, but it plays hell with us trying to hit a target. We'll try some slow flight so that you can see what I mean." Mo was an experienced instructor and had crop-dusted in these aircraft in South Africa.

Camilo went through the routine for getting to know an aircraft: slow flight, stalls, steep turns, reverse chandelles, and wingovers.

"I am covered with sweat!" Q said.

"The air conditioner's working just fine. I'm quite comfortable. I've got the airplane for a minute," Mo said, and Q could hear the smile in his voice, and knew that he was getting a break to settle his nerves. Like all good instructors, Mo knew just how far he could push without wearing out the student pilot.

"You've got the controls," Q said. He leaned back and relaxed his shoulders, then his legs, then his arms.

"Feel a little more at home now?"

"Yeah, I'm getting the feel for it."

"Then it's time for some fun, lad. Turn on the master arm switch."

Q looked to the right upper corner of the instrument panel and saw the large red plastic cover with MASTER ARM engraved into the aluminum above and below. The engineers had chosen that location so that the instructor could see the position of the weapons arming switch from the back seat. Lifting the cover against the spring loading, Q got his finger pinched when it went over center and snapped open. A large toggle switch lived underneath, and Q clicked it up.

"Turn north and tell me when you see the practice area."

Q spotted the abandoned open pit gold mine. It was about three hundred meters wide by a thousand meters long.

"I have it."

"OK. You have the controls. Let's do a gun run toward the old truck on the south edge. Remember, short bursts."

Q lined up on the truck and centered it in his front sight.

"Watch your airspeed. Don't overspeed or you'll have trouble pulling out before you hit the ground." Q jerked the throttle back, and eased in a little left rudder to keep aligned.

The whole plane hummed deeply as both of the three-barreled Gatling guns sprayed out fifty caliber bullets at over a thousand rounds per minute. Q looked past the sight and, watched the tracers. They looked just like red droplets squirting out of a hose. He used gentle stick and rudder inputs to walk the rounds right up to the truck.

"Pull up, my boy. If you concentrate too much on the truck you'll fly right into the ground," Mo said.

Q could feel a little jiggle in the stick. Mo must have his hand resting on his stick in case he needs to take over, he thought. Q's smooth positive pull pushed them down in their seats as they zoomed back to two thousand feet.

"Now THAT was fun!" Q yelled.

"Good shooting. Let's try again. This time, shorter bursts, use your sight and wait until you are closer before you fire. And don't get target fixation."

After three more runs, they were out of ammo. They didn't have any rockets loaded as they were too expensive to use for target practice.

"Now, let's head back for the field, and we'll try a landing," Mo said.

Q turned back to the south, and immediately spotted the brownish red scar of the runway. His experience made him want to touch the transmit button to get permission to land, but they were employing radio silence. Mick said they believed that N'dalu had no radio intercept capability, but they could not take a chance and perhaps give away their presence.

"We are really light, mate. Just like when we return from a mission. Low on fuel, all the ammo burned up. This beasty has a huge wing, and it doesn't want to quit flying, right? All up takeoff weight is 16,000 pounds. We'll land weighing less than 9,000. So hold 'er off until she's ready to land. If you try to force 'er down, we'll bounce back up like an f'ing tennis ball."

Lined up on final, Q felt like he was just floating down. Power was all the way back, and yet the big bird was still five knots above target airspeed. When he got close to the ground, the plane seemed to stop wanting to descend. Q knew the concept of "ground effect" where a wing becomes more efficient less than a wingspan above the ground, but he had never experienced a wing like this one.

"Keep holding her off, lad. Nose straight. Good. Hold it off!"

After floating halfway down the strip, the aircraft finally settled, tail low, onto the main gear. A little swerve to the right, quickly corrected when Q stabbed the left rudder bar, and the plane slowed to a walking pace for the taxi back to the barn.

"Good job, mate. You are now an Air Tractor Instructor Pilot."

Brno, Czech Republic
Saturday Night

Andrew Houston cursed the cold. He was lying on his back inside the big helicopter and the aluminum floor wicked away his body heat. The pilot seat had been removed so that he could stick his head up behind the instrument panel. His upper back rested on a pillow placed on the rudder pedals. He shook his head and ignored his chattering teeth, getting back to work. Andrew's trained eye looked over their work, tracing the wiring bundles to each terminal block. He checked each numbered wire against a folded engineering drawing to ensure that it went to the correct terminal. This project looked close to completion.

February is not the right time to be working in the Czech Republic, Andrew thought. His team had worked around the clock for the last three weeks to completely westernize the cockpit of this Russian workhorse helicopter. All instruments changed to American, all labels in the cockpit changed to English, and all new radios, intercoms, and audio panels.

"What do you think, Boss. Can we go home now?" Ben Willingham IV stood just outside the nose of the Mi-8MTV helicopter, yelling so that Andrew could hear him through the Plexiglas chin bubble. Ben's insulated brown coveralls made him look even fatter than normal.

"Let's go to the fire, son, and look over the schematics one more time." They both hurried over to their work table placed purposefully near the diesel-fired space heater. There they soaked up the heat for a minute before getting back to work. Built in the 1960's, the huge Soviet hangar could house two four engine Bear bombers, had three foot thick, steel reinforced concrete walls to withstand a nearby nuclear blast, but not one shred of insulation. Other aircraft projects and derelicts lined the wall in an organized confusion.

"The work looks good, Ben. Next time I'm sending you out as lead."

"Thanks, Boss." Ben had a big grin on his face, knowing that promotion to Lead Avionics Technician meant a twenty-five thousand dollar raise.

"I'm getting too old to be out on these projects anymore. I've been working in cold hangars all over Europe since the '60's." Andrew looked at his watch. Almost two in the morning. In order to get some time alone in the hangar, the two contract avionics techs faked a problem with the new audio panels.

They both looked down at the wiring diagrams searching for anything that would look amiss to anyone repairing the systems in the future. These drawings, which would become part of the permanent records of the aircraft, did not accurately represent the avionics upgrade that they had just finished.

The "Customer" called them a few times a year to put tags—tracking devises—on aircraft. Sometimes the aircraft belonged to drug dealers, other times foreign corporations, but the best paying jobs involved placing the tags on aircraft belonging to other governments. They installed three inch by three inch black boxes which burst out a tiny packet of code with the aircraft's position, direction of flight, and speed up to a satellite. Everyone in the company knew that they worked partly for the US government, but the technicians were never sure for which agency they worked. All they knew for sure was that they were paid well above scale, and that they had to pass a polygraph every year. In order to get the work assigned, their company often had to bid the work below cost. But the Customer more than made up the difference.

"No way to see that tag, Boss. Anyone following this wiring diagram will see that the box is an audio booster, see the label in Russian, and just go on." Andrew wished that Ben would stop calling him Boss, but even after repeated requests, the young man continued with the name. It must be an Alabama thing, Andrew thought. But he was right. These upgrades included reusing some of the old Russian avionics boxes, and no one wanted to open one of those up unless something was seriously wrong.

"Let's set up the test box, and make sure everything works," Andrew said.

Ben dug out the test box and set it thirty feet away from the helicopter while Andrew plugged a laptop into a hidden port behind the instrument panel. Andrew turned on the helicopter's BATTERY switch and all the avionics, powering up the tag. Using the laptop, Andrew fed in a signal that the helicopter was moving.

"Speed 45 knots, heading 210," Ben called out.

"Good. That matches up. I don't think we need to check anymore. It's just too cold," Andrew said. He powered down the ship and the laptop, while Ben put the test box back in their bag.

"Yes, the boys at the office did us up right. That was brilliant to hide the tag in an old audio booster, and then include it in the schematics. What did you set the position update for?"

"Every hour when the ship is parked, every three minutes when flying."

"Good. I wonder who this helicopter is going to," Andrew said.

"I got a peek at the work order when I went in to tell Danny that we would need to stay late tonight. Somebody named N'dalu down in the Congo," Ben said.

"Ben, you keep this up and I'll see that you go far in this organization." Ben grinned, showing his bad teeth.

Chapter Five

Sunday

Colonel Ashunta Rodriguez. It had a nice ring to it. His promotion last week to regiment commander was a cause of happiness and worry. Rodriguez was now making more money than he had ever made, most going to savings in a Swiss bank. His private living quarters were better than he had ever dared to imagine. So why was he worried?

Like many war time promotions, his was preceded by the death of his superior. During the last raid, the commander stayed at his command post a few minutes too long, and N'dalu's forward observer saw his position. Too much talk, not enough movement. The mortar fire was deadly.

Now these cursed Americans wanted Ashunta to lead another assault against N'dalu. They would be throwing everything at him, hoping to thrust through the town with a small force and capture or kill him while the perimeter battle still raged. He remembered last night's meeting where the crazy plan had been explained for the twentieth time.

"Before dawn, I'll lead in the first group to take out the perimeter guards before they can sound the alarm," Brett said, pointing at the tactical map of Matai. "The main force, lead by Mick, will then attack the barracks and the tank compound, here, supported by the mortar squad and the airplanes." He turned from the map and smiled. "All this will be a diversion to give Ashunta and his team time to spear into the city and capture or kill N'dalu. We are depending upon three things:

- N'dalu's troops will be asleep, and we can take out the guards without sounding the alarm.
- The aircraft can keep the tanks from maneuvering around the main force. We have enough ammo and rockets to take out every tank. They will stagger the flights so that one is always on station while the other is rearming and refueling.
- The distraction of the attack will give Colonel Rodriguez the opportunity to zip into town and cut off the head of the snake at his own headquarters.

It will be different this time, Ashunta thought. I'll have air support to open the road to town killing those devils in their armored monsters. He smiled when he remembered seeing the two tanks magically blow up when the airplane came to their aid during the last probe of N'dalu's perimeter.

He had been up all night getting his assault forces massed at the Highway 6 Bridge. N'dalu did not defend the bridge over the Congo River, but kept his forces close to home to maneuver for crushing counter attacks. Rodriguez hoped that this bit of hubris would be the key to opening up Asgaard like a tin can.

Less than one hour until dawn. He was banking on the intelligence that most of N'dalu's men got drunk every Saturday night. Their hand was forced early when they found N'dalu's spy during a surprise barracks inspection yesterday. That inspection turned up a satellite phone in the possession of a young radio operator.

After some vigorous interrogation, the young man admitted to Rodriquez that he had been calling N'dalu three times per week with news and gossip from around the camp. One of the items he had passed on was that there was going to be a large scale attack against Matai in two weeks. So now the attack was moved up to surprise N'dalu. They were going in two weeks early without the rehearsals and training they needed. Ashunta's fear tasted like metal, and his tongue stuck to the bottom of his mouth.

"Bring that truck up here." Rodriguez was happy that the new funding had given them three large trucks. The main attack force had already been moved close to the edge of the mining area closest to the motor pool where N'dalu kept his tanks. He would now use them to move his troops across the bridge and then into town.

"Sir, we just got the light signal from the other side."

"Good." The light signal meant that the advance team, lead by the American, Brett Descoteaux, had eliminated the soldiers guarding the gate into Matai.

"Move out!"

The gray clouds hovered over the bridge, and Rodriguez gauged the amount of light. He should have at least fifteen minutes until the villagers downstream could see the troop movements. He looked up and prayed that the clouds were not too low for the planes to fly against the tanks.

As the morning light came full upon the bridge, he ran to catch the last truckload of troops. He was proud of his boys. These were his best, selected to go into the hotel/palace and kill N'dalu. So much better disciplined than when the ragtag unit that started three months before. The thick boards of the bridge rattled as the new Chevy five ton rolled across, the young driver rowing through the gears like a Formula One pilot.

Ashunta took stock of his boys. Silent and long faced, they stared at their weapons or out through the gaps in the wooden stakes that were designed to hold back cattle being transported to market. *They are so young. They'll do* fine. They'll do fine. His mantra tamped down his own fear.

In the distance, he could hear the crump of the mortars. *It has started.*

*****

The world was gray and wet for Bixby Wilson, and with the fog, he could barely see the loaders across the ramp as they finished buttoning the top hatch of the first 802. Their Toyota pickup truck rested just on the other side of the big nose and propeller. A load of green metal boxes of fifty caliber shells and long wooden crates filled with 2.75 inch rockets for the second airplane pushed the bed of the truck all way down until it rode on the axle, raising the nose up to a silly angle.

His hope of getting out of the camp before the battle was dashed after the discovery of the spy. Twenty-two years in the Navy had not prepared him for this. He had no idea when he came over to Africa that he would be in an actual battle. While the fighting would be taking place over twenty miles south, he felt a foreboding, like a low cloud hanging over his head. They were going out to wake the giant.

Elmo Struthers walked up behind him dressed in an old South African cotton flight suit. The gray color matched the dawn, and Bixby noticed that he had painted his flight helmet to match.

"Great day for a cruise around southern Congo, don't you think?"

"Listen, you be careful out there."

"We will, 'ay. It's the damned tanks that need to be worried this morning."

Mo climbed up on the step, and swung into the rear cockpit. His pilot, Lieutenant Tando, was already strapped into the front. Mo, being more experienced, was taking the least experienced Congolese pilot. Q would have Colonel Neguma.

Bixby walked backwards as the gray hulk came to life and the whine of the turbine pierced his ears. He was worried that even if their attack was successful, word would get back that the contract pilots had flown combat missions.

"There is no other choice," Camilo had said during the meeting last night. "The Congolese can't even take off and land the plane yet. We've got to go, or the attack will have to be called off."

With a big dose of power, the heavy aircraft unstuck from the shallow red mud, and waddled toward the end of the runway. The loaders swarmed to the second airplane.

Bixby went to get his survival pack and put it in the office. He had been up most of the night putting it together. His job now was to monitor the radios.

*****

Ashunta's troops knifed through the perimeter. The sleeping guards, still drunk from the night before, had been stabbed by Brett and his boys to prevent the noise of gunfire from rousing the other posts. The three trucks rolled into the town. Every five hundred meters, Ashunta put out a five man fire team to keep the road open and to prevent N'dalu's men from circling to their rear. Sending the first two trucks back to support the main attack force, he was now down to forty soldiers.

The men heard the rattle of machine guns as they entered the town. The muddy and potholed streets were deserted with only an occasional parked car off the side. Their objective, the Intercontinental Hotel was only a half mile away when a rocket propelled grenade hit the engine compartment of their truck. The explosion killed the driver, and they swerved into a building, crashing through the metal doors.

"Out! Out! Lima One left side of the street. Lima Two right," Ashunta said, dazed, but still trying to have the right mixture of command and calm in his voice. His two battle groups fanned out in good formation taking cover where they could.

N'dalu's soldiers, many still in their sleeping clothes, were streaming down the street, and Ashunta wanted to panic and run. But he stepped behind the corner of a building, and motioned for his machine gunner to set up.

The street exploded and N'dalu's troops fell or started to run. Where did that come from? Ashunta thought. The gray airplane swooped in low overhead, turning left. Ah, rockets from our friends. The plane was a welcome sight. Maybe this is going to work out after all.

"Move out Lima One."

Twenty troopers moved along the side of the street dashing from doorway to alley, while the other ten watched them and remained ready to fire. After thirty yards, Lima One took up a watch position.

"Move out Lima Two."

Leap-frogging like this, Ashunta moved toward his objective.

*****

Andre Popronov was dreaming about a faceless woman with a gorgeous body. He was just about to kiss her, but couldn't find her lips. He was shaken awake by a huge black guard screaming in French. Andre spoke French poorly, and the accent here was horrid.

How do I say, "What do you want?" he thought. But he heard the explosions of the mortars, and knew that they were under attack. The guard was sweeping his hands back and forth making noises like machine guns and bombs. Andre knew what that meant: It was time to go to work.

Andre had been a gunnery instructor in the Red Army for twenty years, and for the past ten, he had been instructing all over Africa. Most of the time, it was just like here. He didn't instruct anyone, he was there to shoot down the enemy's aircraft, get his bonus and go home.

Pulling on his pants, he jumped onto the flatbed truck, took the gunner's seat, and the driver roared off toward the last known position of the aircraft.

When he first arrived a week ago, he supervised the mounting of the ZPU-4 onto this flatbed truck. The system, used by the Soviets for fifty years, was simple and effective. Four heavy machineguns, firing parallel, were mounted as if on the four corners of a box. The gunner sat in the middle of the box and aimed and fired the guns as one.

The truck stopped in the middle of a large intersection, and Andre nodded liking the clear fields of fire. He could see bodies strewn around and knew that the aircraft must have anti-personnel rockets. He had no body armor, so his first shots had to be good. He could not afford to get into a duel with one of the gunships.

The distinctive sound of a diving aircraft echoed through the alley, and with the sound bouncing off the buildings, Andre didn't know from which direction the aircraft was coming. Fear jumped up his throat and he almost vomited.

The huge gray aircraft came up almost vertically only a block away. It slowed down as it turned on a wing tip for a return gun run. Andre was stunned that a combat aircraft would perform such a maneuver. It looked like the devil flying was crop dusting.

As Andre was mulling these things over, his hands, of their own accord, spun the handles to slew the guns toward the gray gunship. With his sight ring giving him a reference, he pushed the trigger bar, and shot well ahead of the turning aircraft.

For the observers, it looked like the aircraft flew into the line of green tracers. The bullets hit the armor, and they flashed like white strobes. Smoke boiled out, followed by flames. The right wing broke off, and gunship tumbled like a toy thrown off of a boy's upper bunk bed.

Andre started giving instructions to the driver to move closer to the river, not realizing that he was speaking in Russian. But the driver understood hand motions and tone of voice, and drove north.

*****

Ashunta recognized the sound of the ZPU-4 from his fighting days in Angola, and knew that the battle was lost even as the AT-802 crashed in a fireball. He had seen Mig-21 jet fighters shot down by that cursed contraption. The slow gunships didn't have a chance.

He looked down the street and saw the Intercontinental Hotel less than two blocks away, but it might as well have been twenty miles. If N'dalu would come out, Ashunta could surely shoot him dead. It would be an easy shot. If his troops attacked the hotel now, they might get N'dalu, but then they would never make it out alive. Ashunta's plans did not include dying today. However, he needed to warn off the other aircraft. In the quiet after the crash, he turned to his radio operator, selected the command frequency, and keyed the transmit button.

"Reaper Six, Reaper Two. Over", he said.

As he released the button, he heard the squeal of N'dalu's new jamming equipment. He changed to the tactical frequency. It too was blocked. Knowing that he could not coordinate his troops, call for mortar support, or warn the other aircraft, he motioned his men to fall back. There would be no air cover for his retreat. Only speed and doing the unexpected could save him and his men. The successful thrust into town had brought them so close to their objective, but now left them exposed on almost all sides. Each minute that passed, more of N'dalu's troops would come pouring out of their beds. If they came under fire and became immobile, the tanks would come and finish them off at their leisure.

But they could not retreat the way that they had come. With no gunships to stop them, the tanks would surely cut off the road to the bridge. Ashunta pulled out his compass and pointed.

"Sampson, Pierre, take the point. We've got to run for our lives. Lead us due north to the river!" Ashunta looked around at his boys, some wounded, others with panic in their eyes, and he realized that most would not make it. He singled out his four best men, knowing that he was condemning them to death.

"Alou, Henri, Tiny, and Befe. You stay and fight rear guard. That is the only way we can get out." The four nodded silently, and turned back toward the center of town. As they prepared to man the machinegun, they took all of the AK47 ammo clips proffered by the others and stuffed them in pockets for the running battle to come.

Ashunta saw that his unit was already stringing out, the strong running up the street at an impossible pace, leaving the weak and wounded behind. He started after them, and heard the machinegun bark behind him in measured short bursts.

*****

Q didn't feel comfortable with the airplane or the Congolese pilot, so he decided to sit in the front cockpit.

"This is not acceptable. I am a trained combat pilot, and I will fly the aircraft", said Colonel Neguma.

"Then you will fly it without me."

Neguma looked up at the massive gray aircraft, and his pride and indignation leaked out, leaving him stoop shouldered and pensive.

"I am not fully checked out yet."

"You know that if you go alone, you won't make it off of the runway," Q said. "I'm gonna sit up front, and no one needs to know that you were in the back."

"If it is going to be like that, then there is no need for me to even go."

"That's true. I'll tell everyone that you were on board. You just stay out of sight." Q saw the colonel look around to see who was witnessing the conversation. He moved very close, climbed the ladder so that he was next to Q, and lowered his voice.

"I shall wait here for you." Q smiled as the obvious relief washed over Colonel Neguma's face. "If we are found out, then you will say that you left me while I was using the restroom. You received an urgent radio call to take off immediately. Right?"

"Sounds good."

"OK. Then I go to the restroom."

As the colonel walked away, looking proud and erect in his tailored flight suit and spit shined black boots, Q strapped in and put on his helmet. He looked down and to the left at the South African mechanic and they exchanged knowing smiles. Q twirled his finger as the signal that he was ready to start the engine. The mech returned the signal to show that the prop was clear and it was safe to start.

After his preflight engine checks, Q gunned the engine to unstick from the mud and taxied to the end of the runway. Climbing over the tree tops, he was glad to be rid of the colonel. He keyed his radio and immediately heard a squeal in his headsets. That's not good, he thought. Automatic jamming equipment. A high speed scanner picks up a transmission, and the jammer tunes and transmits on the frequency in under two seconds. Newer tactical radios with frequency hopping could easily defeat this jammer, but their operation had only the old style radios.

In less than ten minutes Q spotted the Congo River and the smoke rising from the town. The coordinates for the tank compound were in his GPS, and the moving map showed him on course. No commo with the troops, so I don't know where I'm most needed, but I can't go wrong shooting at the tanks, he thought. He scanned ahead, but couldn't make out anything past three miles in the gloom and light rain.

As he passed over the marshalling yard, he saw the armor moving out and down the road. He banked hard left and came back around for a run.

*****

When the second aircraft zoomed over, Andre was taken by surprise. He started screaming at the driver to head back to town.

So, this guy knows how to use the terrain to mask his approach. We will see who is best at this game. Andre was excited to be hunting a more worthy opponent than the last pilot.

The aircraft reappeared again as it climbed and banked for a gun run. Andre pointed and yelled at the driver to turn left. The young driver nodded and turned left toward the tank yard. Over the wind noise Andre heard the hum of machineguns and the crump of one of the tanks exploding in the distance.

*****

Ashunta heard the truck screaming through the gears and splashing through the puddles as it approached from behind. He yelled at his running troops to take cover. Before they were ready, the truck flashed by. Several rifle men got off a few shots.

Disappointment crushed Ashunta as the truck raced on toward the tank yard, swaying as the driver tried to miss the biggest potholes. He had missed his chance to take out the ZPU-4. So close. He wanted to cry. With a little luck he could have killed the gunner of the ZPU, and his men might have had a chance. Now all was lost. N'dalu would surely launch a crushing counter attack, destroying the few men and women left back at the base.

He pulled out his cell phone and called his woman. She answered on the second ring.

"It's bad. Get what you can carry, and get out. There will surely be a counterattack on the base. I will meet you at our place."

"I love you, Ashunta. I'll be there."

Their place in Goma was a tiny house in the nicer French section where they planned to live after Ashunta made enough money as a mercenary to open a business. But he didn't mention the town, fearful that N'dalu had a way to monitor phone calls.

Colonel Ashunta Rodriguez straightened, shouted orders, and his column resumed its unsteady trot towards the river. I hope we can steal some boats, he thought.

*****

Andre felt like a giant kicked him in the kidney. He saw the blood splashed up onto his sight, and Andre wondered where it had come from. Realization crept up on him, disbelief reigned for a second, and then he was surprised.

"I'm shot", he said in Russian. He looked down at his belly and saw that the exit wound was bigger than a grapefruit.

The truck stopped in the middle of another intersection, and the driver got out and ran. Andre saw the airplane zoom up, and start his racetrack for another gun run.

"I will never see my home again." As he talked to himself, his hands mechanically cranked the wheels, and the guns swung left. The wheels seemed difficult to move.

"My wife. My sons. I will never see them again."

The aircraft was coming in range.

"Is there really a God? Was my grandmother right? This will be a tough shot. The airplane is angling away from me."

A dark mist closed in on him. His vision condensed to small circles in the haze. He leaned on his gun as he pushed the trigger bar. He watched the tracers and knew that he had just missed, firing ahead of the slow plane. He died disappointed.

The green tracers arced up and passed the aircraft on the right, almost parallel to the direction of flight. Each projectile weighed over a half pound and travelled at 2,500 feet per second. Ninety seven bullets passed in front of Q in less than a second, and he saw nineteen tracers. He knew that he should take some evasive action. But before he could move the stick, the last bullet entered the right side, just behind the engine armor and ahead of the cockpit armor. Traveling forward at a twenty degree angle, it tore into the accessory section in the rear of the engine, shattering gears and bending shafts.

Q felt the aircraft shudder, and then the engine stopped with an inner clang and some grinding noises. The engine lost oil pressure, the five propeller blades went to the feathered position, streamlined to the wind. He glided in silence. Less than two hundred feet off of the ground, he had no choice of landing areas.

Floating down between buildings he was committed to land on a wide boulevard. No cars were out this Sunday morning and especially after hearing the combat in the city. He tried to stretch his glide over the street light at an intersection, but the pole caught his right wing.

The plane circled the pole to the right like a boy, who running past a pole sticks out his arm and grabs on. The centrifugal force banged Q's helmet to the left, against the roll cage. The nose of the plane went into a building, and he watched the instrument panel coming toward his face.

Chapter Six

Q tried to raise his head off of the pillow, but the pain shocked him back down. Cutting his eyes to the left, he could see a man close by, on his knees, praying silently. The man, sensing a movement turned and smiled at Q, then came over to the bed.

"I am glad to see that you are awake. You're the pilot? You were flying one of the gunships, right?" Q was captivated by the smooth, rich voice with its southern drawl.

"Yeah. Where am I?" Each word cost Q. Why am I so tired, he thought.

"You are in N'dalu's prison in Matai." Q tried to turn toward the man.

"Ow," he said as the pain hit him. As Q glanced around the cell, he started to remember. "I was shot down."

"That's what I heard. You were brought in this morning, and you have been unconscious all day." The man turned, and walked across the cell bringing back a bottle of water.

Q looked at the man's back. He was trim and fit, but his clothes, several sizes too big, hung on him. His long blonde hair was pulled back into a ponytail and held there by a black ribbon.

"You need to drink some water. You haven't had anything all day." Q realized his tongue was sticking to the bottom of his mouth, and now his thirst raged up into his brain. A long tug on his bourbon bottle this morning was the last liquid that he had had. He struggled to get an elbow under himself and levered his head up to where he could drink. He felt the cool water splash into his empty belly. Three long pulls, and he downed the whole bottle. He fell back onto the pillow, and handed to bottle to the man.

"God, that was good! I never would have thought that water could be so….well, like good Scotch!" The man winced, and Q knew that he had offended somehow.

"I'm Camilo Quartalino. Thanks for the drink, and for looking after me while I was out." Q extended his hand.

"I am Dolph Zimmerhanzel. I guess we will share this cell for a while. All the other cells are filled with soldiers captured this morning. What happened?" Q explained the operation in simple terms, not knowing if his new friend Dolph was really another prisoner, or just a sly interrogator.

"So our mission was to remove N'dalu and regain access to the mining area," Q summarized. "But I guess we failed."

"Looks that way, my friend."

"So, why are you here?" Q asked.

"I am an evangelist, a preacher." At this news Q's face fell. He saw the man give a little smile, used to this type of response.

"N'dalu has been systematically killing off every religious leader he can catch. Witch doctors, imams, priests, and missionaries," Dolph said with a heaviness tinged with fear.

"Are you next?"

"Oh, no. I don't think so. N'dalu likes to talk. He speaks good English, you know. He can talk with me about things that he wants to keep from his staff. I am his sounding board, his conscience. Perhaps even his teacher. As long as I can provide him with entertaining conversations, I'll live." Dolph hesitated, and Q wondered what the man was keeping from him. Perhaps it's just that priestly confidentiality. A scream came up from the basement, long, painful, and without hope.

"What's that?" Q whispered.

"N'dalu has his torture rooms downstairs. It sounds like they are questioning one of your compatriots."

"Did you see any other white men brought in? Hear of another pilot?"

"No, I can't see who comes and goes. This window looks out the back," Dolph said. Another scream, this time much weaker.

"Does this go on very long?"

"No. They'll kill the poor man pretty quickly. A blessing, actually, for him and for us." The man was staring out the window as the sun set.

"Is it still Sunday?" Q spoke to the man's back.

"Yes."

The screams turned to whimpers and lasted into the night, and then abruptly stopped. Q watched Dolph stay on the floor praying all evening. He must be praying for the men being tortured, Q thought. Dolph prayed for a few more minutes, then slid down on the cold stones.

"No, come up onto this bed. There's room enough. Share this blanket with me. That's it."

"Thanks."

"Don't thank me. I'm taking your bed."

Monday

It was almost two in the morning, and Bixby Wilson, Zacheus, and Brett Descoteaux stood outside the operations conex waiting for any stragglers to make it back. Brett, in charge of the advance teams, had stayed in position on the outskirts of Matai during the assault. He was first into battle to take out the guards, and last out to cover the retreat, if needed. But there was no retreat.

They had planned for victory or retreat. No one had planned for a massacre. No one came back to the road, and no one except Brett and his team of ten rear guards crossed back over the bridge. They commandeered a truck, and made it back to the airstrip late yesterday afternoon.

By then, the base was completely deserted, their belongings ransacked, and anything portable and of value gone. When Brett's squad saw the camp deserted, they ran into the bush. Eight hours later, the generator still purred and the big area lights illuminated the perimeter fence and walkways. Fires smoldered and yellow smoke mixed with the fog drifted through the beams of light. Trash blew across the soccer field in a slow whirling dance to settle against the steel buildings like stinking snow drifts. Sunday morning the news of the defeat had somehow gotten back to the wives and whores, and, like a tornado, they had stripped the camp under the veil of the light rain, taking whatever they could carry with them. All day and into the night Bixby and Zacheus stood outside the door of the operations conex, each with an assault rifle, guarding the only items of value left behind, their belongings and the commo equipment inside the command center.

"What should we do?" Bixby asked. "I've always been an analyst. What does one do when everything goes wrong?"

Brett looked over the nightmarish landscape, still looking for Mick Cooper to come striding through the smoke.

"Let's call the Boss for an evac. This thing is blown. They can fly the jet down here and have us out at first light." He turned to the Satcom radio, and keyed the mic.

"Gurka Six, this is Cigar Box. Over."

"Cigar Box, this is Gurka Six. Go." Brett recognized Whitehorse's gravelly voice.

"Boss, we're screwed. Both aircraft are down, all teams are blown, no known survivors."

"Understood. Total loss. We have confirmation from other sources."

"We need to be evacuated. Only three souls and no bodies." There was a long pause.

"We are not, repeat, not coming for you. This is a corporate matter only, and you guys will have to get out on your own. No US Government involvement." Brett was making notes as fast as he could scribble.

"Any hope of a change of heart?" Brett asked.

"Negative. Negative. Word comes from Pipeworks and Logic Green. Close up shop. Destroy and bury that radio far from the site. Your account will be closed. I'm sorry. Good luck."

"Understand all. Cigar Box out."

Brett wanted to scream and curse, but when he looked at Bixby and saw the deep terror in his eyes, he knew that he had to take care of this fat corporate guy. The dark sadness about Mick once again probed into his mind.

Did my bro' make it? Is he wounded somewhere waiting for me to come for him? Brett started stacking up papers to take his mind off of Mick. I must keep my head about me and get my team out, he thought. He looked back up at the other two.

"Zach, you go up ahead and get us a boat to cross the river. We are going south." Brett moved over to the big map. "You ought to be able to get a water taxi about here. Meet us on the main river road. Bixby and I will stay behind and sanitize the site. We'll start out after you. Around day break. We'll have our radio on at noon and at dusk."

"Right. See you later this afternoon." Zach picked up a rifle and his pack, then slipped silently out into the ink of night.

"Who're Pipeworks and Logic Green?" Bixby asked. Brett slumped forward in his chair, his elbows on his knees.

"Pipeworks is CIA Director of Operations. Logic Green is the Ambassador to Congo."

"That's a secure radio. Why don't you guys just talk? Why use code names?"

"Well, we hope it's a secure radio. You never know", Brett said with a sad smile. He started scratching at the papers taped to the wall, tearing down personnel lists, maps, aerial photos of Matai, and even the cartoons taped up for entertainment. Soon he had an armful of paper.

"Open that file cabinet and start shredding all of those files." Brett walked outside and lit the ball of paper with a lighter. Bixby continued shredding until he burned up the motor. He took the rest of the papers out to the burn pile. Brett stirred the clump with a long stick so that all the papers would completely burn. By 0430, they had cleaned out the file drawers and burned everything that might be embarrassing to the US Government or the corporate sponsors.

When Bixby had the burn pile going well, Brett went inside and started erasing the hard drives of the computers.

"Bixby, put some wood on that fire. Make it hot!" Bixby came back a minute later with an armful of brush and threw it on the fire.

After reformatting the drives so that they were erased, Brett tossed their three laptops into the fire. The last thing they did was to burn all the passports except their own. They had delayed in case one of the contractors came back. But now Bixby and Brett were ready to go, and the fire was going out, so they threw them in one by one. Camilo Quartalino. Elmo Struthers. A tear rolled down Brett's right cheek when he threw Mick Cooper's in the fire last. He had to turn away. Bixby stirred to make sure all of the documents were consumed by the fire.

With that done, they picked up their packs and started for the road.

*****

For Chu Lee, drinking tea did more than just keep him awake; it soothed his soul during the long night watches. Now 0233 and he was into his fourth cup. If he drank much more, he would not sleep come morning. A signals analyst at the Chinese embassy in Kinshasa for over twenty two years, he wondered when he would ever get to return to his home in southern China. He cursed the day that he ever decided to study foreign languages.

Reclining in his big captain's chair, he looked down at the letter from his cousin lying in his lap. So my wife has found a younger man, and that younger man is now living in my house and sleeping in my bed. Well, what can one expect? I've not seen my wife for four years. She has needs, and there are so few women in China these days for the young men. Each night for the past two weeks, he re-read the letter, trying to decide what to do.

In his right hand he held the latest denial of request for home leave. Seven times in the last seven weeks his requests had floated around the embassy. Each time they came back denied. This last one contained an additional handwritten note:

Captain Lee:

You are a dedicated and integral part of this team. We cannot function without your skills and knowledge. Please do not ask for leave again. I will inform you of the proper time to put in another request.

General Wu Sing Lao

Having already gone through the shock, anger, denials, and humiliation, his soul longed for something more than work. There is nothing to go home to. What is to become of my life? But I must go home and try to work out something. I'll throw her out of my house. That is what I'll do. At least I will regain some of my honor with my family.

The earphones came alive as he heard Cigar Box calling Gurka Six. He splashed hot tea on his lap as he jerked upright. Turning, he checked that the automatic recorder had started. As he stood up to get some tissues he was jerked back by the cord from the headphones he still wore. Cursing, he pulled off his ear phones.

The US State Department put out a bid two years earlier to upgrade their secure communication systems, and they awarded part of the bid to ASHTAR, a Chinese manufactured secure SATCOM system. The quality was fabulous, their equipment manufactured in a factory modeled on the Cisco plant across town, but the winning factor was the low price.

Unknown to the State Department, this system featured a repeater chip buried in the bowels of each router box. When these systems were installed around the world, China no longer worked trying to break encryption, because most of the secure US radio traffic was repeated, decrypted, to Chinese listening posts over the internet via secure websites.

His cell phone. Where was his fornicating cell phone? He picked it up and called his boss.

"They are abandoning the base."

"Good," said the Chinese general, his voice still thick from too much alcohol. "Then he will not have to counterattack. We want Elder Four to only fight if he has to defend the mines. Message him. You know what to do."

"Yes, my General," he answered in French.

*****

Hurling his sat phone against the wall, N'dalu screamed out the vilest of curses in both French and English. After he ranted, he felt better. He straightened his robe and dismissed his body guards who had sprinted into his bedroom when they heard their boss bellowing. He walked out into his living room, and paced back and forth, planning his day. He sent out runners to call two meetings.

No counter attack. How can I destroy my enemy when I cannot go outside my own compound? He slammed his closed fist on the table, making his laptop jump. Forced to stay in my "zone" by my sponsors, I rot, not being able to fulfill my destiny. I could be king of Congo, and of all the surrounding countries. The wealth of coltan, gold, oil, diamonds and timber could fund my army and even a navy!

He let his mind soar with the possibilities of power and conquest. I can do it. I must do it for the good of the people. I will unite the land, build roads and schools, stamp out the religious oppressors…

A vision of Dolph Zimmerhanzel popped into the forefront of his thoughts. Now there is a good man. But just because I know one good rational man does not mean that religion is good. No! The exception proves the rule. My country would be much better off if I killed every witch doctor, every priest, and every, every…

"My love? Did you send for me?" Startled, he whirled around. She was dressed in a long white silk robe that set off her glowing chocolate skin. Her hair was long and sleep-tousled. Yes, now that I have defeated my enemy, I will concentrate on teaching Angelica to be a better wife, he thought.

"Ah, my Angel. Yes I did," he said in English, their language of courtship. "I know that it's early, but I wanted you to go and visit one of the prisoners. I think that you will be a comfort to him and he to you. His name is Dolph Zimmerhanzel." She was silent for a long time.

"Alright." She turned and started to walk out.

"Angelica." She turned back to him.

"Yes?"

"Take Maura with you. Just in case."

"Yes, my Lord." She walked back to the elevator and was gone.

He loved it when she talked like that. Fleetingly, he considered taking her to bed. But she had been so distant, preferring to sleep in her own room instead of with him these last four months. Besides, it was already 0742. He hadn't showered or breakfasted. He would be late for his first meeting as it was.

"Sir." His favorite body guard, Desiree, stepped forward.

"Yes?"

"Colonel Noel Bunuri here as you requested."

"Bring him in. And do not leave us."

"Yes sir."

Colonel Bunuri came in, as always quivering in fear, knowing that he was hated for being a devout Catholic. The surprise showed on his face to see his general still in pajamas and robe. N'dalu noticed that the colonel's holster was empty, and he gave a small nod of approval to Desiree. She barely nodded her head in return.

"Colonel. Please be seated."

"I cannot sit while my General stands." The colonel gained some confidence as he took refuge in the military courtesies.

"Yes. Quite so. Have you found all of the guerrillas that attacked us yesterday?"

"Yes, my Lord. We killed or capture all of the main force. A small band went north to the river. We killed the majority of them before they were able to escape in stolen boats."

"Good. And prisoners?"

"We have twenty-six. One of the wounded died during interrogation last night." The Colonel shifted his weight and looked at the ground, the guilt of the murder weighing on him.

"Find out any new information?"

"No, my Lord. Only what we already knew. The Americans were using a native militia to drive you out of Matai, reinforced by military advisors and two gunship aircraft."

"And we have one of the advisors in custody?"

"Yes my Lord. He is scheduled for interrogation today."

"Do not interrogate him. I will question him here. He is to be kept in perfect health. Those are my orders. Is that clear?"

"Yes my Lord."

"I want you to take two tanks and reconnoiter the enemy base." The colonel's face turned gray, looking as if all the blood had flowed out of it. N'dalu laughed, and he could see the embarrassment in the old man. I'll have to rid myself of this one sooner than I thought. Is Robert ready to command? After I have cleared away the threat, I will look for a new commander.

"Don't worry, my friend. The base is deserted. We have radio intercepts that they have been ordered out. Not even any support from their own. They are just leaving and getting home however they can. I want you to go in and destroy that runway. Plant cratering charges, burn the buildings. Make it unusable for any other force that may decide that they want our mines. Is that clear?"

"Yes, my Lord."

"One other thing. Two of the American advisors have escaped. I would think that they are headed north to the American Consulate in Goma. Be prepared to move in that direction to capture them. This folder has pictures and descriptions along with identification numbers."

"Yes, my Lord."

******

Angelica and Maura stood before the large wooden doors of the Central Prison. These thick, high doors, built over a hundred years before, were designed so that a large wagon could be pulled inside by horses. In the left door was a smaller door. This personnel door opened inward, and Seko Seki M'Bai, resplendent in his dress uniform motioned the women across the courtyard to the back, towards Dolph's cell.

They walked across the white sand courtyard, and Angelica's mind went back one hundred years. She could almost see the Belgians bringing in thirty prisoners at a time in ironbound wagons. She could almost hear them whipping the black men toward the long stone table on the porch for in-processing. Suddenly cold, she shivered at the brutality, pain, suffering, and death that this building represented in the colonial past and now during her husband's rule. She fought the feeling, but knew that each day she despised him more. Soon, she may even come to hate him.

In the far wall, an iron gate swung open, and she saw a long narrow corridor lined by cells. Angelica hesitated. Perhaps it's a racial memory that gives me this cold chill in my bones when I enter a prison. She smiled to Seko, steeled herself and stepped up into the corridor. The empty cells smelled of unwashed men, and Angelica noticed that each one had been occupied recently.

"Are these men just released?"

Seko smiled, kept silent, and motioned for them to continue. Then she realized that he must have moved these men somewhere else for Angelica's visit. He could not have them calling out rude and sexual comments to the General's woman. She imagined that he would then have had to kill one as an example.

Soon, the three reached the back cell. Angelica could see that this section was newer, larger and cleaner than the others. Also, this cell had a window in the back that let in sunlight. A white man and a black man were inside. The white one was good looking but a bit thin. The black man's face was swollen, he had a bullet head and thick neck, but he had eyes that pierced her soul. These men were different. As was this huge guard. What made these men seem so out of the ordinary?

"Welcome. You must be Angelica. I'm Dolph Zimmerhanzel. This is my cell mate, Camilo Quartalino."

"I am honored, my Lady. My friends call me 'Q'", he said in perfect unaccented French.

"Q? Like the James Bond Q?" she asked.

"No, just short for Quartalino, I guess. I picked up the name years ago."

"I didn't know you spoke French," Dolph said in English.

"You never asked," Q replied in French, and then laughed.

Angelica laughed with him. She couldn't remember the last time that she had laughed, and the feeling intoxicated her. Two handsome and interesting men. Now she knew why these men were different. They are not afraid. Not afraid, even though they are prisoners. Not afraid to look at her as a woman. She could see the desire in both of them as they looked at her. She smiled and a warm glow grew in her belly.

"This is my companion, Maura," Angelica said. Maura stepped into the cell, and Seko closed the door.

"My pleasure," Dolph said as he stepped over to her and shook her hand. His eyes locked onto Maura's, and Angelica could see the immediate sexual attraction. Angelica looked back at Q, and he had eyes only for her. He communicated with his smile and his eyes that soon he would somehow make her his. She felt the heat rise to her face and a tremor that coursed down to her toes.

"Please, let's sit down," Dolph said, breaking the spell. He motioned to the table and the extra chairs that Seko had brought in earlier. The two men sat with their backs to the wall, and the two women across from them, Angelica in front of Dolph.

"Leave us," Angelica said to Seko over her shoulder. He started to protest, but seeing her look, he smiled and backed away.

"Just call out and I'll be back. I am just down the hall," Seko said.

"What brought you to this lovely place, Mr. Zimmerhanzel?" Angelica asked.

"Just call me Dolph. Short for Randolph. I was a preacher. A missionary. Your husband imprisoned me a couple of years ago. By the way, could you tell me the date and day of the week?"

"Of course. It is Monday, the twenty-eighth of February."

"2010?"

"Yes. 2010"

Dolph slumped in his chair.

"I've been here over two years now," he said to himself in English.

"Well." He breathed in through his nose and straightened up in his chair, motioned toward the women, and smiled, savoring the perfume.

"I want to thank you lovely women for coming to see us," Dolph started. "Do you know why you are here?"

"No. My husband commanded that I come. He said that I would find you interesting. And that, so far has been true." They all laughed. Again, the magic. She would have never thought that she could be so comfortable so quickly. Could life really be like this?

"Your husband had me over to his office the other day and asked me to talk with you. He wanted me to give you some instruction on being a happier wife."

At this Angelica's face darkened, her hands made wide gestures, and her words flooded out much faster than Dolph could understand. Maura was nodding in agreement. Dolph put up his hands. He was horrified. He thought that it would be a joke they could share, but he had poked a festering psychological wound.

"Please, please. You must speak slower. My French is not that good!"

Seeing the terror and bewilderment on the two men, the anger fell from her face. Angelica thought it funny that she could frighten these two tough men, and she started laughing. They broke up too, and soon all four were laughing too hard to sit up straight. They caught their breath, and there was silence for half a minute.

"I don't think that I love my husband anymore," Angelica said with hatred in her eye.

Dolph knew then that he would have been better off wandering into a tiger's cave. This marriage counseling had all the earmarks of a disaster. Worse, his desire for this Maura woman was pushing out all other thoughts. Often he glanced toward her. I must concentrate. I must. He paused, trying to frame his next question in the most positive light.

"You loved him at one time, did you not?" asked Dolph.

"I don't think that I ever really loved him. I saw a handsome, sexy, powerful man, and I was lured in by his personality and persistence. I thought I could change him into a good man, and a good leader. I was a fool."

Yes, I could see how that would happen, Dolph thought. What can I say? The silence weighed on him.

"Where do you want your relationship to go now?" Dolph asked.

"I'm not sure. Some days I want to leave him, other days, I want to kill him. Occasionally, I am still attracted to him and even think that I could, even now, change him."

Dolph reached across the table and took her hand. He looked into her eyes, and after a long time he asked, "How do you want to change him?"

"I want him to be more caring for the people. Enact some laws to feed the starving, create jobs, cut down on pollution. You know, be a responsible leader. Someone that I can respect." He could see that she was fighting to hold something back. Dolph squeezed her hand.

"Is that all?"

Angelica looked sideways at the floor.

"I want him to be nice to me." She jerked back her hand, covered her face and began to cry. Maura reached out her arm and drew her mistress close and held her as she cried. After two minutes she sat up straight, and glared at Dolph.

"He is cruel to me in bed. His idea of sex includes tying me up, humiliating me, making me do things that are not natural. I had several boyfriends in college. I am not a prude. When he was wooing me, he was tender, loving, and giving. On our wedding night, he showed his true self. He tells me to learn to enjoy it; that his other women do."

She stared at Dolph, silent, but fire darted out of her eyes. The tears continued to course down her cheeks.

A cold fear gripped Dolph's gut. Should this session continue in this vein, all of their lives could be in danger. This was becoming ten times worse than he had imagined. He glanced over at Q, and saw that he was keeping the emotion from his face. Good, very good. *I should be more neutral, but my hatred of Francois N'dalu is clouding my vision. What can I say to help this woman?*

"Angelica, men do not change. For the most part, the only thing that a woman can do is suppress some of the bad, and accentuate the good. But if there is no good, you will not create it in his life. Only God can change a man. But you, my dear, can change. You must change something. Either you go to where your husband is spiritually, or you must leave him. If you stay when you two are so different, you will never be happy.

"Francois wanted me to teach you to be a happy wife. A happy wife is in tune with her husband. Can you change to be the wife your husband wants?" She leaned forward, her face only inches from Dolph's. She spoke in a fierce whisper.

"No. That will never be. You do not know him as I do." The volume of her voice increased. "He is evil. He steps on his people to grub out the tantulum and enriches himself even while they die. He tortures his enemies, he kills God's teachers." Now she was almost shouting. "I must get away. I must get back to my family. I must escape....I must!" She slumped down and whimpered. Maura stroked her hair and cooed to her in a dialect that Dolph did not know.

Q leaned over to Dolph and whispered in his ear.

"Pray for us, preacher. Make it loud and long."

Dolph looked bewildered at the order. Q spun his finger in the air and urgently and nodded his head.

"Our Father, we exalt you as the Most High God. Your love for us is everlasting. Our requests flow up to you, oh Father…"

Q was impressed. The deep voice boomed down the hall in English, rising and falling, rhythmic, and almost impossible to ignore. He leaned close to Angelica, talking softly.

"We don't know who is listening. You must pretend that you are getting better and better at being N'dalu's wife. If he gets wind of this he could kill you, and us. Also, if you are improving, he will keep these sessions going. If you help us, we can all escape. Get me paper and pencil.

Send Maura later with it." She looked at Q for a full minute.

"What am I doing? If Francois found out, he would kill me," she said to Maura. "But I have to get away."

Maura stared into her eyes giving silent encouragement. Angelica gritted her teeth and nodded, committed.

Q motioned to Dolph, and he cut short the prayer.

"Thank you, pastor. I think that you are right. I can be a good wife to Francois. I will try harder," Angelica said a little too loudly.

"Come back and see me in two days, and we will talk again."

Seko appeared at the door as if he had read their minds.

*****

"Come on. I know you're tired, but we've got to get out of here." Brett pushed aside a palm frond as he continued down the trail."

"Why can't we just get on a bus and go to Goma?" Bixby asked.

"N'dalu is going to be looking everywhere for us. He'll figure that we've either taken a boat to Kinshasa or the bus to Goma. We're going where he doesn't expect us: To Angola."

"I've got to rest. I've only gotten three hours of sleep in the last two days. Just give me five minutes."

"Five minutes."

Bixby sat down and removed his pack so that he could use it as a back rest.

Brett went ahead on the trail for a few feet so that he could look around the bend, assuring himself that no one was coming. Brett looked back at Bixby Wilson and saw him breathing hard. This guy can't take much more of this or I'll have a heart attack on my hands. Brett came back and sat down, pulling his map out of his leg pocket. He studied it for a moment and pinpointed their location. They were right at the ninety degree bend in the trail.

"I figure that we have about ten kilometers more before we reach the crossing. Zach should be there and already have us a boat. He's a good man." Brett realized that he was speaking all this to himself. Bixby sat slumped forward, asleep. They had gotten an hour of sleep just before dawn, but poor Bixby Wilson, the corporate intel analyst, wasn't up to this pace. Well, this is just about the worst place I could pick to sleep, Brett thought.
He shook Bixby's shoulder and motioned to start up again. He handed Bixby a bottle of water.

"Drink or you'll get dehydrated. Drink, you'll feel a little better." Brett fondled his M-4 carbine, and that made him feel a little better.

Why didn't I become a doctor like my father wanted me to? My father has a good practice in Vermont, makes a good living. I could be in a cozy office prescribing valium to middle aged ladies to calm their fears that their husbands have found a younger woman.

He smiled imagining himself in a lab coat instead of jungle fatigues, and wearing a stethoscope around his neck instead of his rifle. A very easy life. My father couldn't understand how I could be fascinated with medicine and helping people, but just as interested in killing the bad guys. Just as comfortable with a rifle as with a blood pressure cuff.

Maybe I'll go to med school when I get finished with this op. It's a little late in life, but someday, if I keep this up, I'll end up like Mick, cold and dead and alone in some third world hellhole. Did anyone bury my friend?

*****

It was the heat of the afternoon when the screaming started again. Awakened from a healing sleep, Q wondered what type of tool they were using to inflict the pain that caused such tormented cries. Were they crushing knuckles with pliers, burning flesh with flame or white hot steel, or, God forbid, mutilating the prisoners' genitals?

I must prepare myself, he thought. I'll be in there soon. The thought of his death almost paralyzed him with fear. So much better to have died in the plane crash. Only one instant of pain, then…what? He smiled sadly remembering his last visit from their pastor, back when he and his wife were going through marriage counseling.

"God and I aren't speaking right now, reverend," he had said as a joke. But it was and still is true. If I am to die today, how do I make peace with God? Can I? His reverie was shattered by another scream, longer and more pitiful than the others. Worse, it ended in the gurgle of death.

Dolph noticed how Q jumped, his eyes wide with fear, and went over to him, placing his hand on Q's shoulder.

"Don't worry, brother. They won't interrogate you. You're with me. This cell is only for the important prisoners. I'll bet N'dalu figures on trading you for something. Maybe a ransom. Maybe a guarantee that he will be left in peace. But don't worry. If you were going to be tortured, you would already be with the others, watching your cellmates. That's how they do it, hoping to break the will of the later ones by letting them watch the pain of their comrades."

"I thought the world had moved past this."

"No, my friend. This is Africa. This torture is not so much to gain information as to punish those captured. N'dalu will let a few go back to the bush. But be sure that they will be missing a hand and a foot. They will spread the tale of the terrible fate that most of the soldiers endured.

That way, N'dalu will keep the people from ever volunteering to come against him again. That's the African way."

Q saw the sincerity in the preacher's eyes and felt a waterfall of relief cool his soul. Only a tiny spike of doubt poked at his brain, and then only occasionally.

"I need a drink." The urge was sudden, overbearing and he frantically reached down into the bottom ankle pocket of his flight suit. He pulled out an airline bottle of Scotch and saw that it was empty. He reached in again, and brought out a second bottle. Some guard must have consumed its contents while he was unconscious.

Q cursed and spun around, swinging his arms. He hammered the air with both fists, filling the cell with his wrath.

"Those sons a'bitches drank my emergency scotch. I kept two airline bottles right here in these pockets. They drank them and then put back the empties." While he continued cursing, he showed Dolph two custom pockets sown inside the lower leg pocket of his flight suit.

"A man who hides his booze, so that he is never without, is an alcoholic," Dolph pronounced. Q collapsed onto the bed, his head hurting from throwing his fit and the bruises from the crash.

"Preacher, I need a drink," he pleaded like a three year old. Q tried to remember the last full day that he had gone without a drink. Scared and ashamed, he finally admitted to himself that he couldn't remember the last day that he had gone without alcohol.

"Don't you have a drink around here someplace? I've got to have a drink." Another scream echoed off of the walls.

"We should use this time to plan," Dolph whispered, hoping to distract his cellmate. "Seko is busy and the screams will keep the listeners or microphones from overhearing us."

"Maura will be back tomorrow afternoon. What should we tell her?" Q asked; now back to the task of escaping.

"If they can get a car up to this back wall, and some type of tool to get through the wall, we can go out that way." Dolph looked longingly out the back window.

"No. That won't work. Look." Q pointed out the front bars. "Our cell is at the end of the main hall. They can see right into this cell from seventy feet away. There's no way we can tunnel or cut bars without someone seeing us. We must get a guard to let us out."

"How will that happen?"

"I don't know. We just have to find the handle on one of the guards. Bribes, blackmail, extortion, sexual favors: All the old levers still work. We just have to find the right one to pull." Q smiled, and Dolph shivered in front of his new cellmate, seeing his capacity for evil.

"NO! No, I will be no part of that. We'd become no better than they. If we must get a guard to help, then it will be because he has mercy on us, or because he will get some reward, or something...I cannot, I must not be a part of these evils." Dolph sank to his knees, and shook, weeping silently. In a few seconds, he spoke again without raising his head.

"I want out of here so bad. So bad. At times I've thought of killing a guard and taking his keys. The temptations are so great that I feel like I'm being pulled into hell. I have no choice, I tell myself. But I pray. I pray, and I'm patient. The right circumstances will arise." He looked to the ceiling and swung his arms up, crying, "My God, don't leave me here!"

Q was open mouthed. He had only suggested the common sense methods taught by all military survival courses. *What a team we make: A broken alcoholic pilot and a crazy preacher. I can't reason with this guy, so I'll play along. But I know his lever. Maura. She can talk him* into anything. I saw the way they looked at each other this morning. I'll talk with Maura, she'll make him see.

*****

The prisoner sat still and silent. Seko suspected he was playing possum to get rest from the systematic amputations. Seko motioned one of the guards forward. The young man gingerly walked through the pools of blood and placed his ear close to the prisoner's mouth and listened for breathing.

"Check his pulse, son!" Seko bellowed. He knew that he was taking his frustration out on the boy named Bobby, but the verbal blow was already struck.

"He is dead, sir. There is no pulse." The boy backed away, looking down, and whispered, "He is already cold."

"Get him out and bury him," Seko said, motioning to the four prisoners detailed to the burial squad. Two riflemen accompanied them as the prisoners dragged their dead comrade out the back to the truck.

"Bobby, take these pieces out to the truck. Wash down all this blood," Seko said to the young guard. This time he spoke more like a father to his son. Seko turned to the prisoners lined along the back wall.

"Back to your cells! I will have mercy on your worthless souls for one night." Seko knew that he should continue torturing and killing these prisoners as instructed by his General, but he was sickened and confused. It was too early to go home, only five o'clock, but he needed to get away from this prison, the screams, blood, and horror. He needed sleep.

In a fog, Seko went to his office, turned off the air conditioning, and walked home. What shall I do? He wished that he had never circled around to the side hallway to listen in on Angelica's meeting. But I had to, he told himself. The General might ask me how things went, and then I would be incompetent should I have to tell him, Sir, I don't know.

I am a soldier. My loyalty is to my Lord General. But I love Dolph Zimmerhanzel. He smiled at the thought of his friend, the quiet soul that had blessed him and his guards for two years now. I am convinced that this spirit man has brought healing, prosperity and peace to my family and my prison.

Until this cursed attack. To torture one or two offenders, that is my job, to inflict fear into the wrongdoers, the enemies of my General. But to bring in more than twenty? Yes, make an example of one or two, and let the rest go back to tell of the punishment for attacking the ruler of Matai. We have already killed three hundred during the battle, say the perimeter guards. We have won a great victory. Can my liege not show *any* mercy?

Now my friend and the General's wife are planning an escape. Should that happen, I will be tortured and my family wiped out. But it is my duty to tell my General. Can I betray my friend, this powerful spirit man? And my princess, Angelica. Could she be telling the truth? What is to become of me? I must betray my Lord or my friend. He noticed that he was walking around the block instead of going inside his house.

I will talk with my woman. She is wise. She will know. He wanted to see his wife, to hold her, and be comforted by her. She will know what to do. He rolled the thought over and over. He straightened up, picked up his pace, and marched toward his house. As he pushed open his front door, he noticed the tiny droplets of blood splattered on his otherwise perfect uniform.

From the kitchen window Oni watched her husband come up the road and then turn the corner. From his gait and the set of his shoulders, she could see that he carried a great burden. Does he know? No, there is no way he could know, she thought. It is something from work. Look, he is home early. She went back to preparing dinner for her family.

In a few minutes she heard the board on the front porch squeak, and knew that her big, strong husband was home. The thought filled her with contentment. Just a few seconds later, he stuck his head into the small kitchen and inhaled through his nose.

"Smells good, woman. What are you cooking?"

"My handsome husband gives me money to buy meat and fresh vegetables, beans, rice and flour. So, we are having grilled chicken, soup, onions, and tomatoes," Oni said without turning around.

He walked into the kitchen, pressed himself against her back, and wrapped his arms around her.

"You are a good wife. What would I be without you?"

"The handsome husband to another woman, I would wager." Oni laughed and turned around in his arms, facing him. When she looked up at him, her smile died. The hurt and indecision in his eyes pierced her heart.

"What is wrong, my love?"

"Is our son home?"

"Not yet. He is still playing soccer."

"I have heard a terrible thing today. Dolph Zimmerhanzel had a meeting with Princess Angelica. They are plotting against the General. They are planning an escape. I only heard part, but I know enough."

"What do you think you should do?" Oni asked.

"I should turn them in, but I love Dolph. I revere the Princess." A moment of panic iced through Oni's breast. If he were to turn her in, she thought, we will all bear the guilt. Besides, my bosses want N'dalu to fall. This will be a blessing to see his bride escape.

"No, my love. You must not turn him in. I don't think this is best for you, for us. You must forget that you heard this thing." She placed her hand on his cheek. "And if it happens, if they escape, you must promise me that you will never tell N'dalu that you heard them planning anything." She looked in his eyes and lowered her voice.

"I know that you feel it is your duty to report her. But it is your duty to protect your family. Pretend ignorance, my honored husband. You never heard them talking." She stroked his face. "You never heard it." Seko was silent as his wife peered into his eyes. She kept stroking his cheek, waiting for him to think out his response.

"It is good advice. I knew that you would have an answer for me for you are a wise woman." He kissed her and held her tight. She could feel his passion.

Her husband left for work before dawn, and soon afterwards Oni pushed her son out the door toward school. As soon as she saw that he was walking around the corner, she went to her closet and pulled out a sat phone. She dialed the number from memory to give a report to her superiors. For six years now, Oni had been giving reports to the DGSE, France's equivalent to the CIA. They were always interested in little tidbits and news about the mining operation. They would be enthralled to hear about Angelica. Perhaps a little bonus to her retirement account in France.

****

Almost dusk, and like every evening, the monkeys, insects, and birds ratcheted up the noise level. Brett walked five meters ahead of Bixby and enjoyed the cool evening breeze. The trail was level here, well traveled, and wide enough for a vehicle. We must be getting close to the village, he thought.

Several times they stepped off of the trail and hid when they heard or saw vehicles, bicycles, or pedestrians. Brett was surprised that there were no soldiers patrolling the road looking for them. May be they were concentrating on the road to Goma and Kinshasa.

"I've got to stop. I've got blood coming out of my shoes," Bixby said.

"Don't look at them. We can't stop. I know you're hurting. We'll be at the boat soon."

"I just need to take my shoes off for a few minutes."

"No can do, my man. You take those shoes off, and you'll never get them back on. Then we're stuck. When we get on the boat, I'll treat you," Brett lied. "You want something for the pain?"

"No."

Brett Descoteaux had those rare qualities that commanders sought in point men: an incredible sense of smell, a keen eye, excellent physical condition, but most importantly, the third eye. Brett had first heard of the ability to see the unseen danger ahead, to feel the ambush, or sense the booby trap when he went to Afghanistan. Soon his superiors recognized the magic, and though he was the medic, he often walked point on patrols.

That third eye started itching, and Brett felt uncomfortable. He motioned Bixby Wilson into the bush along the side of the trail. Quietly, Brett covered them both with palm fronds and they waited. In a minute he heard an individual ease past their position. Brett knew that the man was carrying a rifle from the occasional rattle of metal and plastic. He caught a whiff of Old Spice under the normal body odor, and said in a normal voice, "Zack, is that you?"

"Yeah, boss. It's me. You just about scared the skin offa me." Brett and Bixby came out of the fronds, and they shook hands.

"I got us a boat. Figured it was gettin' dark, and I ought to come look for you. Didn't want to use the radio. Never know who's listening."

"Good thinking, my man," Brett said slapping him on the shoulder. How far?"

"Less than a kilometer. Here, Bixby, let me take that pack. I left mine at the boat."

We'll cross as soon as it gets dark.

****

The flames licked his face and he beat on the side door to escape the cockpit. His best kicks had no power. Framed in the side window, his wife looked back at him with disgust. The hot air scorched his lungs and he could no longer breathe. He saw his flesh char, and he could smell the meat burn.

"You can't even fly an airplane right," she said. Her usual disapproval poured out through her voice and her captivating eyes.

"I'm burning, get me out! Get me out!" She just slowly shook her head. "I'M BURNING!"

Camilo wakened to the vigorous shaking. Dolph was in his face. They were both sitting up in bed.

"Wake up! Wake up, Q. It's alright. I'm here. Are you awake? You were having a nightmare."

"Yeah, yeah." Q looked around, confused, and it took a few seconds to remember that he was in prison in the Congo. Whew. Better than in that cockpit. Here it was dark, cool and dank. Condensation on the stone wall dribbled down to the floor. A mosquito buzzed beside his ear. A guard came by, curious about the screaming, and shined a flashlight inside.

"It's OK," Dolph turned and said. "Only a bad dream." Q was shaking. He could not control his muscles, and a horrible flower of pain bloomed in the space just behind his forehead. He put his hand to the crown of his head, and it took great concentration to sit upright.

"What's happening to me?"

"I think you've got the DT's, my brother. Your body is having withdrawal symptoms from lack of alcohol."

"Get me a drink, Dolph. Please. Please, just one to calm my nerves." He bowed his head and a new wave of palsy started at the crown of his head and, like a slow wave, rattled his chest, hit his stomach, clenched his buttocks, then coursed down to his toes. Now his skin felt tender and painful everywhere his clothes touched.

"I don't have one, brother." Dolph wrapped his arms around Q and held him as he shivered. Sweat poured off of his bald head and dripped on the blanket. In a minute, the shaking diminished. Dolph guided Q back into a lying position, and he relaxed into the sleep of the exhausted.

Dolph eased out of bed, and went to the window. He could see a few stars through the tree, and he prayed in silence for his cellmate, for Angelica, and for Maura. He gripped the bars and closed his eyes before he started, framing his thoughts for his Creator.

My Father, bless my friend Camilo Quartalino. Dolph always believed that it helped him concentrate his prayer when he used full names, even though he knew that God understood for whom he prayed. Camilo is fighting with a demon, Lord. Remove his addiction. Let him see that only you can give him peace.

The visage of Maura rose and he could see her face clearly, projected onto the backs of his eyelids.

Lord, you know that I haven't had a woman in two years. You know that women are my weakness. I am vulnerable, my God. What shall I do? I almost took that woman in my arms this morning. He paused, embarrassed.

I wanted to take her to my bed. Oh God, give me strength. How can I know so quickly that she is for me? We said but three words to each other. How she can see into my soul! I feel her presence when she looks at me. Is she your gift to me or a temptation from the Prince of Liars?

He faltered in his prayer, thinking of her smooth skin, swelling hips, and narrow waist. He smiled and remembered watching her walk away at the end of their meeting. She moved with such grace and poise. But it was when she turned around to look into his eyes, into his soul, one more time, that he knew that he was in love.

Forgive me, Father. I drifted. Give me help! And what of this attempt as escape? Is this why you have kept me here for two years, to guide this man out? Speak to me, Father. Guide me! How can I know which path to take unless you bless me?

And what shall I do with Angelica, my Lord? Divorce is wrong, but do I tell her to go back to a man who is evil? Is my own hatred of him clouding my reason? Of course it is! What should I do? I feel like I am caught in a great river, and I cannot swim against the current.

Dolph's elbows and back pained him as he remained in the same position. Still he prayed to his God. The sky turned gray, and the stars disappeared. Dawn would be here soon. With the singing of the birds, he ended his conversation. An aroma of fresh coffee drifted through the cell, and Dolph thanked God for the great pleasure.

Chapter Seven

Tuesday Morning

Two left turns out of the prison, then sixteen blocks to the south. Q counted the blocks to the hotel and observed everything about the city, and remembered. I must recon, he thought. This may be the only chance I get before we get out of jail. He laughed to himself remembering playing Monopoly as a kid. He always lost to his older sister, but felt good whenever he drew the "get out of jail free" card.

After his fitful sleep, he awakened refreshed, the shakes only a dim memory. The guards gave him clean clothes after breakfast, and now were hauling him to an interview with N'dalu. Still observing his surroundings, he replayed the objectives for this interrogation.

- He wanted to make friends with N'dalu, hoping to keep away from the torture chambers.
- Do not give out important information.
- Do not slip and let N'dalu know that he spoke French.
- Do not give even a hint that he was in love with Angelica and planned to escape with her.

Smiling, he remembered his sendoff. Just before the guards had escorted him out, Dolph had grabbed him by the shoulders and said, "Do not be afraid. I have prayed for you."

What a strange man. But I like him. He's my partner now.

Goose pimples jumped up on his arms when he walked into the air conditioned lobby. The high ceiling, dark red carpets, marble columns, the people coming and going, and the coffee service on a side table reminded him of a life so far away, yet only two weeks in the past. The sun streamed in from windows set high above, lighting the dust mites in the air, yet the mood in the lobby remained dark. Few smiled, and those who did were leering at bought women or talking a big money deal in the bar, already open. His gut cried out for a drink when he saw the whiskey bottles stacked on the wall in back of the bar. He turned, and thankfully entered the just-opened elevator.

N'dalu sat behind a huge antique table that served as his desk, smoking a long, fat cigar. A churchhill, thought Q, recognizing the size named after Winston Churchill who used the large cigar both for his pleasure and as a symbol of his leadership. The smoke brought another pang to Q as he walked to the front of the desk. He looked around as much as he could without turning his head, noticing the trophy case, signed pictures of N'dalu with unrecognized politicians, and what?! Out of the corner of his eye, Camilo saw a long gray rectangle mounted high on the wall, the crazy angle drawing one's eye toward it. He recognized that it was the right elevator from his airplane. It looks much larger indoors, Q thought. Anger and shame started to smoke in his head.

"It is my newest trophy. What do you think, Mr. Quartalino?"

"I am sure that it will give you pleasure, Sir." Camilo struggled to control his face. He thought of himself soon smoking a good cigar, holding a tumbler of scotch over ice, and so he produced a sincere smile to go with his comment.

"Please sit, Mr. Quartalino. We have much to discuss. I have a folder here with some interesting facts. You were a Navy SEAL, yes?"

"Yes sir. Twelve years in service. Honorable discharge."

"And you are fluent in French. But I am comfortable in English, so we can continue. I need the practice. You came to Africa to teach the Congolese to fly your gunships. Why were you flying, and not a Congolese?" Q cursed silently. This guy knows everything about me. What else is in that folder?

N'dalu drew smoke into his mouth and expelled it toward the ceiling.

"The pilots weren't ready, sir. My friends needed air support against your armor, so I decided to fly the mission instead of sending the troops in without anyone to look after them." The smoke drifted toward Camilo and he enjoyed the smell.

"You are a cigar smoker, Mr. Quartalino?"

"Yes sir, I enjoy a cigar now and again."

"This is a 1999 Partagas 150. Cuban. They cost over seventy-five US dollars each. I ordered these cigars when I found out that your force had occupied the old airstrip at Tondo Kivu. I knew that I would smoke them in celebration of your defeat. I just heard from my commander. He has blown up the runway and blasted your buildings. There is nothing left. So now, I can enjoy this fine cigar." The two men were silent as N'dalu took another puff.

"Mr. Quartalino, I know everything that I need to know about you. It's all right here." N'dalu tapped the manila folder with his middle finger.

"That is why you have not been interrogated. But I do know something about you that even you do not know about yourself." N'dalu leaned forward and put his elbows on the table. "You are presumed dead. I can keep you in prison forever, and no one will ever know."

Q held N'dalu's eye and tried to look confident and unafraid. His mind churned. No one would be coming after him. No press coverage. No diplomatic pressure to get his release. No visits from the Red Cross. At least his life insurance would take care of his kids. After a minute, N'dalu laughed through his nose.

"I like you. You are not like most men. You do not beg, you do not tell me about your wife and family, you do not say that you did not know that you were really going to fight. It would be a shame to waste a man like you by letting you rot in prison."

"What did you have in mind?"

"You are a mercenary, Mr. Quartalino. No, no, do not object." N'dalu raised his hand as Q tried to speak. "You have engaged in combat for money. You are not a technical advisor or an instructor. You are a combatant. You and your men attacked me, unprovoked. I have every right to keep you as a prisoner of war, or have you executed for murdering my men." N'dalu stopped and took another puff.

"But I am merciful. I want you to work for me. I intend to develop an air capability and pilots are a rarity in Matai. I need a jet to fly to Europe and a helicopter for local use."

N'dalu paused and puffed. He held Q's eye and leaned forward with his elbows on the table.

"You will train my men to fly my aircraft. Your dossier says that you fly both airplanes and helicopters, no? Work for me, and you will be well paid, have women, booze, cigars, and…" N'dalu turned and looked left, out the floor-to-ceiling window. "You will be out of prison."

Q sat back in his padded chair, let his hands drop to his side, and cocked his head. This is the last thing I expected, he thought. His mind raced ahead. I could be out of jail and earn some big money. I wonder what type of aircraft he is talking about. No, it's not right. He could feel his jaw tighten. He looked up at the ceiling, playing for more time.

I can't change sides. That would not be honorable. However, this is not an exercise. Am I willing to be tortured and to die for my honor? Besides, if I get this job, perhaps I could get Dolph out of prison.

"Come, Mr. Quartalino. You must know that no one from your group will come for you. We have radio intercepts that they wouldn't even come for Bixby and Descoteaux. Even now, we are moving to capture them."

He even knows our names. Is it true that we've all been cut loose to fend for ourselves? What of Angelica? How could I ever have her if I hook up with him? Q looked into the face of N'dalu searching for some clue of his trustworthiness. Only threats, viciousness and treachery flowed out of N'dalu's eyes. But did he have a choice?

"Alright. I'll work for you. What are the terms?"

"You destroyed one of my tanks, so you shall work for the first two months without pay except for a room, meals, and clothing. The third month, you will be paid fifteen thousand euros per month. You will work for me for two years, and then you will be free to go." Q knew that he was in no position to negotiate.

"I need to get some things from the prison."

"All of your personal items will be brought here. Lucy will take you to your room." N'dalu picked up his cell phone, turned back toward the window, and called his mine manager.

Q stood, dismissed like a servant. Lucy grabbed his left arm and led him toward the elevator. Once the door shut, he said in French, "Are you going to the prison for my things?"

"Yes, sir."

"I need you to take a note to my friend in prison, explaining where I am, so that he will not worry about me."

"Of course. That will be no problem, sir." She led him down a hall to Room 822, produced a pass key and slid it in, opening the electronic lock.

"This is your room, sir. The General said to bring you whatever you desire. We have Johnny Walker Red here, but if you would like some other type of liquor, I can get it for you."

"No, please, take that out. Take all the liquor out. However, I could use some coffee." His hand itched to reach out and stop her as she left with the bottle. But from somewhere within a strength glowed like the last ember of a campfire. He held his breath until the door closed. He opened the desk drawer, and found some paper, still embossed with "Intercontinental Hotel, Matai, Congo". A pen lay by the phone. Only a short time to write this. I've got to get it right. No guaranty that Dolph will even see this, but I know that N'dalu will. He smiled, thinking of the Sherlock Holmes quote, "The game is afoot!"

*****

Dolph,

I am OK. N'dalu made me an offer I couldn't refuse. I am now working for him. I will be training his pilots. I'll see if I can get you to come to work with me. Lucy will pick up my things.

Keep praying for me, brother,

Q

Dolph held the letter down and away from him, brought it back up and read it again. Is there a message within a message? Would Q hide some other meaning in plain sight? I have to assume so. First of all, he couldn't reject the offer; that much is plain. Like Joseph working for Pharaoh in the Bible, perhaps God has put Q in a place of authority that will help us all get out.

He still wants to work with me. N'dalu probably used threats to get him to change sides. But what if he really wanted to go to work for N'dalu? What if N'dalu convinced him that the riches of the mines were worth betraying me? What if he is making great money and eating steaks while I rot in this prison!

Dolph knew deep inside that he was envious, disappointed, and afraid, all mixed together into a rancid emotional soup. *I must meditate and sort this all out.* As he positioned himself on his bed and let his mind empty, he recognized that his meditation was not just an asset, but also a weakness. A cave of refuge, but also a place to hide from reality.

And how will this affect the women? Will Angelica still come to see me? And will she bring Maura? He felt the familiar lust course through his veins.

A new scream pierced the afternoon humidity.

"Camilo did the right thing," he said aloud to himself. "We must first survive before we escape."

Chapter 8

A sharp knock on the door woke Camilo from a restless nap. A lifelong habit since his days in the Navy, Camilo learned to sleep whenever he could, not knowing when fate would give him the next opportunity. He glanced at the digital alarm clock. 1130.

"Just a minute," he said in French.

When he opened the door, a small, dapper black man walked in uninvited. He was dressed in a gaudy blue flight suit with captain's bars on the shoulders. His lace up flight boots shone like black mirrors.

"I am Colonel Jesse M'bota. I am in charge of N'dalu's new air force," he said with pride. "You are Camilo Quartalino, our new instructor. I am delighted to be working at you." With a huge smile, he shoved out his right hand, and Q shook it, surprised at how such a small man could have such huge hands.

"Colonel, I am honored to work with you."

"No, call me Jesse. You are not in our military. I want to take you out to see our new aircraft. We speak in English, the language of aviation. I need practice."

Soon, they were bouncing along the pot-holed road that led south to the old airport in one of N'dalu's new Toyota pickups. The jungle heat shimmered on the road ahead, but the cold air conditioning blew hard enough to make Q wish for a light jacket.

"When General N'dalu decided to acquire an air force, he recruited me to buy aircraft, get the maintenance in order, and repair the airport. It was derelict for several years, so we had to cut the grass that was growing through the pavement and patch the runway. But is now very serviceable. We have more than two thousand meters available."

Jesse continued on about the problems of maintenance and procuring parts.

"What type of aircraft do you have?"

"We bought a very nice Falcon 20 in corporate configuration and an Mi-8 helicopter, also with a nice executive interior," Jesse said with pleasure leaking out of his voice.

Yeah, I'll bet it's a twenty-five year old piece of junk that barely made the trip down, Q thought. I may have been safer staying in jail. But then the sounds of the torture boiled back up into his memory, and he said a silent prayer of thanks for escaping the fate of the other militia soldiers.

That's funny. I haven't talked to God since my wife left me, Q thought. That preacher is getting to me. Probably good for me.

They rounded a corner, and he could see the terminal and a small but clean ramp with a new white hangar on the south end. The hangar was a kit-built affair, manufactured in Europe or the US and shipped over in pieces to be assembled in place. The aluminum trusses held up a heavy cloth that served as both sides and roof. Q noticed the electric motor in the entrance that winched the door – a heavy canvas curtain – up and down.

The pair walked in through the personnel door on the side, and Q sucked in his breath when he saw the Falcon Jet sitting in the middle of the brilliant white floor. The white nose towered above him, and a blue ribbon stripe swooshed up and back toward the tail.

Jesse introduced the three maintenance personnel to Camilo. One was Polish, one a Frenchman, and one Czech. They all spoke English in the shop since they didn't speak each other's language. Camilo and Jesse walked around the aircraft admiring the new paint.

"This model has been retrofitted with the Dash Five engines. The interior was completely refurbished by the Falcon factory" Jesse said. "This one just came out of the shop when the stock market crashed. It sat unsold for several months. They made us very good deal. Would you like to see the inside?"

Without a word, Q walked forward to the nose of the jet and up the door on the left side. He turned and noticed the new equipment neatly arranged along the hangar wall: a tug, a ground power unit, special tools in one corner, and then the ZPU-4 parked in the very back. Q laughed sadly.

"Is this the gun that shot us down?"

"Yes, it is," Jesse said after an uncomfortable pause. They stood and looked at it for several seconds before Q mounted the stairs and turned into the cockpit.

Everything was like new, the instrumentation, the Flight Management Systems, the seats, everything. A small ground air conditioner blew cold air into the cockpit through a long hose.

"You know, I've never flown one of these," Q said.

"We will run the checklists today so that you can learn all of the switches. Tomorrow or the next day we fly the plane."

"When was the last time this plane flew?"

"I flew it over with two Americans just after we bought it. We have had it here for over a month seeking another pilot. No one seems to want to move over here," Jesse said.

"So much the better for me."

"I have your Congolese license and your new Congolese passport. I keep them safe while we fly."

Q chuckled through his nose.

"Of course. You've thought of everything." While still smiling, a dark thought coursed across his mind. Of course, you'll keep them safe. Less chance I'll escape if you hold my documents. I feel naked without any way to prove who I am.

*****

After crossing the Congo River, they slept by the side of the road with Brett and Zach taking turns at keeping watch. Just after dawn Zach stopped a southwest bound truck, and paid him to let them ride in the back. After four horrible, bumpy hours Brett, Bixby, Zack arrived at a little mining town called Luiza.

The driver let them off at the largest, and only, hotel in town. Brett sent Zach in to get them a room. He rented the biggest room they had and paid cash in advance for three days. The room had a kitchen, opened to the courtyard, and had another entrance on the street side. As the diamond mining boomed during the last six years, the hotel had grown, adding a new building every two years. The lobby had the oldest rooms adjoining the main hall. Three L-shaped outbuildings clustered around a large central courtyard. Their room was in the corner of the newest building with tile floors and air conditioning.

No one took notice of the rifles and packs the men carried, their torn and filthy clothes, or that they had not bathed in three days. Several other dirty men roamed the streets armed with AK-47's.

"The first thing we have to do is treat your feet, young man," Brett said to Bixby.

"Take these two pills. You'll be in dream land while I fix you up." Too tired to talk, Bixby picked up a bottle of water, and popped the pills in his mouth.

"Go ahead. Drink all that water. You're dehydrated. Good. Now, Zach, I need you to find a drug store. Buy me two liters of hydrogen peroxide, two big rolls of gauze bandage material, and three bars of chocolate."

"Chocolate?"

"I'm hungry."

Brett went into the bathroom to wash his hands and face with the tiny soap bar. No hot water. By the time he got back, Bixby was asleep on the bed, lying on his back, hands at his side. This bed is not a great operating table, but it's better than working with him on the ground, Brett thought.

He pulled out his medic bag, and laid out the items that he thought he would need in a neat row next to Bixby's feet. Scissors to cut away the boots and socks, utility knife to strip any skin stuck to the boots, and tape to close any big tears in the balls of the feet. Like always, Brett started a conversing with himself as he slipped into the role of a combat medic.

"I wish I had my big bag, but it was just too heavy. This bug-out bag will have to do. At least we have a drug store around and running water to wash with. Much better than Iraq." Brett looked at Bixby's jungle boots. Dried blood showed through all of the ventilation holes.

"I'll have to cut these off, my man. But don't worry. It won't permanently damage your feet." He looked up at Bixby's face. The combination of drug and fatigue made him appear almost dead. Only the steady, light snore indicated the presence of life.

Brett sank to his knees, picked up his largest pair of scissors, and went to work on the boots. First he cut the laces, spreading out the tops, and then he cut out the tongue of the right boot. The scissors were not cutting the leather, so he pulled out his folding knife. Slowly and methodically he cut back the leather and nylon so as not to damage the foot.

"Good news, Bixby. The blood hasn't come up very far. Means you haven't torn up your feet too bad," Brett said, knowing that Bixby couldn't hear him.

Zach came back in carrying a small plastic bag and three large cloth bags. "Got what you asked for, and I stopped by a store and got us some food and bottled water."

"You are a genius, Zach." Brett started digging in the bag from the pharmacy and got out his three items. He opened a chocolate bar and took a big bite.

"Wow, what happened to him?"

"I gave him two Zanaflex muscle relaxants. Not an optimum anesthetic, but coupled with his exhaustion, they put him down hard. I don't think he'll feel a thing. Bring that trash can over here, will you?"

Together they worked on cutting off the boots, using the hydrogen peroxide to loosen the dried blood. By propping his feet over the trash can, they kept most of the blood off of the sheets. Putting a towel over the wet spot at the foot of the bed, they wrapped the feet in gauze.

"You shower first while I clean up," Brett said. "And there's no hot water." Zach nodded and moved zombie-like to shower. Brett cleaned his medical tools in the sink, running the last of the hydrogen peroxide over them, and placed them back in his bag. He checked his rifle, and laid it by the bed.

Zack left the water running, and Brett showered quickly, hoping that he would stay awake until he finished. He smiled as he remembered returning to Burkina Faso from a three day patrol in Mali when he had fallen asleep in the shower, only waking when the hot water ran out. Brett dried off, checked the locks and crawled into bed beside Zach.

Brett woke up to the groans and curses of Bixby Wilson and the smell of coffee. The birds squawking in the top of the big mango tree in the courtyard and the sun pouring into the kitchen window made Brett smile. We are alive and well, he thought. Guilt crashed into him as he thought of his friend Mick missing in action. Survivor's guilt. He knew it well.

"What time is it?"

"Around seven. We slept from four in the afternoon until now. I guess we needed some rest," Zach said. He turned back to the stove, and Brett could see and smell that Zach was preparing a big breakfast for them all. Fresh French bread, ham and eggs frying, and fruit laid out in an orderly fashion told Brett that somewhere, Zach had been trained as a cook.

"And how are you doing, my man?" Brett asked Bixby as he came out of the bathroom, groaning with every step.

"Every inch of my body is sore, and my feet are killing me!"

"We'll get you a little something for the pain, and you'll feel better after breakfast." Brett got up and picked up his pants. Wrinkling his nose at the smell, he put them on.

"We've got to get some new clothes today, boys. How much money have we got left?"

Zach thought for just a minute, and then answered, "After renting the boat and paying the truck driver, then renting this room; around a hundred thousand francs. That's a little more than two fifty US."

"That will last us for a few days, but we need new clothes and travel money. Zach, can we get some money from your ATM card? We don't dare use ours. I'll pay you back personally."

"Not a problem. You guys have always paid my expense reports."

"Good. We go shopping today. Bixby! After breakfast you will shower, for you stink."

"I hurt too bad to shower."

"Cut the whine, my man. I'll give you some Tylenol-3. This stuff has codeine and you'll feel much better in just a few." Brett dug in his kit for the drug, and produced two long pills.

Zach, already having set the table, slid the eggs out of the skillet onto each plate, along with a small piece of ham.

"Let's eat." They sat and devoured the breakfast.

"Zach, when did you get all of this food?" Bixby asked.

"The market is just down the street. I woke up first and went shopping 'cause I was hungry."

"Where did you learn to cook? I mean everything came out together, and looks and smells great." Brett asked between slurps of black coffee.

"My folks had a restaurant in Kinshasa and I grew up cooking. I hated it."

"Well, you sure do it well."

Twenty minutes later no food remained. Brett pointed at Bixby, and then pointed at the bathroom. He could tell that the Tylenol and the food had blunted Bixby's pain. Still the man winced, rained out curses when he got up, and moved toward the bathroom.

"There's no clean towels!" Bixby cried from inside the bathroom.

"Get in the shower, you wuss! We're tired of smelling your stink!" Brett winked at Zach who was cleaning up the kitchen. "Zach, that breakfast was wonderful. Thank you," Brett said in French.

"My pleasure," Zach said, his smile saying how much it meant to him to be noticed.

Brett went to the bed, and like any good soldier, used the spare few minutes to wipe down his weapon and check his ammo. When Bixby came out Brett changed the dressings on his feet, pleased that there was no sign of infection.

"Now men we need to have a planning meeting before we send Zach to shop for clean clothes." Brett said. They gathered around the table with fresh cups of coffee.

"My thought is that N'dalu is probably not looking for us, but there is no reason to take that chance. Therefore, we should continue on to Angola," Brett said.

"Don't you think that we should get a message out to our people that we're OK?" Bixby asked.

"No. We don't know who is being paid by N'dalu. We'll stay inside as much as we can. No phone calls, no email. Zach is not as high profile as we are, so he'll buy our new clothes and food. I know that your family is worried, but we can't take a chance until we get out of N'dalu's area."

"How are we going to get to Angola? I can't walk."

"Zach will check on bus service. If no bus, then we may have to hire a car, or pay a truck driver to ride. No airlines into this little place. Let's see, this must be Wednesday. I want to watch those feet and make sure there's no infection. Also, things should cool down in a couple of days. We should be ready to move out by Saturday."

Everyone nodded.

*****

Dolph Zimmerhanzel waited in his cell. Today would be his second session with Angelica N'dalu, the Princess of Matai. He smiled at his small joke. But in the last few days, while wrestling with the dilemma of her marriage, he realized that in a way he was counseling a princess, and that perhaps the rules were somewhat different. A normal woman could divorce her husband. But a divorce meant N'dalu would be humiliated in front of his subjects. He might find it easier to have Angelica killed. Marriage counseling was devilishly hard even without the political considerations. He felt like he was guiding a medieval queen instead of a modern wife. I must help her escape. There is no other way.

Refreshed from his pre-dawn shower and sporting the new clothes Seko Seki M'Bai gave him, Dolph felt ready to meet with Angelica. He wished he could get a haircut. Instead, his hair was pulled back into a ponytail and tied with a string. Would she bring Maura?

What can I say to her? I still have misgivings about how to counsel this princess. My best course is to let her tell me her story. She must come to her own decision. My duty to her is to warn her of the consequences of her decision whatever that decision may be. He laughed a little. She is probably more aware of those consequences than I am.

The knocker on the outer door thudded against ancient wood. A hollow echo ran up and down the halls. Dolph glimpsed Seko hurrying across the big courtyard to open the door for Angelica.

The muttered female voices floated in and his anticipation rose. Maura was with her! His palms grew damp. They rounded the corner, laughing with Seko Seki. The captain of the guard adored Angelica. Yes, just like a princess. She wore a form fitted antique-white long dress, very light weight because of the heat. Maura wore an African dress with a matching blouse made of thin dark blue cloth with big red flowers printed on it. Both dresses did nothing to hide their curves.

Dolph's cell door was already unlocked, and as they came in Seko turned to leave. Dolph was surprised by Angelica drawing close, grasping his left shoulder, and offering her cheek for him to kiss. He could smell her light perfume. Maura was next, with an unreadable smile, but dancing eyes. She too came close for a kiss, but Dolph reached out and put his hand in the small of her back and pulled her close to peck her cheek. He could feel her breasts against his chest, and his mind fogged with desire.

They sat at the table with the women on one side, and Dolph on the other.

"I have so many things to tell you," Angelica said. Dolph put up his hand and she stopped mid sentence.

"Do you speak English?" Dolph said. He spoke so that they both had to lean forward to hear him. They both nodded.

"Good. I have been thinking about your situation, and it could be dangerous for you. The things that you tell me could mean danger for you."

"Yes, it is as you say," Angelica answered in the same low voice. Maura stood up and went to the door, keeping watch to see that no one slinked up to the door to listen.

"Last time, I fear that we talked too openly and we may have been heard. They might have microphones or someone listening. You are in a very dangerous position with N'dalu. If he ever suspects that you might leave him, I don't think that he could take the humiliation. He could do something to hurt you or even kill you."

"Yes, I have thought of that. But our last talk cleared my mind. I have thought about it, and prayed a lot. I cannot stay. I cannot live with a man like him. I've been happier these last two days knowing that there would be some end to my nightmare."

"Does N'dalu suspect anything?"

"No, I told him that I was much clearer after talking with you. That you told me to respect my husband. I have not scolded him or argued with him. One night he approached me to make love to me, but I said that it was too early for that. He hurt me last time, and I told him that he needed to give me a little time to regain my trust. He said that he understood and he left." Tears started down her cheeks.

"He never apologized for beating me." She slowly lowered her head into her hands and shook as she wept silently. Maura came over and put her hand on Angelica's back and rubbed it with small circles.

Dolph sat still, knowing that anything he said would be wrong. In a minute she sat up, pulled out a tissue and dabbed her face. Maura returned to her post at the door.

"I'm all right. Did you know that he is using the bodyguards for his sexual release?" Dolph could understand how those women would be tempting to a man who had such power. His mind's eye saw Desiree glide across the room in her red dress with the plunging neckline.

"They are not happy, but they fear him. They talk with Maura. Those women believed that they were being promoted from the ranks because of their performance and their devotion. Now they feel like whores. But Francois threatened them all so they sleep with him when required." She reached out and grabbed Dolph's hand with such speed and strength that he was startled.

"I must get out of Matai, or I will die trying," she said with steel in her eyes.

"Have you contacted your parents in Kinshasa?"

"Francoise took away my cell phone and cut off my email months ago. I can still get emails, but the servers will not let anything go out."

"Interesting. Your parents must be sick with worry. Have you seen or heard from Camilo Quartalino?" Her face brightened.

"Yes, he is flying our new jet. I have not been able to talk with him, but Maura has checked with his body guard under the guise of perhaps becoming his girl friend." She laughed a little.

"He is doing well and putting his efforts into flying and getting back into shape. He spends lots of time at the hotel gym."

"Is he drinking too much?"

"None at all, the girls say. And he has politely refused the prostitutes that my husband has sent him. I am so proud of him."

"Me too."

"I will see him tomorrow. I am accompanying my husband to a UN sponsored meeting in Goma. We are going in our jet!" She looked for a moment like a precious little girl. Then the skepticism flowed over her face.

"The UN has these meetings every six or seven months to work out how to get everyone to give back the mines to the Congolese government. It is so stupid to think that the Rwandans, the Zims, and the Angolans, not to mention the freelancers, would give up their riches just because the UN asks them nicely. But we all go and agree to whatever, and then everyone goes back to raping the country and fighting amongst themselves.

"Francois has never agreed to go; before he always sent emissaries. But now that he sees himself as the future president of Congo, he will go to this one. I think that he wants the publicity. He sees it as a way to get into the public eye. But at least I will get to see Q." Dolph smiled and tried to think of something intelligent to say, but his eyes kept drifting over to Maura.

"She is beautiful, isn't she?" Angelica said. "She likes you too." Dolph leaned forward and took her hand.

"Angelica, you must be careful. We can get out of here if we are patient."

"Yes, I know that you are right."

They talked of weather and news, Angelica filling Dolph in on the world events of the last two years. They talked of childhoods in Texas and Kinshasa, and dreams of what it would be like when they escaped. Too soon, Seko Seki was at the door. Both women hugged Dolph and thanked him for the advice.

As Seko followed the women out, he turned around and Dolph saw a look of puzzlement on his face.

I wonder if he has been listening, Dolph thought. I'll talk with him about it tomorrow. Perhaps he will tell me something. If he has been listening, it's plain that he hasn't told N'dalu, or the women wouldn't have come the second time.

*****

"Gear down, before landing checklist," Q said. This was the first and only training flight he would get before taking N'dalu and Angelica to Goma tomorrow. He was flying in the left seat and for the last ninety minutes, Jesse had been putting him through steep turns, simulated emergencies, slow flight and now three landings.

This plane flies great, Q thought as he eased the thrust levers back a quarter inch to maintain his reference speed for this last approach. No wonder Falcon has such loyal customers. What an easy transition from the commuter jets I've been flying.

For the last two days Jesse M'bota had taught him about the Falcon 20. Long classroom sessions looking at the training manual together, mixed with cockpit drills using the normal and emergency checklists had given Q a good understanding of the aircraft systems and the confidence to fly it on a trip with Jesse. Jesse had a good knowledge of the aircraft and it would be easy to fly as his co-pilot.

"Three green," Jesse pointed at the gear down indicator light.

"Confirm."

"Landing checklist complete. You are ref plus ten. Looks good," Jesse said.

Q eased the thrust levers to idle and the old jet settled nicely onto the runway. He lifted the reverser levers and saw the lights indicating that the clamshells had swung out venting the jet exhaust toward the front. With light braking, they easily slowed to taxi speed well before the end of the asphalt. Q swung the jet around to back-taxi to the ramp as Jesse cleaned up the cockpit, raising the flaps, resetting the trim, turning off the pitot heats and landing lights.

After shutting down, Jesse turned to Q. "You fly the aircraft very well. N'dalu made a good choice with you." They opened the door to see the three mechs lined up outside like in the military.

"Any squawks?" Danny Vasicek asked, holding a clipboard. He must be lead maintenance tech, Q thought. These are good guys.

"No, everything worked perfect," Jesse said. Two mechanics hustled to hook up the tug and while Danny Vasicek walked around the aircraft searching for leaks, torn tires, bird strikes or any other damage that may have occurred during flight.

"So you are gonna fly left seat with N'dalu tomorrow, right?" Camilo asked as they watched the maintenance crew push the jet back into the hangar.

"Oh, no. You will fly captain. I have several hours in the aircraft, but only as co-pilot. In the air force I flew co-pilot on the president's Gulfstream," he said proudly. Then he looked down at his shoes and held his hands behind his back. "However, I could never pass the captain checkride, so we always had an American captain. The president sent me to Flight Safety in France, but I did not qualify. I was released from the air force last year." He straightened and looked again at Q.

"I am an excellent administrator and a good first officer, but I am not a captain."

"Jesse, we will train you to be captain. But if you wish, I'll fly left seat tomorrow." Jesse beamed, and Q knew that he had hit upon Jesse's secret yearning.

"Your flight suit should be in your room when we get back. You will wear it tomorrow. N'dalu is delighted to be showing the world that he has an all black flight crew. You will please speak French to everyone and tell them that you are Congolese. And there will be armed guards on board. You must be good and not try to escape," Jesse said, shaking a finger at Camilo.

"Don't worry about that."

*****

Thursday Morning

Ashunta Rodriguez pulled down the dark blue sports coat to make the collar even around his neck. The tie choked him. He hated wearing a coat and tie; a battle uniform would have been much better. But he was happy with his new job as Director of Security for the Goma International Airport.

The city was still trying to recover from the 2002 eruption of the Mount Nyiragongo. As if the war and invasion by the Rwandans were not enough, the volcano spit out a river of lava that flowed across part of the airport, then through the center of town, and onward into Lake Kiva. The news services said that 4,200 died, but Ashunta believed that the count was low.

When the lava cooled, the northern third of the runway lay beneath ten feet of rock, effectively cutting off international flights into the shortened runway. After eight years of begging, three aid agencies banded together to restore the runway. They would start blasting next week and hoped to restore full length of the runway by June.

He walked out of his air conditioned office, through the terminal, then out to a shade tree on the edge of the customs ramp. Was it only a few days ago that he was almost killed as a mercenary soldier?

After the failed battle for Matai, Ashunta was one of only a few to escape into stolen boats and cross the Congo River. He ditched his rifle and ammo on the far side. After changing into the civilian shirt he kept in a vacuum packed bag, he hopped a bus, and by eleven o'clock the next morning rolled into Goma.

From the pay phone in the bus terminal, he called his woman who was working at her mother's upholstery shop.

"Annette. I am in Goma." He held the receiver away from his ear as she squealed with delight.

"Yes, it was bad. But I'm alive. I'll be home in an hour or so." He tried to interrupt and finally got to talk.

"No, you just stay at work. I know where you keep the key. Anyway, I need to sleep before I see you." They laughed.

"Yes, my love. Don't mention to anyone that I am back yet. See you this evening. Kisses."

Next he called his CIA contact in Goma, to make sure that he got his last paycheck. This month's pay was more money than he normally made in a year, and if the Americans thought that he was dead, they obviously would not wire any money. Rodriquez knew that he would have to get debriefed, but it was the only way that he would be paid. Besides, it would be better to let his old bosses know that he was alive than for them to find out weeks or months later. Who knows, they might assume that since he didn't check in, he must have been working for N'dalu, and that he shared some of the blame for the disaster.

"American Consulate. Commercial Attaché," the secretary answered.

"Billy Wright, please. This is Ashunta Rodriguez."

"Just a minute Mister Rodriguez." A pause, then a click.

"Wow, it's good to hear from you, my friend." Billy's French was terrible, so much so that it caused Ashunta to wince in pain when he heard the accent. "Can I buy you a drink tonight?"

"No, I have plans for tonight. But I'll be in town for a while. How about breakfast tomorrow?"

"Sounds good. See you then." Ashunta hung up the phone with a smile on his face. Whenever the two met, there were two places and two times. That way no one had to mention any information over a possibly compromised telephone line. Billy would meet him at Ebele's Restaurant at 0530.

It was good to be home. He walked out of the bus terminal and headed south, the opposite direction from Annett's house. He turned into a narrow alley lined with tiny shops. After two blocks, he paused to check something in his backpack, then turned abruptly and started walking quickly the opposite way. He searched every face that went by, looking for anyone who might be following him.

He entered the bus terminal again and stood in line at one of the booths to buy some chewing gum. Just before he got to the front of the line he moved rapidly toward the south door watching for any reaction. Now that he was pretty sure that he had no tail, he turned north toward Annett's house. Still he checked behind him at irregular intervals until he hailed a motorcycle taxi. Giving the rider four hundred francs, he got on behind, and rode to his lover's little white stucco house.

The next morning he left Annette's house before dawn. He smiled as he remembered her pleading for him to stay and make love to her again.

"No, my love. I have to go to work. I'll see you tonight." He leaned over and kissed her forehead, and he felt his way out of the darkened bedroom.

He trotted down the alley, stopped at the street to see if anyone else was out this morning, then crossed into the shadow of a high wall. Working his way south, he found the narrow opening that he sought.

The grey morning light did not reach this far down into the tiny, dirty alley, so Ashunta had to use his small flashlight to weave between the garbage cans and find the back door to the restaurant. He pushed open the door and slid unnoticed into the warm kitchen.

At 0525, with the restaurant opening in five minutes, the two cooks were busy with preparations for the morning rush. The espresso machine gurgled and an automatic juicer wobbled on its stand, eating two oranges at a time and dribbling out the fresh squeezed juice at the bottom. Ashunta smelled something good in addition to the fresh bread, and while he cocked his head and tried to place the smell, the fat cook closest to him turned around.

"Oh, my love, you have returned for me!" She wiped her hands on her greasy apron, swooped over and gave him a big hug and a smacking kiss on his cheek.

"You know that I couldn't stay away from your charms, my princess," he said as he held Ebele back and looked her up and down. Her name meant "mercy", but God had showed her none for she was definitely the ugliest, fattest African woman that he had ever known. But, off and on for several years, Ashunta had eaten breakfast in this restaurant, trading sexual innuendo and playful declarations of true love with the fat owner.

"I need my normal table, my love. I am having a meeting."

"Of course, my dearest. I'll have your coffee right out."

Ashunta pushed through the flimsy aluminum double doors and took the booth closest to the kitchen. Due to the high seat backs, the other clients could not see who occupied the booth unless they wandered down the hall.

Billy Wright came in at 0535, waved at the hostess, and ambled back to the booth. He had once been a powerful man, but his muscles had all gone to fat. Dressed in the usual CIA uniform, khaki pants and a blue button down shirt, anyone who cared to notice could see that Billy was a government man. Ashunta didn't want anyone to see them together. That made this restaurant a perfect meeting place.

"Colonel Rodriguez. It is good to see you in one piece," Billy said, shaking Ashunta's hand. "I am glad to see you alive. We've heard terrible things about your unit. We need to find out what happened."

"I know. I'm available anytime."

"There's a new safe house. Here is the address. Come in the back way. Tomorrow? 0900?" Billy slid a business card across the table that advertised a tailor shop specializing in clothing repair. The address was not far from Annett's house.

Ashunta nodded.

"Now, about my pay…"

"Yes. Yes. I have that all taken care of. Right after you called I sent a message out to remind the guys that you needed to be paid. It'll be transferred at the next pay day. I think that is in about six more days. Full pay to include the days during debrief."

"Thank you," Ashunta said sincerely. He had not expected things to go this well.

"But I have something else we need you to do for us, Colonel." Of course, that is why the American agreed so quickly to pay me, Ashunta thought. Always a catch. He did not say anything, just continued to look at Billy Wright's big square head.

"The airport is going to hire a security manager. They're gonna try to start international air service again. We have a little influence on the choice, and we want you in that position. You would earn a normal salary, plus we would pay you a good bit to send us occasional reports of the comings and goings. It's an easy job."

Ashunta remained silent. He knew that Billy hated silence, and would continue to rattle on, often revealing more than he had intended.

"We can't pay what you were making as colonel. How about two thousand five hundred US per month sent to your Swiss account?" Ashunta pursed his lips.

"How about two thousand five hundred euros a month," he said as a statement, not a question.

"OK. We can do that," Billy said. Ashunta slowly nodded his head as he thought over the offer. No more combat. That is good. A regular salary. That is good. Sleeping with Annette every night. That is very good.

"Who do I need to talk to?" Ashunta asked.

"I'll arrange everything. I'll give you the details at debrief. I'd better be going. See you in the morning." Billy got up, bumping the table with his leg and sloshing Ashunta's coffee. He pressed a fat tip into the hand of the hostess, thudded into an incoming customer, and was gone. So much for being low profile.

The debrief had been fairly painless, Ashunta's recounting of the battle matching the imagery gathered by satellite and the radio and phone traffic picked up by the listening stations.

Now, two days later, he stood in the shade in his new suit, uncomfortable, hot, and worried because his first security task was this UN meeting. Lots of warring parties coming for a "peace conference", and, of course, they would all show up armed.

Zimbabwe's new leader, George Tsvangirai, had already arrived this morning. The young nephew of Morgan Tsvangirai had seized control from Mugabe through a bloody coup just last month, and showed no signs of moving out of the gold and diamond fields of southern Congo. Ashunta made notes on the weapons, uniforms, and comments of the guards. He never got close to the new president so as not to raise suspicion. But he did manage to talk with the British pilots. He got some good stuff for his report such as the pilots' impression of the social and economic conditions in the new Zimbabwe.

Francois N'dalu is due in next, he thought. Each arrival was scheduled so that none of the warring leaders would be on the ramp at the same time. One never knew what might spark a confrontation or even a gunfight if two or more heavily armed contingents jockeyed for the best parking spot or raced to be first through customs and immigration.

Ashunta heard the roar of turbine engines and looked up to see a sleek swept-wing jet fly directly overhead ninety degrees to the runway then bank steeply left to parallel Runway 01. A sweeping 180 degree turn brought the jet to a perfect final approach. Ashunta lost sight as the jet descended behind a line of trees. Three minutes later the Falcon 20 rolled up to the Number One parking spot, just vacated as the Zim's jet was towed into a hangar.

N'dalu's security team, sent up on busses yesterday, trotted out in precise formation and surrounded the jet. The airport staff unrolled a small red carpet and the cabin door lowered. A short black man in a blue flight suit descended the stairs, held out his hand and helped a gorgeous black woman step smoothly down to the red carpet.

This must be his wife, Angelica, Ashunta thought. He hummed his appreciation as he studied the cut of her white pantsuit, her flowing hair, and the striking face.

"Mmmmm...perfect," he said to no one in particular. N'dalu then came out, paused at the top of the steps, and looked over his security team. He seemed pleased. He wore a formal military uniform of subdued green without any hat. Coming down the aircraft stairs like an emperor, his precise, smooth movements shouted out his power and confidence. He took Angelica's hand and, with the senior UN representative, walked inside to customs and immigration.

She is even more beautiful than the rumors, Ashunta thought. He ambled over to the aircraft to talk with the pilots to see if he could elicit any information. As he climbed the stairs, he could see the copilot in the right seat filling out some kind of book. The captain backed up the aisle dragging a large suitcase from the baggage compartment in the aft of the plane. In the back of the cabin sat a female armed guard in a pressed combat uniform and beret.

"Oh, excuse me. Let me get out of the way," Ashunta said in French. There was a hesitation, and then the captain turned around. Mutual recognition was instantaneous. As Ashunta took in his breath to speak, Q held up his hand and cut his eyes toward the cockpit.

"I'll need to speak with the captain when you get a moment," Ashunta said, his eyes never leaving Q's. Q nodded. Colonel Ashunta Rodriguez climbed back down the stairs and walked to the rear of the aircraft where the large trees gave some shade.

Thoughts cascaded through his mind. So Quartalino made it. He must have been captured and pressed into N'dalu's army. Did anyone else get out alive? I doubt it. I must tell Billy Wright.

In a minute, Camilo came over accompanied by his copilot and the gorgeous guard with an AK47.

"I am Ashunta Rodriquez, the security manager for Goma International Airport. Could I see your papers please?"

Jesse had papers for both of them. Ashunta looked over the passports, visas, and pilot licenses.

"Everything seems to be in order. Where will you be staying tonight?"

"The Hotel Ihusi," Jesse answered.

"Good hotel. Be wise, men. There are many loose women in that part of town, and many thieves. I advise you to stay indoors after 2200 hours." Ashunta was hoping for some sign from Q, but he kept his eyes lowered the whole time, letting Jesse talk.

"Have a safe stay in Goma, friends. I will see you tomorrow." Ashunta watched them walk away. He reached for his cell phone. No time to wait for a written report; Billy Wright needed to know now that Camilo Quartalino was alive and in N'dalu's employ.

Chapter 9

Angelica opened her bag and put her clothes in the closet and drawers. Even though she was only sleeping in the hotel one night, she refused to live out of a suitcase.

"I am so glad that my pig husband is staying in his own room," she muttered, throwing the last of her underwear in the drawer and slamming it shut.

"I don't even have a servant here," she said aloud. "No room for Maura, he said. Yet he made a way to bring his whores up here! Does he think that I don't know about those two women he sent up on the bus? Has he no respect for me? Here we are at a huge international conference, and he has two—two!—women for his amusement. The international press will find out and I'll be a joke among the leaders of Africa. If I could, I would claw his eyes out." She gritted her teeth and felt her nails dig into her palms. "Someday I will. For humiliating me, oooh, I swear I'll see him suffer."

Guilt swooped in over her like a dark cloud. I am no better than he if I keep thinking these things. Christ said forgive, but it is so hard. How can a woman forgive her man after he has betrayed her, beat her? We are supposed to be as one flesh. The husband should love his wife as his own body. She felt the hot tears well up in her eyes.

Why did I ever marry him? Why? My father was so right. He warned me. Oh, did he warn me. But Francois was so handsome, so confident, so rich. It was the power that snared me. I wanted the power to change the world for the better. Yes, I wanted to be the wife of the next president, too. Now look where it has gotten me. I am just a prisoner in a golden cage.

She went to the window, and from her tenth floor room, she could see Lake Kivu in the distance. Perched on the side of the huge lake like a fisherman sitting beside a pond, the city depended on the lake for everything, transportation, food, and water. She marveled at the sky-blue water reflecting a brilliant white thunderhead, and beyond, a lush green carpet of forests and farms. What a gorgeous country, and look what we have done with it. Tears rolled down her cheeks as she cried in silence for her country and even more for herself. She tried to think of something positive.

At least I got to see Camilo. He looks so good, even in that ridiculous flight suit that Francois makes them wear. Why didn't Francois ask me about colors? That blue is hideous. They need to be dressed in nice black pants, white shirts, and ties. And he can fly that airplane. So smooth and confident. Thinking of Camilo made her stomach flip and her face feel warm. Humming a tune from "The Fiddler on the Roof" she turned back to her unpacking.

Only her toiletries remained. She took out a large zippered pouch, walked into the bathroom, and started to lay out her razor, shampoo, and moisturizer. Near the bottom of the bag she felt a firm piece of folded paper. She picked up the bag and peered inside. On the tightly folded sheet of heavy stationery she recognized the logo of the Intercontinental Hotel in Matai.

A note from Camilo! How smart of him to stash this where only I would find it. Her hands shook so that she had to steady them on the counter to read the note.

> Ah, my love,
>
> It seems like years since seeing your lovely face and hearing your sexy voice. I could find no other way to communicate with you. I am still committed to escape when the time is right, and I will not leave you behind. My love for you continues to grow, even when we are apart. Do not lose hope or put

yourself in any danger. I am fine. This is a good flying job.

Be patient. We will get out. Not to worry.

Kissing you in my dreams,

Q

PS: Destroy this note now. Tear it to small pieces and flush it down the toilet. If you can, leave a blank piece of paper in the same bag. Then I will know that you still love me and miss me.

Relief and joy swept Angelica into a whirl around the room as she crushed his note against her breasts. She read the note again, then started to tear it but stopped. One more time, I'm going to read it one more time. She tried to memorize each word and interpret each pen stroke. Only then she ripped the note into tiny pieces. Half the pieces went down with the first flush. Half the pieces went down with the second flush. Just to be sure, she flushed again.

Happy now, she pulled out her gym outfit. She would go to the hotel fitness center and work out. I need to look good the next time that Camilo sees me.

*****

"Fools! I am surrounded by fools. We leave here immediately," he yelled at Angelica. The elevator doors opened and they stepped out, Angelica turning left toward her room, and N'dalu turning right. "Be ready in thirty minutes."

"Yes my dear," she said sweetly. Walking into her room and shutting the door, she allowed herself to smile while she replayed the opening press conference in her mind.

Francois had been maneuvered by a series of questions from a BBC correspondent into admitting that he occupied Matai and the adjoining mines without permission from the Congolese or the sanction of the international community. There had been issues raised about torture, pollution, and expropriation of private property. As N'dalu answered each question he dug himself in deeper and deeper. Finally, N'dalu fled from the stage, unable to stand the barrage of questions.

Yes, it had been lovely seeing Francois squirm up there on the podium, unable to escape the traps laid by the international press, Angelica thought. Now the mighty Francois N'dalu was going home after being here only four hours with RCD's status lower than a prostitute's credit rating. But would this make him act better or more paranoid? Definitely more paranoid. I may be in even more danger if he decides to completely ignore international conventions.

Practical matters first. I must put that paper in my makeup bag. She opened drawer after drawer looking for some hotel stationery. There must be some paper in this room. What if I can't find any paper? He'll think that I rejected his note. He might think that I've changed my mind. In a minor panic, she started to tear around the room.

"Wait. I've got to settle down. Take deep breaths," she said aloud. "They must have some writing paper in here." Working systematically around the room, checking every shelf and drawer, she came to the entertainment center. Then she noticed a notebook on a shelf above the television. Opening the notebook she found hotel propaganda, a menu for room service, and a phone directory. Finally, she found some blank paper in the back pocket. She took out a sheet and folded it exactly like the one she had torn up. Fighting back the desire to write down her love for Camilo, she put the paper in the bottom of her kit and piled her makeup on top.

Am I being a fool hoping for a stranger to rescue me? What do I know of this man, Camilo Quartalino? What other choice do I have? Yet I know from the short time with him that he can take care of me. He is not especially handsome. He is not rich or powerful. What is it that I see in him? He is confident, almost arrogant. But he has none of the hardness like Francois. He is happy where Francois is angry. Thinking of the bald bullet shaped head with the big smile, she hugged herself. Now, I must pack.

*****

Camilo Quartalino sat up from his nap instantly awake. His guard picked up the room phone on the third ring. After grunting into the phone twice, the guard said, "You must be ready to leave in thirty minutes. General N'dalu has decided to return to Matai."

"Great." While pulling on his boots, Q wondered what had happened, but a career of answering the bell left him with no real curiosity about the circumstances of the change. Jesse would take care of the flight plan and fees. Camilo picked up his still packed bag, adjusted his now-rumpled flight suit while he checked himself in the mirror, and smiled at his guard.

"Let's go."

Arriving at the aircraft, Q started to make ready for the departure. First, he started the auxiliary power unit so that the air conditioner could cool the cabin. He then ordered fuel and bought a bag of ice for the onboard drinks. While he walked around the plane and checked it for any damage or leaks, he hoped to run into Ashunta again. Now that I'm alone, I can talk with him without raising any questions. Surely he'll tell someone that I'm still alive. Hope swelled inside his head.

Thirty minutes later N'dalu came out of the terminal striding toward the aircraft, his face a mask of rage. Jesse scrambled behind. Even further back, Angelica and two baggage handlers brought the luggage. Q rushed forward and took N'dalu's bag first. While the passengers waited outside, he threw the first bag up the stairs and, using its rollers, zipped it down the aisle to the rear baggage compartment.

The second larger, heavier bag belonged to Angelica. He lugged it up the stairs, and since it was too wide to roll down the aisle, he dragged it sideways and stashed it behind the rear restroom. This gave him a few seconds out of sight. He reached into the bag and found the makeup kit on top. Zipping it open, he dug around. Why do women always pack so much? What do they do with all this crap? I'm sure she will have a paper there. Nothing. One more time through. Go all the way to the bottom. There it is. He eased the hard white square into his chest pocket and zipped the zipper.

After an uneventful flight, Camilo greased the landing at Matai. When they parked N'dalu was first to the door. Opening it, he stormed down the stairs, pushed the driver away from his Land Cruiser, and got in.

"Where are the keys?" He screamed out curses until the driver managed to dig them out of his pocket. N'dalu sped off, squealing tires and spitting gravel. Angelica, the guard, and the baggage were left stranded.

"What was that all about, my Lady?" Jesse asked Angelica.

"The first press conference went very poorly. You can probably see it on CNN International at the hotel this evening. The General thought it better to come home." She tried, but could not keep a smile off of her face.

"Yes, my lady." Jesse looked away to cover his embarrassment. "You can use our truck, and the driver will bring it back. We will then deliver your luggage."

"You are more than gracious, Colonel M'bota. Thank you." She turned to get into the waiting Toyota. Only a glance toward Q. He quickly moved in front of Jesse and held the right hand door open. As she slid into the seat, she smiled up at Q. Her white skirt rode up her thigh, contrasting with the perfect milk chocolate colored skin. Camilo kept his face closed and only nodded, since Jesse could still see his face. As she drove away, Q fingered the folded paper in his pocket.

*****

As part of his job, Chu Lee watched CNN International in English. The coverage of the UN peace meeting in Goma made the lead story, and Lee was proud that he had the foresight to record all of it on the DVR for his boss's viewing and later transcription into Chinese.

This will not be good, he thought. The press conference had been horrible, but then the damage multiplied when N'dalu ran from the meeting like a guilty criminal. All of the other parties piled on as well as the international media. The spin came out that there was only one party who refused to negotiate: N'dalu and the RCD. This unrepentant dictator invaded the city, expropriated private property, and stole the mineral wealth of the Congo.

Worse, they enumerated N'dalu's "crimes against humanity": slavery, torture, and even more delicious for the news media, destroying the rain forest and polluting the Congo River. Not that the Zims, Rwandans, Angolans were any less guilty of these same crimes, but by directing the press at N'dalu, they could get the spotlight off of themselves.

And where did N'dalu get that jet? We did not authorize a private aircraft for him, Chu thought. General Wu will not be pleased. Chu rehearsed in his mind what he would say over the cell phone, knowing that the call would be monitored by at least three other governments and two oil companies. On the fourth ring, the General picked up his cell phone.

"Yes, what is it, Chu?" Lee heard the annoyance in his leader's voice and the low roar of the cocktail party in the background.

"Sir, we have a very big problem with Elder Four," Chu Lee said in English.

"I am busy right now," Wu said quietly, almost spitting into the phone.

"Sir, I suggest that you return here immediately."

"You had better be correct." The growled threat hit Chu Lee in the back of his knees, and he had to sit before pressing the "END" button on his cell phone. Even as his dread bent him over in the chair, he knew that he had done the right thing.

This windowless room, the endless hours listening to English and French telephone traffic, and now his wife living openly with a younger man. Shaking his head side to side, he said aloud, "I must get out of here. I must escape. If I stay here, I'll surely go insane."

But one item caused a smile to brighten his face. Bixby and Descoteaux were safe in a hotel in Luiza.

When the report came in Wednesday that Zacheus Girard's ATM card was being used in Luiza, Chu automatically listed the item in his log. The Chinese paid watchers at the Kinshasa airport and had pictures and a dossier on Zach, and knew that he was an employee of the American CIA. It was a reasonable assumption that he was still with the two Americans and they all were living off of Zach's credit card.

During the last month, Chu had become very familiar with Brett Descoteaux's dossier. The handsome American kept a lovely wife in Maine, volunteered during his off time, and was a highly decorated combat medic. It would be a shame to let N'dalu find him.

Yet N'dalu pressed him every few hours for information about the missing American advisors. Just hours after finding out Descoteaux's location, Chu found himself lying over the sat phone to N'dalu about their whereabouts.

"I have reports that they have been seen in Katanga," Chu said, delighting in the lie. Somehow, he felt as if this were a blow to both his boss who would not let him go on leave, and N'dalu who always spoke to him like he was worse than a slave.

Still chuckling over his small victory, Chu busied himself with the transcription of N'dalu's news conference for the files even though his boss spoke French and English fluently. He watched the interview again while another television broadcast the reactions on BBC and Africa Now, Congo's national news station.

Chu interacted with few Westerners and did not realize that his ability to watch three televisions and monitor phone calls while transcribing a conversation into Chinese was a rare and valuable talent. And so, he labored on in his personal prison, only smiling when he saw once again the multiple gaffes and pomposity of Francois N'dalu during the endless loops on the different news channels. Within an hour, General Wu pushed through the door, wobbling a little from the evening's cocktails.

"What is so important that you called me during the German ambassador's birthday party?"

"Sir, you need to sit and watch this." Chu Lee had the interview queued up and pressed play. The interview came up on the center and largest screen. As the press conference proceeded, the General started to curse and point at the television.

"He has no ability with the press. No one has taught him to deflect a direct question, to remain on his talking points. A thirty-one year old standing before the cameras. Just a boy. I'm a fool for not giving him a press secretary." He cursed in French, then Chinese. Sitting back in the chair, the General flicked his right hand at Chu, signaling to stop the recording. The central screen went blank, but N'dalu still spoke on several other TV sets.

"It is over, Chu. We cannot afford to be linked with N'dalu. The propaganda damage could be greater than I wish to imagine. How much tantalum have we?"

Chu picked up the production printout, glad that he had thought to have it ready for this meeting. He started to read the figures aloud, but General Wu just grunted and held out his hand. Chu Lee passed the papers over.

He looks so old and tired tonight. How old is he? Chu wondered. Perhaps sixty-five. He won't last too much longer if he keeps on drinking like this. General Wu has been working this project for three years now without a break, and now it is starting to show. Chu felt pity for the General. And for the thousandth time he wondered why such a high official would be in charge of a backwater operation like this one.

"It will have to do. We will just have to buy the rest of our tantalum on the open market from now on." The General passed the papers back to Chu. "It has been a good run, Captain Chu," said the General with a small smile, speaking Chu's rank for the first time in months.

Chu sensed a drunken mellowness in the General and pressed in, seeking the reason for this messy operation.

"Well, we have enough tantalum for our electronics industry for several months. A large advantage over our commercial competitors," Chu said with a big smile.

"No, Captain Chu. This tantalum is not for our electronics." General Wu looked over at Chu with delight in his eye. "One of our engine manufacturers has found a way to friction weld a coat of tantalum alloy on the interior parts of jet engines. This allows our aircraft, tanks, ships—anything with a turbine engine—to run at higher temperatures without damaging the engines. Higher temps, higher power. No, the tantalum is a strategic advantage in our military buildup against India."

The whole operation opened up to Chu Lee as his nimble mind put it all together. The recruitment of N'dalu, the equipment, arms, and intel. Such an investment, but such a reward!

They both sat in silence, staring at the repeat of N'dalu's stupid assertions that he was the rightful ruler of southeastern Congo. His handsome face splashed across three different television screens.

"No one elected me," N'dalu raged. "I am the born leader who will bring my people to a better future without the crutch of religion. No more witchdoctors, no more priests, no more missionaries. We will be an example of logic and reason to the rest of the world."

A gorgeous reporterette stood, shouting out her question. "But, General N'dalu, no one in your district has any freedom to come and go as they please. There is no free press, no right to a trial. Reports come out of your district that there is widespread use of torture…"

"I want to speak to that," N'dalu said, pointing his finger at the camera. "People need a strong ruler to guide them. I am that man. I am like a father to my subjects. I know what my people need. Sometimes a people must be disciplined. Sometimes a society must be cleansed."

"Turn it off. I cannot bear to watch this fool. How could we place such an idiot in power? Why did I think it was a good idea to let him attend that peace conference?" General Wu bent forward in his chair and put his head in his hands. He looked at the floor for a long time. "Put Senior Four in effect," he said.

"But, sir, we have…"

"I said, 'Put Senior Four in effect,'" the General stated slowly, rising from his chair and straightening his expensive tropical suit. "Now, I must get back to the Ambassador's party."

*****

Bixby Wilson cursed and hobbled around the room. "We've got to contact somebody to let them know that we are alive." The supper dishes sat drying in the plastic rack on the counter. Brett pulled the tooth pick out of his mouth, and smiled, trying to mollify the older man.

"Come on, Bixby. No need to get all riled up again. Zach just fixed us a great dinner. Have some more wine."

"I don't see why we can't use the Iridium phone to call home. My wife must be worried sick."

"We don't use the sat phone because someone might be monitoring the phone call. You know that call comes in from the satellite then goes through normal phone lines to your house. You never know who's listening. You can bet N'dalu knows who we are and has phone taps on our homes. We'll just hole up here until your feet get better and we can scoot out to Angola.

"Look. We have proof that N'dalu doesn't care about us." Bixby started counting on his fingers.

"One. Zach's been out in town talkin' to the locals and hasn't heard a thing. Hell, these people haven't even heard about our attack and defeat!

"Two. Zach ain't seen no soldiers.

"Three. We're low on money.

"And four. We've got to get out of here. I'm going crazy in this hole!"

Bixby turned to Zack sitting over in the corner, and spat out another vile expletive.

"And quit cleaning that gun! You make me nervous."

"Just a habit, man. You never know when I'll need this weapon," Zack apologized.

"OK. OK, just settle down, Bixby. You know, there's no reason to curse your teammate," Brett said. I've got to do something or Bixby's going to blow a gasket, Brett thought.

"Sit down, Bixby. You act like we've been here for two months instead of two days. However, you are right, we've seen no soldiers. And we need money." Brett thought about his pretty Colombian wife back in Portland, Maine, and smiled involuntarily. She's a trooper, but it would be nice to get word to her. Zach's tapped out his bank account, and I don't dare use my US ATM card.

"You're probably right that N'dalu's not chasing us. But I'm alive today because I've never underestimated my adversary. We still won't go out, but Zach…"

"Yes sir."

"Go to the internet café and send a message to Whitehorse. Use the emergency email."

Zach waited until dark, and then slipped out into the street, walking away from the internet café. Everything looked good. No one seemed to notice him. He smiled and spoke to a pretty young woman cooking round cakes and mystery meat on a sidewalk grill. She came around to talk with him, standing very close. Taking her upper arm, and pointing to the burnt offering, he maneuvered her so that he could look over her shoulder and back down the dark sidewalk.

No one hanging back. Looks like I don't have a tail. He flirted with her for a minute and took her proffered cell number. Thanking her, he left the disappointed woman and headed back the way that he had come. He scanned all around looking for anyone paying too much attention, or not enough. Crossing the town square, he turned into the open front of the internet café.

An empty booth in the back beckoned him. The computer was dirty and ancient, the keyboard was a variation for a Spanish speaker, or maybe Portuguese, and the broken plastic chair pinched his skinny butt. For all that, he was delighted to be able to communicate again.

I'd sure like to check my email, he thought. But he pushed down the temptation and fell back to his training. Bringing up the team's emergency email account, **darkheart701@swingers.org**, he found an email from **ima36dd4u@swingers.org**. Ah, there's Whitehorse right there.

>Are you there?
>Winny

Of all the email servers available, Zach still wondered why Whitehorse still insisted on using this swinger site. Perverse sense of humor. Zach answered, trying not to put too much into the message that might alert a government monitor.

>We are looking forward to seeing you. B,B, and I are here. But we lack funds to travel.
>Butch

Zach waited for an answer. This email should buzz directly through to Whitehorse's Blackberry. Six minutes crawled by. Maybe Whitehorse doesn't have his Blackberry on.

    Call me. All my love,
                Winny

This is so gross, thought Zach.

Attached to the message was a jpeg image. Zach gritted his teeth and slowly shook his head as he opened the attachment. After a long download the picture popped up. A fiftyish English woman, nude and slightly overweight, smiled out of the picture at Zach.

"Not as bad as the last one he sent," Zach said under his breath. He called up the software service they subscribed to and hit the DECODE button. The service used a powerful encryption algorithm to encode messages into photos. One needed the keys from both sender and receiver to decode the hidden messages. The printed message appeared underneath the image.

    Zach,

    Good to hear from you. Let me know your position. We just heard that Mister Q is OK and still in Asgaard. Remain in position for possible aid in recovery.

    I will wire some operating funds into your account. And a bonus.

    Be safe, W.

Zach pushed the ENCODE button and wrote in the message block:

> We are concerned about families. Any way to notify all that we are OK? In the Amazula Hotel, Luiza. Room 131.

Less than two minutes later:

> Can do. We will contact all families. Talk with you tomorrow.
>
> W.

Zach ran a counter-surveillance route through a different part of the small downtown, ending up on the other side of the hotel than where he left. Coming around the corner into the dim light of the courtyard, he saw Brett sitting at the picnic table enjoying a cigar.

"You know, the smoke keeps the mosquitoes away," Brett said, looking lovingly at the big stogie. He had found it for sale at the drugstore. No telling how old it was.

Zach sat down across from Brett and watched the smoke curl up around the low hanging branches. Several moments passed, and then Zach briefed Brett on the message traffic and the instructions to stay. Brett nodded in silence, watching the cigar burn.

"Brett, I've had to work very hard to keep from taking Bixby outside and beating his ass," Zach said.

"Whoa, there boy! Where did that come from?"

"Who does he think he is bossing me around and cussin' me every few minutes?"

"Zach, easy. Easy." Brett put his hand on Zach's forearm. "Just take a look at him. He's never been out of an office, let alone been in a field operation. He's in horrible physical shape, doesn't know how to cope with isolation, and he's just trying to compensate for his shortcomings. Don't be too hard on him. We don't know how hard his journey's been."

"Bixby is out of place here. Don't you think we could ship him home?"

"Nope. He is part of the team. The money men sent him in, and he needs to be able to report everything back to them. He'll be alright. Have a little patience."

"Just keep him away from me then," Zach said, with no little menace in his voice.

****

Friday

0330

As he sought sleep, Dolph Zimmerhanzel listened to the echoes from the footsteps of another guard passing by his cell. For the last two days his mind ranged over the possibilities that Q might be working for N'dalu, that Angelica could have told Francois that she no longer loved him, or that he could be turned in for planning to escape. Everything could be ruined. He could be tortured if they found out, or worse, he could spend the rest of his life in this hole.

Each time he tried to discipline his thinking, to pull himself out of his mental mud hole, the dark clouds of doubt and worry pounded through to shake him back into that quiet panic. What is to become of me? His whole body jerked, each muscle fighting the other until he sat paralyzed. He screamed silently, his head vibrating from the tension.

For the first time since his wife's death, Dolph could not pray. Many times during the day, he knelt, intending to talk to God, but nothing came. It's a lack of faith, he told himself. I must believe and trust that He will care for me. But what will I do about Maura? I cannot lose her. I've already lost one love.

For the first time in several months, grief again cut into his guts. He vividly saw his wife's smile and with his mind's eye looked down and noticed the small bulge in her belly. His child, their first, grew inside of her. Then that horrid image appeared, her face twisted by the cerebral malaria as she rested in her simple casket.

He wept, turning to the corner. "Oh God, why have you taken away the only thing that mattered to me? Why have you left me in this prison to rot?" Realizing that he was talking once again to the Lord, he poured out his doubts, then his anger. Railing against the Lord for the injustice of the last two years, Dolph beat on the stone wall. His anger burned.

"I have been your servant, and you have treated me like I'm your enemy. Why haven't you answered me? Why haven't you delivered me?"

Not knowing how much time had passed, he found himself lying full length on the floor on his belly. His hands were sore from beating the stone. He felt emptied, but better. Just like vomiting after eating a rotten fish, he thought. Aren't they the same, rotten fish in the stomach and rotten thoughts in the brain? They both must be vomited out. Both cause pain and use up huge amounts of energy. But what a relief once a person has purged himself.

Then he remembered a scene from his boyhood. He sat in a crowded unairconditioned church listening to a skinny West Texas preacher. The heat forced the preacher to slough off his suit coat. Drops of sweat popped off of the old man's bald head.

"Tell God what is wrong with your life. Be angry with God. He can take it. We don't understand his ways, but He wants to hear how you feel. He will answer you."

That would make a great sermon. I must write this down and add it to my series on prayer. Dolph pulled out his spiral notebook and pen, the latest in a series that Seko always bought for him. On a new page, he wrote of his anger with God, his lack of faith, and his conversation with the Father. For the first time in two days, Dolph smiled. He climbed into his bed, readjusted his mosquito net, plumped his pillow, and instantly fell into a peaceful sleep.

Seko Seki rattled the barred door. "Wake up, my friend. Lord N'dalu would talk with you this morning."

"Good morning, Colonel." They both laughed at Dolph's old joke of promoting Seko three grades. "Do I get a shower before my important audience?"

"Of course." Seko threw a large, thin towel at Dolph, watched him wind it around his waist, and then followed him toward the officer's shower where there would be a little hot water.

"And how is Lord N'dalu this morning?"

"Not well, my friend. I have been watching the news. You know, on satellite television. At the UN peace conference in Goma, the General did very poorly during a press briefing in front of the television cameras. The foreign journalists made him look the fool. Worse yet, the General fled the peace conference, making him seem guilty of all the charges that they brought."

Dolph ripped off the towel and stepped into the shower without any hint of embarrassment about his nudity. Seko turned away and kept talking.

"The princess is confined to her quarters, and N'dalu's fury shakes the foundations of his army. Many are afraid."

"But not you?" Dolph asked.

Seko laughed, deep and resonant.

"I have done nothing wrong. Our God protects us."

"Amen, my brother. I didn't know that you're a believer."

"There is much about me that you do not know. Your clothes are here on the rack. I will wait outside."

What will N'dalu want to talk about? Why me? Barely noticing that his pants and shirt were pressed this time, Dolph tried to prepare himself for this interview. This could be the most important of the series. Unable to verbalize his sense of foreboding, he prayed quickly for wisdom and courage as he checked himself in the mirror behind the door.

Dolph walked out and two soldiers flanked him and guided him to the waiting Land Cruiser. It is much earlier than my other talks with N'dalu. The growl in his belly reminded him of his lack of breakfast. Perhaps the General will have another bowl of fruit. Deserted streets and shuttered store fronts stared back at Dolph as he looked out the right side of the truck. Just a shell of the city where I once came for supplies, he thought.

Once inside the headquarters, the chill of the air conditioning brought goose bumps to Dolph's skin. The clacks from the soldiers' boots echoed through the empty foyer, and Dolph marveled that N'dalu's rage could paralyze the city. On the elevator ride up, he noticed the guard's watch. Only 0645. No wonder everything seemed deserted.

"Welcome, my friend," N'dalu said with a big smile. Dolph's mental defenses went up. N'dalu has never been friendly to me before, he thought.

N'dalu came toward Dolph and offered his hand. Warily, Dolph shook hands. The crisp uniform, the shined boots, and his electric energy could not hide the deep fatigue on N'dalu's face. Dolph guessed that the general had been up all night.

"Come and have breakfast with me. I have been looking forward to talking with a reasonable man."

The table was spread with fresh fruit, scrambled eggs, hot waffles, fried ham slices, a cheese tray, and two insulated pitchers of coffee. Dolph stopped two feet from the table enjoying the aroma.

"Sit. Enjoy."

As soon as Dolph's butt hit the chair, the female body guards came forward, pouring coffee, loading his plate with food, and asking him if they could get him anything else from the kitchen.

"This is quite unexpected, my Lord," Dolph said.

"I have need of your advice, and seeing that I had such a full day today, breakfast seemed like the best time for us to talk." They ate in silence, and Dolph longed to ask a million questions.

But he remembered his father telling him years ago, "The first one to talk in a delicate situation is the loser." So, he worked on his crisp waffle floating in butter and syrup.

"Well, I went to Goma yesterday for a meeting brokered by the UN. Several parties were there. All of them my enemies or rivals. During the opening press conference, I made a fool of myself. My pride got the better of me, and I said many things that the foreign press used to make me look like a monster."

Dolph was astonished but kept his eyes lowered. He thoroughly chewed his piece of waffle, then concentrated on cutting a slice of his ham. He bought himself a few seconds to compose his thoughts.

"I am not used to hearing you admit any weakness," Dolph said reaching for his coffee cup.

"I find it hard to tell you this, but one must face the truth. The greatest sin is lying to oneself, don't you think?" N'dalu's smile barely turned up the corners of his mouth as he peeled his tangerine.

"The reason I asked you to come have breakfast with me is to get some advice from a man whom I consider to be quite wise." The formality of speech gave Dolph a small insight. This talk cost N'dalu the humiliation of admitting to a large mistake. He is spending a huge amount of emotional capital. What does he expect back from me in return?

"Sir, the wise man is most aware of his own shortcomings," Dolph said.

"Yes. Reverend, this press conference has damaged me." N'dalu leaned forward, and Dolph saw some of the old fire return. "What can I do to get back some of my respect? How can I keep my patrons from abandoning me?"

Patrons? I never thought about N'dalu having patrons or anyone that he answered to. Dolph sipped his coffee, letting the silence deepen.

"Sir, I didn't know that you had a patron. However, I reckon we all have someone we answer to. Like any boss, it'll be best for you to go to them first. Collide with the criticism before it reaches you. Let the bosses know that you understand your mistake and how you intend to rectify the situation."

"Yes. I see what you are saying. However, the stakes in my business are life and death. My bosses will not stand by and see my policy errors painted onto their shields."

Dolph was a little annoyed that he was not being allowed to enjoy this sumptuous breakfast because of

N'dalu's personal problems. Guilt swelled up in his heart, and he realized that his mission to influence this leader rated much higher than a breakfast.

"What do you see as your options?" Dolph asked. N'dalu got stood up and paced.

"I could simply ignore the situation and hope for the best. I feel that this is the most childish and damaging of my options. It would surely result in my termination." He walked to his desk and stared out the window.

"I could take my riches and run, taking refuge in Switzerland or Monaco. I see this as my most cowardly option. That would be such an empty life. No purpose." He turned back to Dolph and smiled. "Besides, this option would never get me to the presidential palace in Kinshasa.

"My other option is to fight." He strode toward Dolph. "I would root out all the operatives of my patron, change body guards, use my own money for operations and sell all the minerals that I produce on the open market."

"It seems to me that you've already made up your mind."

"What else is one to do in the great game? If I go off of the offensive, I must either retire from the field of play, or I will be killed on that same field one day soon."

"You could be killed while you are on the offensive," Dolph said.

"Yes, that is the downside. For the next few years, I would have to have increase vigilance, worrying everyday that someone will shoot me down."

"I would hope that a wise ruler would take into consideration what would be best for his wife and his subjects."

This took N'dalu back. Dolph could see that he had never considered that angle.

"What is best for me is best for my wife and for my people!" N'dalu came and sat down. He picked at his food for a moment.

"Reverend, I am going to fight. I have made up my mind. But I need help. I need advisors. I especially need a press secretary. The other world leaders have a 'face' that talks to the press and prepares the leader's speeches. Someone who can stand pressure when in front of a crowd. Someone who is persuasive and a good public speaker.

"You have speaking ability. You have kept your balance in our, shall we say, contentious discussions. You have put forth ideas that are repulsive to me, but with such tact and reason, that I have actually considered your point of view. This is why I have asked you here this morning. Would you consider being one of my advisors?"

Shocked into silence, Dolph studied N'dalu's face looking for something there. Why is he asking me? I am just a prisoner. Then Dolph realized that the pool of people that N'dalu had from which to choose was rather shallow. Not many press secretaries lived in Matai, nor would any wish to move here to work.

"I will give you a room in the hotel, clothes, food."

"General N'dalu, I don't want clothes and food. I want to go home."

"Think about it, Reverend. You can serve me for two years, and then I will release you with a large cash bonus. You will have input into my council. You will be my face to the press. You will be able to do good."

"Why? I don't understand."

N'dalu's enthusiasm increased. He leaned over the table toward Dolph and, with at confident smirk, he counted off the reasons.

"You will be loyal to me. You will never participate in a plot to assassinate me. You will help me transform my kingdom into something admirable to the world. You are wise, and you will be a great presence in front of the press."

Dolph wanted to say a million things. He wanted more detail, more information. But his past conversations with N'dalu infused him with caution. Tempted to say yes to escape his prison cell, he instead put down his fork and wiped his mouth with the cloth napkin.

"Well, what do you think?" N'dalu looked hopeful. Almost like a little boy.

"I need some time to pray about this," Dolph said.

"You have forty-eight hours. We must get to work soon."

Chapter 10

Friday
0920

     Michael Stauffer arrived at work a little late, as usual. He hoped his boss could not smell the alcohol on his breath from last night's party. No one around, I guess they're already out at the mines, he thought. He remembered the prostitute still lying in his room. What women they have around here. That mixture of French and black produces some of the world's most gorgeous and exotic females. But I am getting too old to stay up drinking and whoring like I did when I was twenty-five.

     A stack of papers sat in his inbox. Some were handwritten and some computer generated. He looked through the parts requests while filling his huge insulated mug with the black ink the shop foreman called coffee. He took a sip and his stomach rebelled. I should have eaten some breakfast, he thought. Walking slowly across the office, he realized that he was still a little drunk. The computer seemed like an ugly enemy sitting on his corner desk, but he forced himself to sit and start typing the orders into his laptop. The mines needed a thousand things to keep the big machines growling and eating into the red dirt and rock. After he got warmed up, his long fingers blurred across the keyboard. He barely saw the items as he typed; as if there was a direct connection from his eyes to his hands without going through his brain.

     Then he noticed the request for pistons, bearings, and a gasket kit. Someone blew an engine, he thought. Probably one of the pumps that empties the water out of the mines. He looked over the list after he printed it out for his files. Cases of grease, needle bearings, gears, seals, shafts, universal joints, paint, tires, barrels of hydraulic fluid, and scores of cutting teeth. This list was short. No major breakdowns.

Opening the internet connection, he attached the list to an email. The parts would be pulled tonight in Rotterdam and placed on a KLM airliner to Kinshasa. There, an Antonov An-32 freight airplane would bring the parts, along with food and booze to the airport in Matai.

After receiving a confirmation from the Caterpillar parts distribution center, he went to his personal email. This was the first time he had checked it for several days. Seeing the message marked *Grüner Kopf* caused his sack to contract. Relieved to see that the message was from last night, he opened it. As with all the "Green Head" messages, it was in German.

> Your mother is very sick. Call home immediately.

His hand trembled a little as he pushed the reply button. He typed in the phrase that would signal his acceptance of the assignment.

> Can't call today. Give her my love.
>
> Michael

And so, the time has come.

At first, Michael Stauffer hated his job as a parts clerk, but it was the only one he could get in the city. He had no experience in mining. Only because of his language abilities did they offer him employment. Since the maintenance techs came from all over Europe and the US, the language of the shop floor was English as were the parts manuals, but he needed his French to live on the economy. Strangely, after the seven months here, he had come to enjoy his life as a lowly clerk. No responsibilities, fun women, good food. And the pay he earned was like a bonus added to his monthly retainer. Now he must revert to his primary mission.

As he considered his next move, he automatically walked toward a jumbled pile.

Two types of parts came through his warehouse: Normal wear parts that were automatically reordered and the hot parts that were special ordered. The latest shipment of normal wear parts lay in the middle of the warehouse floor waiting for him to sort and store them in their rightful bins and shelves. Already, the hot parts, those for broken machines, had been separated out and carried to the mines. Those that remained were auto re-orders. He inventoried the parts, checking them against the order form, and placed them in the correct areas of the warehouse so that he could come back and lift the parts onto the correct shelf and into the correct bin.

But his mind worked on another task, pulling the plug on Operation *Grüner Ausgang.* Who thinks up these stupid names anyway, he wondered. I guess it doesn't matter as long as I get paid. He took the small parts to a chest with twenty wide shallow drawers. Starting to place the small gaskets in their proper drawer, he whistled "Strawberry Fields Forever", proud of his tone and vibrato.

I wish I could've brought my clarinet. But then it would have been too easy to make that connection to my real past. His ruminations ceased as he concentrated on lifting a short shaft up onto a waist high shelf.

"This thing must weigh thirty kilos," he said in German. His skinny arms barely got one end onto the shelf so that he could lever up the other end.

"First chair clarinet in the Prague Conservatoire orchestra, teacher of French, and here I am stacking bulldozer parts in darkest Africa." Then he thought about his fee, and it brought a large grin to his long face, showing his perfect teeth. Musician and language teacher had been great cover jobs for his true profession of GRU officer. But now that the USSR was gone, one must take whatever work there was.

Michael Stauffer got back to his apartment at 1820. After he showered and changed into his shorts, a short walk brought him to the hotel pool. A gorgeous mixed-race waitress wearing a white bikini and a wide brimmed white hat served drinks on the other side. He chose a seat in the shade of a palm tree and waited. When she turned, he caught her eye and motioned for her. She smiled and went to the bar. Soon she glided over to his chair with a Long Island Iced Tea in her hand.

"Hello, Christina, my love. Is that for me?"

"You know it is, Michael. How's my lover boy?"

"Just wonderful. When can you come by my room tonight?"

Christina frowned and looked around to see if anyone was close enough to hear. She pulled a chair close to his and sat down. He could not help but stare at her large breasts barely held in by the two white triangles and some string.

"I heard that you found another girl for the past couple of nights."

"Never, my love. Only you."

"Yeah, right." She laughed a little, but her eyes betrayed her true feelings. "I get off at eight. Do you want me for the whole night?"

"Of course. I'll leave the door open for you."

Michael sipped his drink and watched the sun go down. His eyes kept lighting on Christina, noting the contrast of the white bikini and her café latte skin. He paid his tab with a big tip for Christina, and got up to walk back home.

Now that the sun was gone, the cool air felt good on his legs. Lots of the old timers scolded him for wearing the short European-style shorts, calling them 'Malaria Specials', but he enjoyed the freedom and the style. He whistled a soulful rendition of "Blue River", happy that he now had the lever to move Operation Green Exit to the next level—Christina's sister, Desiree Musa.

Just a little past eight, a light knock on his door pushed it open and Michael jumped to his feet. He was excited at the coming bout with Christina, but even more so at the prospect of the quarter million euros waiting for him as soon as the termination hit the papers.

"Hello, my love."

"How is my favorite boyfriend?" Christina wore a short white silk dress, clinging so that it gave the distinct impression that she worn nothing underneath. Her long black hair was pulled back into a thick ponytail. But the biggest effect on Michael was her smell. A light, sweet perfume rode on the healthy scent of a freshly bathed young woman. They kissed in the doorway, and he guided her inside the one room efficiency apartment.

About ten o'clock she got up and padded nude into the bathroom. Michael turned on the bedside lamp and pulled on his pants. When she came back out a few minutes later she was wearing the little white dress. Michael sat at the small kitchen table smoking a cigarette. He watched her eyes go to the short stack of money sitting on the table across from him. So much for true love, he thought.

"Have you had a chance to speak with Desiree about our proposal?"

"Yes, but she has some reservations." Christina pulled out a chair and sat at the table across from Michael.

She scooped up the money, uncounted, and secreted it in her bosom.

"I'm listening."

"How will you guarantee that our family will get to Europe? What if we are stopped?"

"Once N'dalu is killed, it will be every man for himself. I am sure that there will be looting, raping, and rioting when these soldiers realize that there will be no further paychecks." Michael snubbed out his cigarette and leaned back in his chair. "Then we'll put you in a car and drive to the dock at Bumba. There you can catch the executive boat to Kinshasa."

"What should make us think that you will keep the bargain? What if we don't get a ticket to Brussels?"

"You and your sister name the date, and I will get you both and your mother tickets and a little traveling money. I've already gotten all three of you resident visas in Belgium. That should show you my seriousness in this matter."

"Many bodyguards have killed their bosses in Africa. I know of none that have made it out of the country. When the new government comes in, they kill the old bodyguards claiming that they could not be trusted."

She is a good negotiator, Michael thought. She could work at any multinational company, but in this hell hole she has to be a prostitute to survive.

"But my dear, there will be no new government. You will all escape during the confusion."

"I have a proposition to make, Mr. Stauffer, or whatever your real name is," Christina said.

"Go on."

"We decide upon a date. You will be my hostage until we get paid for the job. As soon as we receive tickets and confirmation that the money is in the bank in Brussels, we release you."

Michael struggled to keep the smile off of his face and almost succeeded. The idea that this beautiful woman could hold him hostage caught him as very funny.

"Actually, that will work out rather well as I intended to accompany you to Kinshasa on the boat since I will have no more need to work at the maintenance shop."

"Then you agree?" The look of amazement on Christina's face made Michael Stauffer laugh.

"Yes I agree. You see, I want to see this succeed. I am sincere, so I have no problem being your hostage until you are paid. By the time that we make Kinshasa, about three days, the money will be in your bank. But what guarantee do I have that your sister will go through with the job?"

"My sister almost killed the bastard the other night. She was hired and trained as a body guard. But two months ago, N'dalu raped her. Oh, she fought, but she was no match for him. After he beat her, he raped her again. He demands sex from her now every week or so. She is in fear for her life."

Michael nodded. If I had known that, I could have offered less. But what is seventy-five thousand euro to the Chinese? Just expense money. I would normally do this kind of job myself. After all, that is my specialty. But N'dalu is a hard target. He travels everywhere in his Land Cruiser, probably armored. His soldiers are everywhere. He hardly leaves the hotel. Too hard for me to get him and still get out alive. This girl's sister is the perfect weapon.

"Pick any date. The boat leaves Bumba every morning around six. Give me some time so that I can be sure to have a car ready," Michael said. They both stood and shook hands.

"No kiss?" he asked.

She shook her head with a sad smile as she floated out the door.

*****

Saturday
1400

Camilo Quartalino felt the heavy vibrations through his shoes and knew that the General's new helicopter had landed. A little sorry that he had missed the approach and landing, he pushed open the office door and walked out onto the ramp.

The Mi-8MTV sat like a huge insect on the ramp, its rotors still whirling while the crew went through the shut down checklist. New white paint with a blue sweeping stripe could not disguise the ugliness of the helicopter. The most popular rotorcraft in the world had never caught on in America. The design beliefs of American and Soviet engineers differed too much. While the Americans designed a helicopter as an aircraft that could land anywhere and haul people and things, the Soviets believed a helicopter was just a flying truck. This philosophy ran throughout both families of designs. American helicopters were elegant and beautiful; Soviet ships were ugly, rugged, easy to maintain, simple, and overpowered.

Q walked up to the front door as the rotors creaked to a stop. A smiling, gray-haired man slid out of his seat and bounded down the stairs. He towered over Q as they shook hands.

"Greetings. I am Vladimir Wilk, factory training and demonstration pilot. I am your instructor to fly this fine helicopter." Q could understand his flowery English, even with the thick Russian accent.

"Camilo Quartalino. Glad to meet you. Let's go to lunch. You must be hungry."

"No, sir. We stopped for lunch in Katanga. If you don't mind, I would like to find restroom, then start your instruction. I am told that you are a military helicopter pilot." Q guided him toward the offices. He noticed the two flight mechanics already had the cowlings open, checking the engines for leaks.

"Yes, I am, but it's been several years since I've flown a helicopter."

"Just like swimming, sir. It will come right back to you. You have been studying the manuals I sent you?"

"Yes, we have."

"Then you will check out in the helicopter this afternoon, and I can get back to Kinshasa on the cargo flight tomorrow morning."

After a short break, Vladimir took Q on a walk around the aircraft. He pointed out fuel tanks, exposed air lines to the brakes, and the operation of the rear clamshell doors. Then Vladimir invited Q inside. The wide cockpit felt more like a small sun porch with twenty windows than the front of an aircraft. A wide console squatted between the pilot and copilot seats, full of navigation and communication radios, the autopilot, and gauges telling fuel quantity, fuel pressure, oil pressure and oil temperature.

"As you know, sir, starting a flying machine is the hardest part of piloting it. By the way, what is your rank that I may properly address you?"

"Captain or Q will do just fine."

"Q?"

"Yeah. Just Q."

They sat down in the pilot seats, Camilo on the left, and Vladimir on the right.

"Good. Call me Vlad." His hands moved in a deliberate quickness around the cockpit in a flow from left to right, then to the overhead panel, turning on most of the switches. A whine from up top told Q that the auxiliary power unit was spooling up.

"While the aircraft can be flown single pilot, I would recommend against it. Always take your flight mechanic along with you." Q looked back to see a short, thick man unfolding a jump seat from the door jamb.

"We are leaving Peter here with you to train your mechanics and to fly with you. He will keep you out of trouble. Listen to him. He has several thousand hours in these machines. After you are checked out, I recommend that he sit right seat until you have at least two hundred hours. Then you can train one of your own copilots."

Monitoring a pressure gauge in the overhead panel, Vlad waited until he had enough air pressure to start the first engine. Q knew from reading the manuals that this aircraft made use of compressed air for a number of functions.

Vlad pushed a button that released high pressure air into a small turbine that spun the first engine. He introduced fuel, and monitored the start. Soon the other engine came on line, the rotors came up to speed, and Vlad told Q to taxi out.

"Release the air brake and nudge the stick in the direction you wish to go. The castoring nose wheel will let you turn whichever way you push the stick." Vlad sat back in his seat as if to tell Q that he had complete trust in him to control the aircraft. Like most big helicopters, the Mi-8 has large wheels so that the pilot can roll the helicopter around the ramp without damaging other aircraft with the massive downdrafts caused by hovering.

The big machine lumbered to the left and Q guided it to the runway and faced into the wind.

"Pull pitch and let's go," Vlad said.

Q pulled gently on the long horizontal lever on the left side of his seat. Upward movement of this lever, the collective, increased the bite of all five main rotor blades evenly. Pulling up on the lever caused the rotor to develop more lift, and lowering it decreased the lift. Out of the corner of his eye he saw Vlad bring his hands to the matching flight controls on the right. He smiled. Not as confident as you pretend, he thought.

Noise level increased, dust swirled away in all directions, and in slow motion the monster rose four feet into the air. Q's hover bobbled a little. Loosen your grip, Camilo, he told himself. A big smile came over his face. He never would have guessed that he could still hover after all these years. After all hovering is one of the most difficult skills in aviation.

"Lower the nose, and take off." Q pushed the stick between his legs toward the nose, the monster tilted forward and began to accelerate almost parallel to the ground. At forty knots, he eased back on the stick and the machine climbed like an elevator without cables.

After almost two hours of airwork and approaches, Vlad finally let Q taxi to the ramp. Together they went through the shutdown checklist. Q's clothes were soaked with sweat.

"I don't think that I am quite comfortable with start-up and shut down procedures," Q said.

"Don't worry, Peter will be there to get you started and to properly shut down the machine. You are a fine pilot, Captain. I will now sign whatever license you need for your country," Vlad said as the rotors slowed to a stop.

"I don't think that there are any documents for this part of Congo." They both laughed.

"I completely understand. Then I suggest that we meet at the bar for a vodka."

An hour later, Q walked into the club, showered and wearing clean blue jeans and black polo shirt. He saw, and smelled, Vlad. The big Russian stood at the bar holding an impossibly large tumbler filled with clear liquid. He still wore his flight suit, and had not yet showered.

"Ah! You are late. Peter and I have already toasted your city several times. Here, I have a glass waiting for you." Vlad slid a tumbler toward Q.

"No, this is too much. I only want a shot," Camilo protested.

"To the General's health," Vlad yelled, adding a long, indecipherable line in Russian. Everyone in the bar held up their glasses, and they all drank.

A tiny shaft of light pierced his eyelids as the beam of sunlight coming through his window moved so that it shined into his right eye. The pain shot through Q's neck, his muscles spasming all down his back. He fought for a minute with whomever had him pinned, and then realized that he was alone on the floor. Taking inventory, he tried to determine the position of his body. His head twisted to the right, his legs bunched up and bent left. He could taste copper in his mouth and knew that it was his own blood. Gasping because of the pain, he lifted his head. An odd-shaped pool of blood dried on the tile floor. Sunlight streamed through his window.

At least I am in my own room. Must be nine o'clock, he thought, judging the angle of the shadow. He struggled to his feet, using a nearby chair as a crutch. Flashes of light zapped his eyes every other step, accentuating the pain in his back.

"I've got to get some water," he said aloud, but his ears told him that his thick lips and tongue were not working well enough to enunciate the words. He pulled a bottle of water from the refrigerator, and drank a swallow. He drank again, this time a long pull. I need some aspirin, he thought, holding his head.

I've heard about this. An alcoholic gets drunk after some time off the juice and his body can't handle it. I wonder what I did last night. Did I get in a fight or just bang my head on the floor when I came home? He looked in the bathroom mirror to check that he still had all his teeth. The left side of his face was bruised, but his hands were not cut up.

Good. I hope I didn't hurt anyone. He drank the rest of the water, got undressed and ran a hot bath. It took all of his concentration to climb into the tub without falling. For the next ten minutes he lay in the tub, soaking away some of the pain and vowing never to drink again.

"I must be an alcoholic. I can't even handle one drink," he said aloud. Shame crashed down on his head.

He closed his eyes, and the memories of his life played like a movie in his head. With a clarity brought by pain, he saw that at each major junction of his life, alcohol played a part. He realized that his marriage broke up because he chose Scotch over his wife, because he loved booze more than his family.

"I'm an alcoholic. I am an alcoholic."

Camilo Quartalino started to cry. Silent sobs convulsed his muscular body sending waves spilling over the top of the tub.

*****

Sunday
1000

Dolph Zimmerhanzel sat on his bed, once again dressed in rags. Even though he had unsuccessfully chased sleep last night, he felt no fatigue. Instead his mind whirred, wrestling with the problem of General Francois N'dalu. He hoped that regimentation would bring comfort. So he started this morning like so many identical mornings as a prisoner. Up at dawn when the birds started squawking. Exercise. Breakfast. Prayer. And now meditation.

Unlike the other mornings, Dolph could not find the peace he sought. His heart thudded and he wondered if he was close to a heart attack. His mind raced and he could hear the blood rushing past his ears. What would he do about N'dalu's offer? If I take his offer, I am helping a murderer, a tyrant. What could he want from me, anyway? I am only a preacher. I know nothing of politics. He wants me as a figurehead to show his tolerance for religion. I will be a show piece in front of the international press.

But I would like to get out of here. Wear nice clothes, have a bath every day. And eat. I could eat all I wanted every meal. Never to know hunger again. Then in two years, N'dalu would release me.

What a fool you are, Zimmerhanzel. He'll never release you. How can you trust a man who would imprison you for two years just for preaching the gospel? Dolph longed to be able to think logically and to stay on one side of the argument for more than few seconds. He knew that his brain was jumping from side to side based on his emotions of hope of release and fear of torture. What does God want me to do? As he looked inside his soul, his fear pushed him back to the endless ping pong match of self argument.

But if I refuse, I could be tortured and killed. Oh God, I don't want to go through that. Dolph shivered remembering the unending screams of the men tortured to death. Those three days were hammered into his brain, punctuated by the horror of cries for mercy, and the reek of urine and blood. I could not face that, he told himself.

I'll help N'dalu just to get out of here and keep my hide, but I'll seek to escape. That's what I'll do. He felt better having made his decision.

Three big booms echoed across the courtyard and down the corridor. Someone was beating on the door. Not with the knocker, more like a rifle butt being thumped against the door. Dolph stood and looked out his door to watch the commotion.

"It's the General!" The cry floated down the hallway from one of the sentinels on the wall. Feet clattered and Dolph could hear the lock turned and formal greetings given by Seko. Now the footsteps echoed measured and rhythmic as N'dalu and his retinue marched toward Dolph's cell. When Dolph saw them turn into his hallway, he retreated to the middle of his cell.

Seko Seki opened Dolph's door and N'dalu strutted in, his wide-brimmed hat at a jaunty angle. Several officers stood outside the door watching. N'dalu wore a forest green formal uniform with shimmering black cavalry boots: ribbons on his chest, a gunbelt around his waist, and his Colt .45 auto pistol gleaming in the morning sunlight.

"Well, Reverend, I am here to take you out of this place." He stood ramrod straight and gestured with a sweeping hand.

"Come with me and we shall work together to expand my kingdom until we rule all of middle Africa!" Unlike their other meetings, N'dalu spoke in French.

Dolph stared, standing straight and mute. A strange tightness squeezed his head, his teeth clenched, and all that Dolph could think about were the scores of preachers, imams, and witch doctors murdered by this thug. This pretender, who came in here dressed in his ridiculous uniform to impress his officers. An anger burned against this man who had imprisoned him without cause, spoken down to him, teased him with food and women. Without thinking, Dolph answered in French with a loud measured voice.

"I could not, would not, ever, ever work for a murderer such as you."

N'dalu jerked forward, bending from the waist, the surprise on his face hidden from the men behind. He smiled and switched to English.

"Come now, Reverend. We can work together for both our sakes." A pause. "With your help I can make life much better for all the people of Matai."

Dolph only shook his head. The General glared, forcing his will upon the ragged preacher.

"I can force you." Menace poured out from his voice and stance.

"No, you can kill me, but you cannot force me to work for you."

N'dalu stepped closer to say something, but Dolph retreated, keeping the distance.

"You will be sorry, Reverend."

"My God will protect me, and if he doesn't, he will carry me to his bosom."

N'dalu's face contorted with rage; his fisted right hand shook in front of his chest. He wheeled, said something to Seko Seki that Dolph could not hear, and stomped down the corridor and out of the prison. His officers scurried to keep up.

Seko caught Dolph's eye as he locked the door. Seko frowned and shook his head slowly. Dolph noticed the sadness in Seko's eyes.

Dolph sat down alone on his bed.

"My God, what have I done?"

Peace then descended on Dolph Zimmerhanzel. His heart slowed and he lay down on his bed and slept.

*****

Angelica heard about Q and the drunken party from Maura. Being freer than Angelica, she could wander the hotel/palace gossiping with guards, maids, and prostitutes.

"Yes, my princess, he drank with the men who brought down the new helicopter. The barmaid said that he drank vodka like it was water. When he could no longer stand, his guard and another soldier carried him to his room. The guard was still posted outside his room this morning when I went up to check on him."

"How goes your 'romance'?" Angelica felt a tiny stab of jealousy that Maura got to talk to Q as she faked an effort to become his girlfriend. He passed long notes through Maura, as if he and Angelica had an old fashioned long distance romance. But she knew that it was their only method of communicating. She loved the way he wrote. Those notes were her lifeline to sanity.

"He only wants to talk of you." Maura said with a quiet smile.

"When can you see him?"

"The guard said that he was still asleep. I will try back in about an hour."

"Maura, I need to see him." Maura moved behind Angelica and rubbed her shoulders and neck.

"Be patient, my princess. We will get out of here. And then you two will be together forever."

*****

Desiree looked at the new schedule with horror. She was up for tonight. I hoped that I would have a few days to get ready, she thought. Now, I only have four hours before I go on duty. I must get word to Mother and Christina that we are on for tonight. The dressing room served all N'dalu's female guards, and from the sympathetic looks of the other girls, they had already seen the new schedule. Whenever one of the girls drew night duty, it usually resulted in bruises and humiliation for the female bodyguard. One woman who had refused to have sex with N'dalu was beaten and an arm broken before she was dumped in the women's prison.

Befitting N'dalu's penchant for order, the rotation of bodyguards never changed. Until today. Does he suspect something? Desiree had a paranoid nature, honed by a life in Congo. Knowing that N'dalu's men listened to cell phones, especially the guards' calls, she must talk to her mother in person. Her mom would then tell Christina. So she walked out of the building and turned towards her mother's cafe.

Desiree did not look behind since she already knew that she was being followed. Two blocks south of the hotel, Desiree turned into her mother's café, "The Black Cat". Maria came around the counter to hug her daughter. As they embraced, Desiree whispered in her ear.

"It's tonight." Her mother's body tensed.

"Can't it wait until we get ready?"

"No, mother, I cannot take another raping from that snake. I'm going to kill him tonight," Desiree said through clenched teeth.

Maria broke the embrace and held her daughter at arm's length, a hand gripping each shoulder. Desiree could see the pride in her mother's eyes. Desiree's determination soared. She must free her mother and her sister from this evil man and this evil place. Two years ago, when N'dalu tripled the taxes on all businesses, Maria and her daughters sought permission to leave the city. But the General enjoyed "The Black Cat" and saw it as good restaurant for his men, so he refused. Cost of food skyrocketed, but N'dalu instituted price controls, squeezing out any profit. Her sister Christina took up work as a prostitute to help with the taxes and lay aside money for their escape.

"Alright, my daughter. I'll tell your sister. Do you want something to eat?"

"Thanks, mom, but no."

Maria hugged her daughter so tightly that Desiree couldn't breathe. She whispered in her ear.

"I am so proud of you. God go with you." When they broke their hug, Desiree stared at her mother. What a strange thing for her to say. Her and her sister had been raised as atheists, her mother always decrying the corruption of the church and the foolishness of the witchdoctors.

Desiree walked outside, turned back toward the hotel and took up a rapid pace. She caught sight of a soldier, her watcher, jumping up from a sidewalk café across the street, trying to pay for his coffee. She smiled at his problem and increased her speed.

How will I do it? I haven't had time to smuggle a weapon into his room, and there is no way to defeat him in unarmed combat. Desiree knew about the fighting knife he kept behind his pillow, attached to the headboard a little below the level of the mattress. She had been briefed about it when she trained as his body guard. But to use that dagger, she would have to get to the head of the bed. She would have to let him... No she must think of another way. That will never happen again. I will die first.

Desiree showered, then strolled nude across her room to her make-up table, deep in thought. From a small drawer she pulled out a black leather sheath. A thin boot knife lived inside. With a black blade and handle from the factory, the boot knife measured just over eight inches.

"Who knows when you might need this," Christina had said as she presented the dagger to Desiree last Christmas. "I always keep one like this in my purse and another in my nightstand."

Desiree immediately took her new blade to a welding shop and told the boss what she wanted. He used a belt sander to grind down the handle and guard to barely thicker than the blade. At home she worked the handle with sandpaper until it fit her hand, and then spent hours sharpening the double-edged blade until it could shave hair off of her arm.

This would be the first time that Desiree would use the weapon. But how? She placed the sheath on her inner forearm, and imagined wearing something long sleeved to cover it.

No, that will never do, she thought. The guard will find it too easily.

How about if I wear it on a necklace so that it hangs between my shoulder blades? She stretched her arm back trying out that position for the knife.

No, too slow to draw. Then she saw the roll of duct tape lying on the top of her dresser.

Last fall, when Christina heard that Desiree was required to attend a state dinner, she gave her the tape. She then helped Desiree tape up under her breasts for more support. N'dalu had been impressed when she showed up in a slinky, backless, black formal dress, her cleavage perfect. He had, after all, instructed her to come and look ravishing while protecting him from any possible assassin. She smiled at the memory of that dinner. Then her face darkened thinking that it was only three months later that N'dalu had first raped her.

Desiree set her face, ripped off a length of gray tape and applied it vertically to the upper inside left thigh. She placed the knife against the tape, point toward the floor, hoping the cloth would protect her skin against the sharp edges. Then she taped over the knife, securing it to her thigh.

She put on a tight black dress with nothing on underneath. The hem reached just above her knees, and the dress hugged every curve. The modest neck line and hem only accentuated her femininity. She applied a little makeup, brushed her long wavy hair, and put on her black high heels. A little perfume spritzed on her cleavage finished her preparation.

The four hours had passed like four minutes. Desiree wished that she could pray to some God right now. One of the reasons that she had been chosen for the inner guard was her profession of atheism. A small voice deep in the back of her conscience wondered about eternity. Will I die? If I succeed, will I go to hell for murdering a man?

No, she thought. This man has raped me repeatedly, as well as other guards. He deserves to die. I am only ashamed that I didn't rid the world of this cockroach several weeks ago.

*****

    He still burned with fury about that cursed preacher. N'dalu had not been able to get rid of the image of that superstitious fool defying him. Even while that preacher was still in a prison cell, he had the gall to defy me.

    "He humiliated me in front of my staff," N'dalu said aloud. Barefoot and dressed in a dark blue silk robe that reached his knees, he took another swig of twenty-six year old Glen Albyn scotch. He glanced at the bottle and saw that it was almost empty.

    Nancy, the evening body guard, lurked in the corner of the dim room, and stared at him, not understanding the English monologue. He just glanced back and her and continued to pace. The day was ruined, wasted. At least it was over and he would have some diversion from his favorite, Desiree. Changing the schedule went against his sense of order, but he needed her tonight to help him forget. His manhood stirred thinking of her beauty and how he would dominate her.

    "I will take my pleasure with pretty Desiree tonight, then in the morning I will go to the prison and visit the Reverend. We will see how proudly he talks with my pliers crushing his knuckles."

    N'dalu searched his heart for the glee that he hoped to find at the thought of bringing hot revenge upon his enemy. Instead, a faint, heavy sorrow leaked to the surface. He took another drink.

    "I must punish him for shaming me in such a public manner. I will show him who is king of the Congo! No one defies me. No one," he yelled. He stared at his trophy wall and in a smaller voice said, "But then who will I talk with when I want some intelligent conversation?"

    N'dalu could see Nancy, the guard, trying not to notice that he was conversing with himself in a strange language. He smiled, then grunted through his nose, and laughter bubbled up as he imagined how silly he must look. Here I am babbling to myself as I walk around and around this room dressed only in my robe.

While he was laughing, the elevator door opened and Desiree and Brulo, his male body guard emerged. N'dalu glanced at Nancy, the other guard, and she ducked into the elevator even as the other two exited. N'dalu watched the counter making sure that it counted down to the first floor. Now I shall have some privacy, he thought.

N'dalu sat down on his couch and watched as Desiree walked toward him with small steps and swaying hips. As she came into the circle of light thrown out by his lamp, he let out a soft low whistle. Now this woman is perfect. Look at her bearing, her strength. N'dalu took another sip of scotch and nodded. Brulo started to frisk Desiree. She glared down at him as he obviously enjoyed the search. N'dalu looked on approvingly as Brulo's hands moved roughly over her breasts and buttocks. She would be alone with him, and he wanted no hidden weapons. N'dalu could see the loathing in her eyes, and that aroused him. Her athletic body gave her the strength to resist, and her spirit, never broken, would give her the courage to bite and claw at him.

I love that tight dress, he thought. The black tactel fabric clung like skin to every curve. He could smell the light perfume. Black, sharp-toed high heels adorned her feet. She enjoys the battle also, he thought. Else why would she dress so for me? With a flick of his hand, he dismissed Brulo to the far side of the room. He stood up and realized that he must have consumed a little too much scotch. But he got himself squared away and led Desiree into the bedroom, closing the door.

She stood in the middle of the room, arms at her side, tall and straight, fearless. N'dalu turned off the main light. Now only the lamp on the far nightstand gave light to the room. I love this one, he thought. No begging for mercy. No telling me to be tender and loving. She understands how a real man treats a woman. He walked around her, never more than six inches away, and his eyes never leaving her body.

Standing close, face to face, he reached around her for the zipper down her back. She batted his arm away, and in a flash N'dalu slapped her hard on the left cheek. The small telegraph of her shoulder movement triggered his automatic response, blocking her right hand as she tried to claw his face. Catching her wrist with his left hand, N'dalu twisted her arm, forcing her to turn around. Jerking back on her hair with his right hand, he arched her back so that she could not bite or hit him with her other hand. She tried to muffle a cry of pain.

"You look so good tonight, Desiree. Take off that dress for me."

"No, you bastard. Oww! You're pulling my hair out."

"Take it off, I said." He jerked hard.

"Alright," she yelled. He released her and turned her around.

"Take it off."

"I need to go the bathroom first," Desiree said, head lowered.

N'dalu felt mellow from the liquor, so he made a face and dismissed her with a wave of his hand. She moved a little too slowly for him so he slapped her hard on her bottom. She turned and her eyes shot fire at him. He laughed as she shut the door.

"Don't take off that dress in there. I want to see you take it off out here."

"Yes, my Lord."

As soon as she closed the door, Desiree kicked off her heels and pulled up the hem of her dress. She wiggled her hips to get the black dress up over her thighs. If this skirt hadn't been so tight, Brulo would have surely found my knife, she thought. Her heart pounded in her chest, and she could not catch her breath. Remembering the first time N'dalu raped her, she gathered the force of her resolve, and calmed herself for the kill. She pulled the skirt back down. Taking the knife, she cut a ragged gash up the right side of the skirt all the way up to her hip, just nicking her skin with the point. She cut another on the left side. Now I'll have room to fight.

"What's keeping you so long, my love?" N'dalu called out.

She did not respond. Putting the knife in her right hand, she held it point up, so that her hand and forearm shielded the weapon from sight. She opened the bathroom door with her left hand and slid out, leading with her left side. She tilted her head down, her long black mane hiding her face. She tried to douse the knowing smile from her face. N'dalu sat on the end of the bed more than ten feet away. *I should have plenty of room to move*, she thought.

"Now take off that dress. Slowly," N'dalu said.

"No. You'll have to take it off of me." She saw N'dalu's grin and knew that he had misinterpreted her smile. *He thinks I want to play his game.* Hoping to keep his attention away from her right hand, she stroked her hair with her left hand as N'dalu sauntered toward her. Still presenting her left side to him, Desiree shifted the knife to a saber grip, point down.

Just a little closer, she thought. *Can't he see me shaking? I'll have just one chance.*

She stepped forward with her left leg and swung underhanded at N'dalu's stomach. Taken by surprise and slowed by the scotch, his right-handed down block came late, but he managed to move the blow to the side.

"Ahhh!" he yelled as the point cut into his right side, and he could feel the burn. Like a machine he continued to spin all the way around, his right foot coming up to deliver a devastating blow to Desiree's right ear.

But the intoxicated kick missed low and hit her in the right shoulder, throwing her onto the floor. She watched her knife glint as it rotated end over end in its flight to the corner of the room.

"I'll kill you, now, you whore," N'dalu yelled. Then in a soft, vicious voice, "But I'm going to get my pleasure from you first." The fight, the blood, and seeing Desiree cowering on the floor all pushed his exhilaration to a new level. He checked the cut on his side, pleased that a few stitches would fix him up.

"I've never had a woman with your combination of beauty, courage, and danger. This is the greatest," N'dalu said. He reached down and jerked Desiree up by her arm. Whirling her toward him with his left hand, he ripped her dress down the front with his right. Desiree gripped his shoulders as he stared at her naked breast. His face softened when he looked upon her exposed beauty.

She brought her right knee up into N'dalu's crotch so hard that she lifted him three inches off of the ground. He doubled over and she moved her hands to the back of his neck. Using her knee again, while holding down the back of his neck, she smashed his nose. She heard the bones break in his face.

He fell on his side to the floor, still in the fetal position. Her hatred consumed her and gave her strength. She thought of going for her knife, but instinct told her not to leave her enemy for even a second.

N'dalu rolled to his back, clutching his broken and bleeding nose with both hands. Desiree aimed her right heel between his elbows and stomped N'dalu's larynx, crushing his airway. She then ran for her knife and came back to deliver the *coup de gras*. But seeing N'dalu unconscious and turning blue, she knew that he would soon be dead.

Remembering Brulo outside, she started yelling, just like the times before when she had visited this room.

"No, no, ahhh! Stop, you're hurting me!" After turning down the sheets, she wrestled the body up onto the bed, grunting loudly for Brulo's sake. Then she yelled again.

"Oh no-o-o-o. Stop. Stop."

Oddly, I don't feel any joy or sadness at having killed my first man. Only emptiness. What do I do now? How will I get out of here? Continuing the noises that she could remember making the last time with N'dalu, she moved around the room taking inventory of what she had available.

The blankets and bedspread lay folded on the sofa. She arranged the body so that the bloody nose faced away from the door, then spread the blanket on the bed, making it look like N'dalu was sleeping. That's not right, she thought. Too orderly. She rumpled the blanket and threw a pillow on the floor. She left the lamp burning.

I need a shower, she thought. Going into the bathroom, she reached inside the shower stall and started the water. No, that isn't how it happens. N'dalu throws me out still stinking of sex. She turned off the water, and picked up her shoes. She hid her knife in the left shoe. Taking inventory before she walked out, she saw that the front of her dress was ripped, exposing her left breast. Good. That fits the part. She looked in the mirror and saw her face bruised and swollen from the slap and from her fall. Unknown to her until she looked in the mirror, tears flowed down her cheeks. Good. That fits, too. What do I say to Brulo? Nothing. I am always embarrassed when I leave, so I say nothing to him.

She opened the bedroom door, holding her dress to keep her breast inside. Brulo grinned at her. She looked at the floor and closed the door behind her back. The open elevator beckoned, but she made a conscious effort not to run.

"Sounded like you two had a great time," Brulo said as he leered at her exposed breast.

"He beat me."

"Yeah, but you know you're his favorite."

She walked into the elevator and pushed the button for the first floor. The door closed, and Desiree slumped against the side.

Michael Stauffer watched the front of the hotel/palace from a side walk café across the street. There was no sign of trouble. No troops running yet. He needed to skedaddle right now, but his curiosity kept him stuck at the cafe. I figure that I have two hours from the start of Desiree's interrogation, he thought. She will hold out, if she wasn't killed, in order to save her mother and sister.

His Omega Speedmaster clicked past 2230 hours. She's been in there with him for thirty minutes. Did he kill her? How will I get to him if she has failed? My bosses want him out of the way by the end of this week. This could be real trouble.

"Messier, we must close up. It is already thirty minutes past time for us to close. I am very sorry."

"Yes, I'm sorry to keep you. I thought my friend would show up by now." The waiter gave him a knowing look.

"Women. They are trouble. I am sorry, but here is your bill." Michel could tell that the waiter knew that it was bad manners to throw a customer out, but the owner was probably in the back wanting to go home. And he was the last customer. I need to go anyway, he thought. I stick out badly here alone. He gave the waiter a generous tip, and received another apology.

As he ambled toward his truck, Desiree stumbled out of the front door and down the wide steps holding her torn dress with her right hand and carrying her high heels with the left. Michael trotted across the wide avenue and steadied her by holding her elbow. Wordlessly he guided her toward his old Toyota Land Cruiser.

After they started to drive away, she looked at Michael and smiled.

"Where are my mother and sister?"

"They're waiting for us on the edge of town." They drove on in silence. No longer able to stand the suspense, he said, "How did it go?"

"The son of a bitch is dead," she said looking straight ahead with her head held high.

"Good girl," Michael said with admiration in his voice.

"How will we get past the guard post?"

"We're going through Mine Number Three as if I am delivering some urgent parts. In a few minutes, you'll need to get in the back, under that stinking tarp."

"I'll do that right now." Desiree climbed between the seats and into the back.

Mine Number Three produced the most tantulum and thus it ran twenty-four hours a day. While it was not usual, sometimes Michael had to make multiple runs to bring urgent parts to broken pieces of equipment. The mine was so large that no one really knew much about equipment breakdowns in other parts of the giant pit.

Michael rolled up to the guard shack; the sleepy soldier recognized him and waved him on through. In the pit below, he could see the giant machines scurry about in widely separated pools of light. Michael drove the perimeter road, sometimes slowing to five miles per hour due to the thick pink dust. At one point, he had to go down into the pit on a steep lane hoping that a big dump truck was not broken down and blocking the road in the sea of darkness below. The rest of the drive was easy since the pit opened on the other side as the land sloped toward the river.

Michael stopped beside a copse of trees on the far edge of the mine and killed the motor and lights. Maria and Christina came out dragging a small suitcase each. Desiree got out of the truck and hugged her mother for a long time. Then she hugged her sister.

"Come on, women. We've got to go. Throw your bags inside. Desiree, you get changed."

Her mother tossed Desiree a plastic shopping bag with a pair of jeans, a pullover shirt, and her tennis shoes. While she changed, Michael used his flashlight to find his bag hidden under a tree. He put on a khaki photographer's vest. After packing into the truck, Michael drove them out the back road toward the highway to Bumba. The boat for Kinshasa left from there at 0600. While it was dangerous to drive at night, it would be worse to stay in Matai. Ironically, it was N'dalu's patrols that kept the bandit population down in that area.

"There's one more checkpoint ahead. Let me do the talking." They all agreed.

Within two minutes, they spotted the tiny shack on the left side of the road. A yellow pipe, hinged on one side, stretched across the road blocking the way. A large concrete counterweight just outside the shack helped when the guard raised the barricade.

Michael slowed to a stop and a soldier sauntered to the car, swishing a rag to and fro to keep the mosquitoes away. His AK47 was slung loose across his chest, and everyone in the truck could smell him from twenty feet. As he bent over to talk to the driver, Michael pulled a .22 pistol out of the inside of the photographer's vest and shot the guard in the face three times. He crumpled without a cry next to the driver's door.

Michael tried to open the door, but it was blocked by the fallen body. He backed the truck up so that the door would clear the dead man. He jumped out and threw his whole weight down on the counterweight. The barricade levered up, and they bumped over the body and roared onto the highway toward Bumba.

Chapter Eleven

Brulo struggled to stay awake. He tried walking the perimeter of the grand room, looking at N'dalu's trophies for the hundredth time. How does a man get so much power above his fellows? Why is he so much better than we who are his servants? If I were king of Matai, I would rule differently. I would have twenty wives and a hundred offspring. He smiled at the thought of being king.

The phone buzzed in N'dalu's room. Brulo straightened his uniform, in case N'dalu emerged from the bedroom after the phone call. After many rings, the bedroom phone was silent. Now the phone on N'dalu's desk began to ring. Brulo was confused. Should I answer it? I am not qualified to speak on that phone. But if the caller hangs up and an important call is missed, I could be blamed. He stared at the ringing phone, and then glanced over at the clock. Two in the morning. This cannot be good. No good news ever comes at two in the morning. Like moving in glue, he picked up the slim black receiver.

"Yes?"

"General, this is Colonel Bunuri. We have an incursion, my Lord."

"Uh... Uh. The General is asleep, my Colonel," Brulo said in his best formal French. "This is his body guard."

"Well, wake him, you fool! We have a guard murdered on the perimeter. Someone is inside Mine Number Three and may be inside the city."

"Just one minute, sir."

Brulo dropped the receiver, clutched his submachine gun and scanned the room for any enemy. Then, backing toward N'dalu's bedchamber, he opened the door, letting the light from the big room spill in. N'dalu sprawled on the far side of the bed, and, judging from the state of the bed clothes, he must have had a great time with Desiree.

"General. There is an important phone call for you, sir." Brulo shook the bed. No movement. He reached for the light switch.

As he walked around the bed to shake the General, he saw the blood on the sheet where it had flowed from N'dalu's nose. He felt N'dalu's cold neck and knew that he was gone.

"Oh, no." He lowered his head and shook it from side to side. "I am a dead man."

*****

The morning sun painted the clouds orange and pink. Dolph wandered to his window to better see the sunrise. He could see a long expanse of sky if he looked out of the upper left corner of his window. A light south wind brought in the drier air and the taste of the desert. The lower humidity felt like air conditioning to Dolph. A female street sweeper moved through the alley behind the prison towing her orange oil drum lashed to a two-wheeled dolly. N'dalu made sure that the streets he frequented were clean while garbage piled up in the rest of the city.

Dolph Zimmerhanzel readied himself for the torture that he was sure would be measured out for him this morning. Last night had been devoted to prayer. While worry had poked its head in during his talks with God, Dolph had found it easy to push it out and continue. The overarching emotion Dolph felt was one of pride that he could do the right thing in the face of evil.

"I thank you, God, that you did not let me dishonor myself during the test. Oh, Lord, strengthen your servant during this next trial. Give me a swift death." Dolph was sure that he could call upon the friendship of Seko Seki to kill him relatively quickly.

Peace was upon him.

The faint rattle of automatic weapons fire barely reached his ears. Then it stopped. Did I hear gunfire? Dolph started to dismiss it. I must have imagined it, he thought. Then a longer burst echoed down the alley, closer this time. What is happening? The force Q fought with had been completely destroyed by N'dalu's counter attack. Who could this be?

He went to his door and peered down the hall in the gloom. Only the widely spaced lights across the courtyard shined through the darkness. Then he heard the guards running for the walls. Prisoners across the central courtyard were shouting, "What's happening? Let us out of here!"

Seko Seki strode down the hall. Dolph knew it was him, even though he could not see him. No one else in the prison walked with that royal stride. As expected, Seko materialized out of the blackness.

"Good morning, my friend. I have good news for you." Seko's smile lit up his whole face.

"I am not expecting good news, Colonel."

Seko laughed. He put down a cloth sack and took the large key ring off of his belt. Dolph could see that Seko was having trouble finding the key to Dolph's cell in the dim light.

"I know. My instructions were to wait for the General, and then help him torture you this morning for refusing to join him."

"That is the good news that you have for me?"

"No. No." Seko swung the door open wide, and looked directly in Dolph's eyes. "The General is dead."

Dolph stood in the exact center of his cell. A world of possibilities exploded. He would live! Dizziness swirled in his brain. Nausea gripped his gut and disbelief tried to make him fear. He could no longer stand, and reached behind for his bed and sat.

Seko came into the cell and sat next to him.

"Dolph, you are a good man. I struggled all night with what I would do this morning. My wife begged me to do my duty, for the sake of our family. And so, I came here two hours ago to prepare for your torture. You cannot know the joy that I felt when they told me that one of N'dalu's body guards murdered him last night."

Dolph held to the side of the bed to keep from falling. It's a dream, he thought. It must be a dream. He knew that he should not be joyful at the death of his enemy, but elation and gratitude boiled up from his chest. Seeing Dolph's weak smile and far off look, Seko turned him and gripped his shoulder.

"You must listen to me, my friend. We have so little time. Are you listening?" Dolph lost his smile, focused on Seko's face, and nodded.

"At least two colonels are fighting for ownership of Matai. Bunuri has the upper hand. He received the news first and rallied his troops. They are on the east side moving this way. I don't know what will happen, but there will be fighting. You must leave here." Seko shoved the bag at Dolph. "This is your chance to escape. Here are your good clothes. You will find some money in the pocket. No, do not protest. Let's just call it pay for the English lessons for my son. There are two loaves of bread and some fruit. Go, my friend, and keep your head low. We will meet in heaven one day."

"God bless you, Colonel. I will never forget you."

"Go with God, my friend." Seko hugged Dolph and kissed his cheek. "You will never know how your dignity during captivity inspired me to be a better soldier, a better man. Now, I have to go. I must get my men together. Colonel Robert is my commander, and I must take my men to the barricade."

Seko turned, and with great stateliness walked out the open door.

"God bless you!" Dolph tried to yell it, but his voice did not work. He brushed the tears off of his face.

*****

Q opened his eyes, but did not move in his bed. Something is wrong, he thought. Reaching to his left, where he kept his pistol in a holster attached to the bed in his home, he realized where he was.

I have no weapon.

He listened for a moment, not knowing why he woke up. Thank God my headache is gone. A day of sleep, plenty of water, some healthy food, and a light workout last night seemed to work a miracle. He looked at his table clock. Five forty-five. Then he heard a soldier yelling on the street below. Kicking off his blanket, he sprang out of bed and went to the window. Soldiers milled around, and a military truck groaned down the road loaded with troops. A small group stacked sand bags on the street corner, setting up a machine gun emplacement.

Q went to his door to ask his guard what all this meant. When he opened the door, his guard was gone as well as the one at the end of the hall. He closed the door silently, and tried to think. Adrenaline pumped through his veins as he went into combat mode. He heard automatic weapons fire.

Someone is attacking.
I have no weapon.
I am defenseless in this room.
It will be daylight soon.

His mind tumbled over data and possibilities. I must find Angelica. I can't leave her. Will it be better now, or in the confusion that will come during the regular attack?

As he pondered, his body found clean clothes. He dressed in his "uniform", as the guards liked to tease him:

Blue jeans, black tee shirt, black running shoes. He had no ID, no money, and worst of all, no weapon.

He quietly opened his door, and stood barely outside. He closed the heavy door behind his back, wincing at the clack when it shut. He fought the temptation run. Trying to act like a normal guest, he walked down the hall toward the elevator. When the stainless steel door slid open, Maura stood inside.

"Get in," she hissed. "I was just coming to get you." The door closed and she punched the button for the tenth floor. "N'dalu is dead," she said in a normal voice, her face barely holding back her glee.

"What happened?"

"His body guard killed him last night. Good riddance."

Q's brain heard the news and started planning contingencies. No time for emotion. Those troops must be fighting other N'dalu troops. Fighting for the riches of the mines. This city will be ablaze in a few hours. He frowned. The puzzlement on Maura's face made him smile.

"We're going to be OK," he said with a confidence he did not feel. The elevator stopped, the door opened. Maura held him back and stuck her head out first. She turned and nodded, then led him by the hand down the hall to a corner room. With her key she opened the door.

He saw Angelica first, and ran to her and they kissed for a long time. He pushed her away, looking at her with adoration. She was still in a see-through robe, and he admired her assets.

"Do you have a pistol or a knife?" Q asked. She laughed long and hard.

"Camilo Quartalino, in my dreams, when we finally got together, I imagined a thousand things that you would say to me. But 'do you have a pistol or a knife?' was never one of them."

"Yes, I know. But do you have a weapon? I feel naked."

"Yes, Francois gave me a knife for a present last year."

"I know where it is, princess," Maura said, moving to a cabinet beside the television. "Here it is. Will this work?"

Camilo looked for a moment at the ivory-handled Randall fighting knife, admiring its seven inch blade. Hand forged, mirror finish, this knife must have cost over a thousand dollars, he thought. He replaced it in its sheath.

"Oh, yes. This will work. Nice knife, but not exactly something that I would give my wife," Q said, threading it onto his belt. "Now get dressed my love. Wear something that you can run and walk a long way in. We're getting out of here."

He went to the corner window, pulled back the curtain to see how the soldiers were deploying. The two windows met at a steel corner post giving the room a panoramic view to the north and west. He could see the smoke from the first engagements to the north. The airport was south of town.

"Do I have time for a bath?"

"You really are a princess," Q said, never turning from looking outside. "No, my love, no bath. And tie your hair up. Things will be getting bad before they get better." She gave a little pout, then smiled and went into her bedroom.

"Do you know the way to the prison?" Q turned from the window.

"Yes. Yes, I do," Maura said. Q marveled that she could keep her voice so level all the time.

"We need a car. We need money. Do you have any food? Bottled water?"

"We'll have to steal a car. We have no money. N'dalu bought everything. He would never let her have any cash. No food, either. Angelica has her meals delivered. But we have several bottles of water."

"Good. Drink one now. We'll need it." He downed a half liter bottle with one long drink.

"Now, we need money. We'll have to buy fuel and food. Does Angelica have any diamonds or gold coins?"

"Yes. Right over here." Maura walked him over to an inlaid mahogany jewelry chest with seven small drawers. She opened each drawer in turn and together they picked out pieces. A necklace with a miniature gold bar, another with a large emerald pendant, gold chains, diamond earrings.

"This should be enough to get us out of here. Put them in a purse or bag."

Angelica emerged from her room in a white long-sleeved shirt and khaki pants tucked into knee high riding boots. A huge smile on her face, she lifted her arms and turned around.

"Those boots won't cut it, girl. Don't you have some running shoes? We could be walking for miles, and those boots will blister your feet in ten minutes."

She made a face and turned back to her room.

"Do you know the roads here?" Q asked Maura. "Which way should we go?"

"The roads to the north become dirt trails a few miles north of the river. Since it is the rainy season, there could be washouts. To be sure, we will have to wait at Bumba for the next boat. It leaves early each morning."

"No, we can't do that. Angelica is too big a prize for us to wait anywhere."

"The road south to Angola is paved. I have relatives just a few miles across the border," Maura said.

"Alright, that's where we are headed, then."

Two minutes later Angelica came out of her room. This time she wore a pair of white Nike cross trainers. Q nodded, and they moved out without a word.

The three of them rode the elevator down to the underground parking garage. Q felt they ran less risk running into a guard than if they used the stairs. Stepping out of the elevator, Maura pointed to the parking attendant's hut.

"You lead the way," Camilo said, hoping the dim light would hide the knife on his belt. The guard came out to meet them and recognized Angelica. He gave a slight, nervous bow.

"We need a car," she said as they continued to walk closer. The young guard gripped his folding stock AK47.

"I am sorry, my Lady, but Colonel Robert…" From behind Angelica Q lunged at the guard, burying the knife in his solar plexus. The guard looked surprised. Q jerked upward on the knife cutting into the heart. He turned the dying guard and dragged him to the far side of the booth. He withdrew the knife and wiped it and his hands on the guard's shirt. With a smooth movement he lifted the AK47 and slung it across his own shoulder.

Maura had already gone in the booth and found the key box. She came out with a key to one of the four Land Cruisers parked along the wall.

"Get all the keys. It will be harder for them to follow," Q said.
They loaded into the white SUV closest to the exit with Q driving, Angelica in the right front. As he closed the door, he noticed that this one was not armored. No time to look around. All the armored cars are probably out already, he thought. Speed and surprise. That's what I need to get out. Q revved the motor waiting for everyone to buckle in.

"We're going south. Which way do I turn?"

"But first we are going to the prison, right?" Maura said as a statement.

"Yeah. Sorry. Which way do I turn to get to the prison?'

"Come out of the hotel and turn left."

"OK. Here we go."

Q gunned the motor and sped up the ramp, scraping the wall. He turned left onto the wide boulevard, squealing the tires. He could see that the machine gun faced the wrong way to fire at him. Several soldiers stared, but none raised their weapons. Q laughed, releasing his tension.

"We caught them by surprise," he said. In two blocks Maura hit his right shoulder from behind.

"Turn right. Right here!" Maura said.

Less than a half mile down the deserted road, they saw a white man walking toward them. Camilo slowed. Yes, it was Dolph trudging toward the hotel, dressed up like he was going to church.

"It's him! It's him! Stop!" Maura screamed.

She opened her door before the SUV stopped and ran over to a stunned Dolph Zimmerhanzel. Throwing her arms around him, she kissed him passionately. So that is where she's been hiding all that emotion, Q thought. He turned to Angelica, and they exchanged a lover's gaze.

"Come on. Get in," Q yelled out his window.

Maura, again composed, got in and fastened her seat belt.

"We can turn left here. Stay on this street and we will parallel Highway 4," Maura said. Q looked at the vehicle's compass after they turned, satisfied to see that it indicated South. For the first time, Q looked at the gas tank. Full. What a great guy, that N'dalu, he thought.

Within a mile businesses no longer crowded the road. The houses then began to thin, with more weedy lots and hovels. Looking ahead, Q could see the jungle overcome the narrowing street.

"We need to turn left and get back on the highway," Maura said.

Q took a dirt road to the left and bumped over to the highway. He hit the gas and sped down the road, trying to miss the potholes. Coming around a gentle curve, Q saw the hasty road block set up by two soldiers. They had picked their spot well. Trees grew up like a wall on both sides of the road, and they had one lane blocked with their truck. If he turned around, they had plenty of time to shoot at the vehicle.

Probably stopping cars, robbing the passengers and killing them, Q thought. Then after they get enough money, they'll desert. The chaos has started. Every soldier for himself.

"We can't stop. At soon as they see Angelica, they'll kill us and turn her in. I'm going to slow down like I'm stopping, then blast on through. When I speed up, everyone get down." Q gripped the wheel. He applied the brakes to show the soldiers that he was going to stop. One soldier ambled out into the middle of the road.

As he got to within thirty yards, he downshifted and hit the gas, aiming for the soldier in the road. The teenager raised his weapon and fired. The soldier had a second of indecision; keep shooting or move. He decided to move, and barely made it to the right side of the speeding SUV. Q looked in the mirror and saw the other soldier unsling his weapon, raise it to his shoulder and fire at the back of the passing truck.

The back glass shattered. Q felt a couple of thumps as bullets hit the back gate. A burning punch struck Q in the left side of his back, just above his pelvis. Keeping the speed up until he reached the next corner, he slowed down just enough to make the turn. With his left hand he reached behind and felt a small entry wound, but no exit. Blood flowed onto the seat.

"Is everyone alright?" Q looked around and the shocked civilians all nodded.

Smoke started streaming from the edges of the hood, and he glanced down at the engine gauges. The temperature needle pegged over the red line. Oil pressure was falling. Now the engine missed just for a second. That soldier in the front must have shot out the radiator, he thought. This car isn't going much farther. With a metallic groan, the engine failed and the Toyota decelerated. Pushing in the clutch, Q used the speed to get off of the highway and nose the SUV into the brush.

They all sat in silence for a minute.

"OK, let's get out. The airport is only a mile or so from here. Maybe we can steal another car." Camilo winced as he opened his door. *That pain is only going to get worse*, he thought.

Angelica saw Q having some trouble getting out. She ran around the car and stopped in horror. She screamed and threw her hands up to her mouth as she saw the blood oozing down Q's left buttock. Dolph came over and bent down to take a look.

"You got dinged there, brother. I don't think the bullet hit anything vital. I guess it slowed down after going through the door. Maura, look in the back and see if there is a first aid kit or a survival vest." Dolph guided him deeper into the brush. Maura returned with a military first aid kit. Dolph found a pressure bandage.

"Look deeper and see if there is a clotting sponge in there," Q said. "Yeah, that's it. Put that over the wound. Now put the pressure bandage over it and tie it on tight."

In a minute, Q stood, grimacing in pain. "Bring the first aid kit, the water, and the jewelry. Dolph, can you carry the rifle? You range ahead and make sure that we don't run into any bad guys."

Dolph picked up the rifle, and shuddered. *I can't use this evil*, he thought. *But I'll carry it*. He instinctively knew how to shoot the weapon, having gone hunting and target shooting as a teen. *But this is different. This is for killing another human*.

Now out of the air conditioning, the African heat scalded his shoulders and burned the top of his head. Occasionally, a truck rumbled down the winding road, but hearing it afar off, the group plunged into the thick foliage before they were seen. At first they made good time, then Q started to slow.

"I'll bet there's some pain killers in that bag," Dolph said.

"No, no, I need my wits about me." Dolph watched Q's face as he fought the pain down with his will.

The end of the runway came into view. They could see the hangar and the helicopter a few hundred yards away. Q pointed out a big tree. Anything to get out of the pounding sun.

"Let's stop here and see what we need to do," Q said, breathing heavily. "We need to get closer so we can have a look. They normally have a couple of guards out around the hangar."

After resting, Dolph and Q left the women, the water and the bag of jewelry under a shade tree. For the next ten minutes they crawled through the tall grass toward the ramp. No breeze reached them and within a minute both were soaked with sweat. Q could not catch his breath. He rolled onto his back and rested for a minute while Dolph kept watch. He could see the waves of pain pass through his friend, and he thought about just staying for a few minutes. No, we've got to get going. We can do this, he thought.

"Come on, brother. We have to keep moving."

Q gave a weak smile, and they crawled again.

As they reached the crest of a small rise, Q pointed out a bush to crawl under. Thankful for the shade and a slight breeze, they rested again. From their vantage point they could look over the ramp and hangar area.

"There don't appear to be any vehicles available," Q said, surveying the empty parking lot.

"What do we do now?"

"Hey, what do you think about taking the helicopter to Angola?" Q asked. The both of them smiled and nodded. Dolph watched a shadow come over Q's face and he wondered if Q had some doubts about starting and flying that big crate by himself.

"Looks like we have two guards patrolling the ramp," Dolph said. "How do you want to handle that?"

"We'll need to take them out."

"You mean just kill them? Not even give them a chance?" Dolph looked at Q in disbelief. Camilo stared back, not understanding.

"Those guys are our enemy. They stand between us and freedom. They die or we die," Q said through clenched teeth.

"No. No, I can't be a part of that." Dolph shook his head.

"This is a black and white matter. What are you thinking, Preacher?"

Q ground his teeth and Dolph could see that he considered threatening Dolph to do it his way. Shaking his head, Q just looked at the ground.

"We're a team, Preacher. We're a team. We need each other. We'll make it through this." They sat in silence for a few moments.

"OK. I'm open for suggestions," Q said.

"If we went to them and talked to them, you know, explained that their boss was dead, and that you had a rifle trained on them. Maybe then they'd let us take the chopper."

Q couldn't help himself. He laughed, trying to muffle the noise.

"That must be the stupidest thing I've ever heard. I'm sure they're posted here to keep anyone from taking or damaging the aircraft. If they let us go, their boss will kill them. And torture them first." They sat in silence for another minute. Dolph studied Q's face, and saw the set jaw and far off stare.

I can't be part of this murder. Those two men are God's creation, living souls. If I take their lives, I'll be a killer, a murderer.

"And what about the women? Have you thought about the women? We put them at risk if we negotiate with these guys," Q said. The question burned Dolph's soul.

"I will not lose my love again," he mumbled. His eyes glazed over, and he looked upwards, pressing his lips together. What shall I do, Lord? I have never killed anyone. I can't. But I am responsible for these women now that Q's wounded. If I allow these guards to live, I condemn Angelica and my love to death, or worse. I must be strong. I must fight for their lives.

"Brother, you're right. We owe it to these women to get them out. Their lives are more important than those soldiers'. It is the lesser of two evils. God forgive me."

Q nodded and slapped Dolph on the shoulder.

Having moved forty meters to the left, Dolph stood up and called out to the guards in French. As they had planned, he became the distraction that would draw both men together. The guards pointed their rifles from the hip and walked across the ramp. Fear pounded him, and he wanted to run. But off to his right he could see Q sighting down the short barrel of the AK-47. Dolph knew enough about rifles to wish that Q had a long rifle in .308 NATO caliber. The short AK round did not have a flat shooting trajectory, and the sights were too crude for an accurate shot past a hundred yards.

The guards moved out from in front of the helicopter, so now Dolph had accomplished his first objective. If Q missed, or the rounds passed through the guards, he didn't want to damage their magic carpet out of here. Just a little closer, he thought. The guards started yelling and motioning for Dolph to come toward them.

Dolph started walking toward them, pretending he didn't understand. In broken French he asked how to get back to town. The one who looked like the leader cocked his head, trying to understand why a sunburned white man would pop up out of the grass and ask directions. He instructed the younger guard to go and get Dolph and bring him over.

"What are you doing here? This is a restricted area!" the younger guard yelled as he walked closer.

"I got lost and I'm trying to make it back to Matai," Dolph said, realizing that he just lied to draw a man to his death.

The older guard raised his weapon, and Q squeezed the trigger. The ugly rifle jumped against his shoulder and blood spewed out of the first guard's neck. Dolph started running toward the nearer guard. Q fired again, hitting the remaining guard in the upper left leg. The man struggled to stay upright, but fell onto his side, his rifle falling out of reach.

Dolph was on him in a second, and started to kneel to help the man. But then he saw the young guard reach for the pistol on his right hip.

"Don't do it," Dolph said with all the menace he could muster. The young black man's eyes locked with Dolph's as he fumbled with the flap of his holster.

Dolph kicked the downed man in the mouth with his loafer. Still the boy moved his hand back to the holster. Dolph kicked him again, this time a vicious blow to the nose. The soldier's hand inched and jerked again toward his weapon. Dolph picked up the guard's AK-47 and shot him in the head.

Silence enveloped Dolph. His ears rang, and nausea swirled in his gut as the adrenalin faded. I have killed a man, he thought. I am a murderer.

"I can't believe you did that," Q said, suddenly beside him. "Great job! I would have never imagined that you had it in you." Even though Dolph could not speak, his mind remained in a state of super clarity. He noticed how heavily Q limped now, and that, in the heat of the moment, he had forgotten the first aid kit.

"I told him to stop, but he kept reaching for his pistol. I told him to stop. I told him." Tears dripped onto the ground. The sobs came like a storm through him.

"It's OK. You had to. He forced you." Q put his arm around Dolph and turned him away from the two bodies. He saw the two women running through the deep grass toward them. Dolph straightened up and brushed away his tears.

"Let's get out of here," Dolph said as Maura came up and hugged him with a huge smile on her face. Angelica helped Camilo. The stress of combat had left him and now the pain threatened to plunge him into unconsciousness. Dolph could see the blood running down Q's leg, faster than ever now.

"Maura, run up to the helicopter and pull off all those covers. Everything that has a red piece of cloth hanging down," Q said. "They keep the bugs out," he mumbled as she ran toward the big machine. "Sharpen up," he told himself. He shook his head and tried to concentrate.

The door of the helicopter was locked with a hasp and padlock that looked like it belonged on a farm shed instead of an aircraft. Wordlessly, Dolph put the muzzle of his rifle against the thin part of the hasp, angling the weapon so the bullet would go toward the back and away from the flying machine. He turned his head away and pulled the trigger. One more shot and the lock flew off.

"Push that red button. Now turn the handle down. Be careful, that door is heavy," Camilo said. Angelica helped Q in and he sat down hard in the left seat.

"Sit in the back. Find a seat and strap in. Dolph sit up here with me." Q looked at the overhead panel trying to remember what the big Russian had done to start the engines. He found the BATTERY switch and Dolph saw lights come on with a reassuring hum.

A white line surrounded the section marked APU on the overhead panel. Q hit the start button and a nice whine filled their ears.

"Let's see. Where's that RPM gauge," Q said. He pushed the short fuel lever forward. WHOOSH. "There's light off. The APU is up to speed. Now we've got air pressure."

The noise level rose too high to talk. Q pointed at the headset hanging on a hook near Dolph's seat. They both put on their respective headsets but still could not hear each other. Dolph could see Q's mouth moving, but no words came over the headphones. Q scanned the overhead panel and saw a section marked AVIONICS and outlined with a white border. He flipped on the AVIONICS MASTER switch and since his hand was there, he turned on all the other electronics switches. The tag came alive and sent out a data packet to the overhead satellite.

"Can you hear me?"

"Yeah."

"Dolph, your job is to keep me awake. If I start to pass out, hit me. Keep me awake." Dolph just nodded.

Now Dolph could see Q's confidence rise. His hands moved over the panel in a blur as he moved a lever here, pointed to a gauge there, and nodded his head. The big blades overhead started to move and the whole helicopter rocked. All of this, just to be killed in a crash. And this is my first helicopter ride, Dolph thought.

The second engine started and came on line, matching RPM with the first. Camilo scanned the instruments. The beat of the rotors vibrated the cabin as they passed 175

RPM. In just a few seconds, the needles on the RPM gages married showing the rotors were now up to speed.

"Hey, we're moving," Dolph said. Q squeezed the hand brake and they jerked to a stop.

"Sorry. Forgot to set the parking braking." Q did not take time with the pre-take off checks. No telling when the guards' replacements would come. He looked down and left to check the collective friction, and saw the growing pool of his own blood on the aluminum plate floor.

He pulled the collective lever on his left and the helicopter leapt into the air. He pushed the stick forward and got some airspeed.

"Definitely unsat," he said.

"What's that?" Dolph was looking at him, white as a sheet.

"Oh, in flight school when you didn't perform a maneuver correctly, the instructor would tell you 'unsat' for unsatisfactory. That takeoff was unsat." The little bit of conversation settled Q, and he brought the helo around to a compass heading of southwest. The GPS showed they were making 115 knots over the ground.

Wind blew through the vents cooling their sweat, and Q started to shiver. I'm going into shock, he thought. He checked his rotor RPM and airspeed. Altitude is good. We've got plenty of fuel.

"We are out of the woods now, my friend. We're gonna make it."

Dolph just nodded.

"Hey, are you OK?" Q asked.

"I've never been in a helicopter before. There's way too many windows up here. I feel like I'm gonna fall out the front."

"It's OK. Really." Q relaxed in the seat a little trying to escape his pain. He settled into the pilot's routine of monitoring the ship and navigating. The minutes dragged by.

"Hey, wake up!" Dolph was shaking him hard. My eyes are so heavy. I just need to rest a minute, he thought.

"Camilo! Wake up!" Q looked outside and saw that they were in a bank to the left and descending. He straightened up the aircraft and shook his head. Dull, heavy pain pressed down on every fiber.

"I'm OK." He scanned the instruments. Everything in the green.

"Talk to me, Dolph. Keep me awake." According to the GPS, they were now forty eight miles from Matai.

"What are you going to do when you make it back?" Dolph asked.

"I'm going to date and marry the princess. And I am NEVER coming back to Africa again." They both laughed. "Can you close those vents? I am really cold."

"Yeah, let me figure out this thing. There. Is that better? Is that better? Camilo answer me!" Q could hear him, but he was having a hard time responding.

"I'm...OK." The edge of his vision was a little gray. "I think we need to land so that I can rest a minute, OK?"

Q did not hear Dolph's reply. I have to get on the ground before I pass out. My legs are numb... There. That's the field where we need to land, he thought. He lowered the collective and started a steep descent.

The narrow plowed field lay alongside a small river and was about a thousand yards long. Huge trees bordered three sides and a bluff rose up across the river.

The helicopter dove into the valley. Too steep, too steep, Q thought. He pulled back on the stick and fed in some collective. The nose pitched up hard and the airspeed slowed to 30 knots. The nose swung from side to side but he could not feel the rudder pedals to damp it out. Now with the descent stopped, he started a slight climb. The end of the field passed underneath.

I still need to lose two hundred feet. He lowered the collective again and held the stick back slowing even more. As he came into ground effect, the dust made a 360 degree cloud. He pulled the collective up to the hover position and stopped the descent. Too many things were happening for Q now. The nose swung wildly and he fought the controls. He realized that he was running out of room and the trees at the end of the field loomed out of the dust.

He lowered the collective again and hit the soft ground while drifting slowly to the left. The left wheel caught and swung the nose hard left. The aircraft hit hard and rolled forward into the trees at a fast walk. The rotor blades cut off tree branches and saplings, but as the helicopter continued forward they shattered against the tree trunks.

Dolph saw Q slumped in the seat. He looked out his window at the mammoth tree trunk just six feet ahead. *I could have been killed. Thank you, God, for your protection.*

Now what should I do, he thought. He saw the two red levers in the ceiling marked FUEL. Dolph remembered that Q had moved those forward when he was starting the engines. He repeatedly tried to pull them back to the OFF position, but they were stuck. Then he noticed that he first had to move each lever sideways, out over a detent, and then back to cutoff. First the left, then the right. In a few seconds there was silence.

He unbuckled and walked around to Camilo. He felt a weak heartbeat at Q's neck, but his gray skin felt like a cold fish. He went to the back to see how the women made it through the crash. The electric instruments continued to hum. The tag sent out another data packet.

*****

Still set on "vibrate only", the satellite telephone buzzed and danced around on the small table by the window. Even though he had placed it there so the antenna could see the satellites, Brett never really expected to receive a call. The last four days were like a pleasant vacation. Zach was an excellent cook, they had rented an extra room for Bixby, and even met some wood carvers.

Brett was the one who had thought up the cover story that they were American businessmen looking for authentic African handcrafts. The wood carvers in the city bargained with them to open a line of imports to the United States, bringing samples and negotiating prices.

Brett picked up the phone and looked at the number. No one he knew. He pushed the green talk button, and leaned toward the window to get the best reception.

"This is Brett."

"Brett, Whitehorse Jackson."

"Hi, Boss. Nice of you to call."

"Hey, we've got news. N'dalu is dead. Killed by one of his body guards last night."

"Great! So we can go home now?"

"No, buddy. The whole city has exploded into a civil war. But that's not our business now. N'dalu's helicopter has taken off and landed close to your position. We believe that Camilo Quartalino is the only helo pilot they've got. My guess is that he stole the helicopter and was using it, trying to get to Angola and ran out of gas. Anyway, it landed close to your position. The tag is still marking its position, so I know he didn't crash. I want you to go check it out. If it is him, bring him in."

"No problem. We'll get a rent car and go get him." Brett copied down the coordinates that Whitehorse read out, and then hung up. Brett looked at the paper for a long time wondering how he was going to make this happen. Staying in the hotel was relatively safe and comfortable, and it took a big push to get into the mindset of going back out in the bush where there was a good chance that he would be killed. He lowered his head and shook it slowly.

"But I sure would want Q coming after me if things were reversed," Brett said aloud. That did it. The energy flowed to his legs and he jumped up and opened the door. Zach sat reading a French paperback novel under the mango tree.

"Zach. We need a rent car. Preferably a four wheel drive SUV. Q's escaped, and we've got to go get him. Zach was already trotting out of the courtyard, his novel left upside down on the picnic table. Brett knocked on Bixby's door.

"Hey, man. N'dalu's dead. We're going to pick up Q. He is only about forty miles away. We think he stole N'dalu's helicopter."

"OK. I'll be here when you get back." Brett was taken aback by that answer.

"No, we're all going to get him."

"Look, you don't need me. I don't know anything about what you're going to do. I'll just be in the way."

Brett stared at Bixby and considered his argument. A teammate is down, and you're willing to sit on your fat butt in an air conditioned hotel room letting other people risk their life to pick him up. Maybe it is better if you don't go, Brett thought.

"Alright. You stay here." Brett said, fighting hard to harness his rage. He turned and walked back to his room shaking his head. I drug that office puke though the bush and took care of him even though all he's done is complain. Never even got a thank you.

Putting all of his gear into his backpack, Brett put his medic kit on top. He no longer had a uniform. They threw out their old clothes after buying civilian attire five days ago. He laced on his boots, and checked his rifle. Only three magazines of ammo. Less than one hundred rounds. Zach had the same.

Zach roared up in an old beat up Land Rover. The faded green paint peeled near the edge of the hood, and one could still see the outline of the diamond mine logo where it had been sanded off. But the tires were good, the A/C cold, and the engine sounded strong.

"Just a minute and I'll get my gear," Zach said. He dashed inside and made it back out just as Brett finished loading his big pack in the back end.

"Where's Bixby?"

"He's not going," Brett said. "He told me that he would be useless on a mission like this. I agreed with him."

"Pretty ungrateful of him. We hauled him here, but he's not willing to help out someone else."

"Let's not talk about it. I've got the coordinates programmed into my GPS. Do you have a map of the area?"

"No."

"I guess we'll just do the best we can. We need to look for a road heading north and east."

*****

The three of them got Q into the shade and laid him on his back. Though still unconscious, Angelica talked to him in a low, soothing voice. Dolph propped up his feet and covered him in a thin curtain torn from the helicopter interior.

"It's going to be alright, darling. We'll just lay you right here in the shade where you will be comfortable. Help is on the way." She reached down and stroked his brow.

"I can't do anything to help him right now," Dolph said. Many times he sat vigil with dying members of his congregation, and then with his wife. He knew the look of death. Camilo would go soon.

"I know. You've done your best," Angelica said with a sad, faint smile.

"Let's get the water out of the aircraft," Maura said, laying her hand on Dolph's shoulder.

Dolph turned around and marveled at their good fortune. Camilo could have passed out and we'd all be dead, he thought. Instead, he fought until he landed safely. Dolph looked back down the field and saw that by landing parallel to the furrows their tire tracks were almost hidden. A few pieces of rotor blade lay here and there, but the main body of the helicopter was in the trees, shielded on three sides.

A brown bluff jumped up sixty meters across the river, and the terrain rose steeply on their side after the narrow field. We couldn't have picked a better place to hide, Dolph thought. But then, how will anyone be able to find us and rescue us?

Maura went up the stairs, and Dolph followed. He could not help but notice all the blood in the cockpit and dribbled down the door. How can one man have so much blood in him? He searched the helicopter for food or anything else that might be useful to them. Maura brought out the purse with the jewelry and a white box with a red cross on it.

"I found this on the back wall. It's a first aid kit."

"Good work. Let me see it." Dolph dug in the notebook sized tin box. Band Aids, gauze, aspirin, and burn cream. Useless, he thought. But he picked it up along with the rifles and they went back to Q. I don't have any way to pull out the bullet or stop the bleeding, Dolph thought.

Q was awake and had his right hand on the back of Angelica's neck as they talked. Dolph came close and saw that Camilo didn't have much time left.

"You got us one the ground safe, my friend," Dolph said.

"Brother, pray for me. When you get back to the states, look up my family. Tell my wife and daughters that I love them. Tell them that I'm sorry." He grimaced as another storm of pain tore through his body. Dolph could see Q struggle to speak, using the last of his energy. "You have to take these women to safety. Be strong. Shoot first."

"I will." Dolph reached down and squeezed Q's shoulder. He nodded, the fire in his eyes going dim. His eyelids fluttered and he went unconscious.

"Isn't there anything you can do for him?" Angelica looked over at Dolph, imploring him.

He could not speak, so he just shook his head.

"We must look around and plan for tonight," Maura said softly, pulling on Dolph. They left Angelica to keep vigil with Camilo.

After they walked to the edge of the field, Maura turned to Dolph.

"Camilo is dying. We need to move before one of the roving bands of militia finds us. If they take us, Angelica and I will be raped and taken as prisoners and slaves. You will be killed. Do you understand this? We must make it to a town. There is little time, my love."

"I know." Dolph felt overwhelmed. "You're right. But I want to bury him before we go."

"How will you bury him?" she asked with a matter-of-factness that surprised Dolph. "We have no tools. We have no time. Even Christ said that there are times to 'let the dead bury their dead'." Dolph looked at her with amazement that she knew the scriptures. Her wisdom pounded home. He nodded.

They walked back to the front of the wreck and saw Angelica weeping, bent over close to Q's face. Dolph touched his neck, feeling for a pulse, even though he knew that Q had passed. Dolph stood and looked around for stones or something to put over the body.

Pieces of broken rotor blades lay scattered on both sides of the helicopter. They were eighteen inches wide and three to four feet long. He started by picking up one end of the nearest piece and dragging it towards the body. Maura placed her hand under Angelica's armpit and gently moved her away. Dolph laid the rotor blade long ways on Camilo as neatly as he could. Heavier than they looked, Dolph hoped that they would deter the scavengers. As Angelica wept, Maura helped him drag over three other pieces. He felt guilty to have survived and wondered why he felt no grief. That will come later, he thought.

Dolph stood at the feet of Camilo and lifted his eyes and his dirty, bloodied hands to heaven.

> "Oh Lord, we thank you for the life of our friend and brother, Camilo Quartalino. Because of him we are free from Matai. Just like us, Father, our friend was not perfect. But we have faith that, by your mercy, you will take our brother into your bosom. Comfort him. Console us. We will miss him.
>
> "Now, oh Lord, we go on without him. Guide us and protect us. By the powerful name of Christ, we offer this prayer. Amen."

They moved to pick up the two rifles, the purse, and their bottles of water. The late morning sun beat down on them as they climbed up out of the field and onto the road that paralleled the river.

Chapter 12

Chu Lee looked at the ringing phone and recognized Michael Stauffer's sat phone number. He punched the blinking button and the call came in over his headset.

"Senior Four. I say again, Senior Four."

"Understood." Chu Lee copied the time and subject of the conversation in his call log.

"When can I expect confirmation of transfer for our contractor?" Michael asked.

"That is not a subject for this telephone." *What does he care when the contractor gets paid? I'm surprised that she survived.* Chu was so sure that the woman would be killed that he had not even started the paperwork for her payment.

"I know that, but I am with her, and she did us a good job."

"Of course, sir, your money is in place already. But for her, these things take time."

"Then I am on my way to collect personally." Chu felt a shuddering contraction in his sack. Mr. Stauffer had a reputation in this business."

"I will see that the transfer is done this afternoon. She should see the funds tomorrow." Chu tried to keep the tremor out of his voice.

"When can you email me the confirmation number so that I can check with my bank that the funds are on the way?"

"That will be on your email this afternoon also."

"Good." The line went dead.

*****

Dolph Zimmerhanzel felt the familiar hunger pangs. *Where did I leave that food that Seko gave me? I must have* left it in the car. I haven't eaten or slept since yesterday afternoon. His legs refused to work any longer, and he stopped. Cramps hit both his calves. Two years in captivity had taken their toll on his legs. I guess those exercises didn't help prepare me for this long walk, he thought. The two women turned around and looked at him. Trying to take up the pace again, he stumbled and fell into the powdery dust.

Maura dug the last water bottle out of the sack and gave it to him, but he was too weak to break the seal. Wordlessly, she took it back, and opening the bottle, helped him drink. She and Angelica lifted him to his feet and took him off of the river road to sit him against a tree in the deep shade.

Angelica stood up and looked up and down the road. "Are you sure we're going the right way?"

"This road parallels the river... And we are headed downstream... There will be a town soon... This is the right way," Dolph said between pants.

"I'm sorry I can't keep up. I was awake all night waiting for my torture," he said.

"What are you talking about?" Angelica asked.

He told them the story of N'dalu's offer of employment, his decision to work for N'dalu, and then his refusal at the meeting.

"N'dalu threatened me and told Seko to be ready to torture me in the morning. So, I stayed up all night praying. Couldn't sleep thinking about the end of my life, hoping that it would be quicker than all the soldiers tortured after the battle." Maura hugged him. They rested for several minutes.

"We can't make it on foot. Let's stop the next truck and we'll use some of the jewelry to pay for a ride into town," Angelica said. Maura and Dolph nodded their agreement.

"Wait. I have some money," Dolph said, remembering Seko's gift.

"No, we'll use that for later. I think I can get us a ride," Angelica said with a smile and a hint of promise.

Twenty minutes later, they heard a truck lumbering down the road. Angelica got up and stood in the middle of the dirt lane and waved her arm. The old Russian pick-up truck stopped. Angelica walked around to the driver's side and started flirting with the huge black driver. In a minute she ran over to the other two.

"There's a big town just forty miles up the road where we can catch the bus. He's going all the way." She looked back at the driver, smiling and waving. "Maura, you keep that rifle on the driver. I don't trust him."

With Angelica in the front seat and Maura and Dolph in the bed sitting on boxes of fly and tick spray for cattle, the old truck lurched through the gears and wallowed its way toward Luisa. The heat rose from the exhaust and mixed with the beat of the sun. Dust clouds flowed over then each time the truck slowed for a pothole.

As they crested a small rise, Dolph felt the truck slow. He looked forward through the hole that once held a rear window and saw a Land Rover pull across the middle of the road, blocking the truck.

"Do you think they'll rob us?" Angelica asked.

"No," the driver said. "There are too many of us and we are armed." He pulled a Makorov pistol from a hidden holster and set it on the dash. "Tell your friends in the back to show their rifles." Angelica nodded. As they got closer a skinny young black man got out and walked over to the now stopped truck.

"Sir, I am sorry to bother you, but we are looking for a helicopter that might have landed or crashed close by. Did you happen to see anything?"

"No sir, we haven't seen anything," the driver said. The three passengers maintained silence. When the skinny black man stared hard at him, Dolph tried to hide the dirt and blood on his shirt.

"You are American, aren't you?" Zach asked in English. Getting no response he continued. "Have you seen a bald, muscular, black American walking down the road? He is our friend, and we are trying to rescue him."

"What is his name?" Dolph asked.

"Why don't you tell me his name?" Zacheus said. Dolph saw the white man in the Land Rover shift just a bit. I'll bet he has a rifle on us right now, he thought.

"I had a friend named Camilo Quartalino. If that is who you're seeking, I'm sorry, he's dead," Dolph said. Hearing the words aloud, Angelica bowed her head and wept.

"Come with us," yelled the white man in the Land Rover. "We'll get you home. Camilo was my friend. We worked together."

Zach paid the truck driver. He drove off, and they all got into the Land Rover. The air conditioning hit Dolph's body like a cool drink.

"Are you sure he's dead?" Brett asked.

"Yes. Very sure," Dolph said. "He was shot in the left kidney and bled to death. No pulse. I've seen death many times, and he was dead. Otherwise we would never have left him."

"Can you take us to Camilo's body? We need to recover it."

"Yes," Angelica said.

"Boss, what do you think you're doing?" Zach said in English. "There's just been a giant vacuum created in the power structure around here. All the militias are moving right now to get whatever they can. Without the authority of N'dalu hanging over them, there will be plenty of stealing and raping tonight,"

"He's right, sir," Maura said. "We must get away. Should anyone guess that we have N'dalu's wife..."

"What! You're N'dalu's wife?" Brett asked.

"No, I am... Well, I was," Angelica answered.

"We've at least got to try and recover Q's body. How far is it?"

"Less than ten miles," Dolph said.

Brett motioned ahead with his hand, and Zach started driving toward the wreck. Dread draped on Dolph like a black storm cloud, and he shuddered. They rode in silence until they reached the single lane descending into the field. At Dolph's direction, Zach turned left, bounced down the road for a hundred meters then stopped as the field came into sight.

Two hundred meters down the hill, to the left front, the tail of the helicopter pointed out of the woods. Four long canoes were stuck to the river bank and more than twenty men and boys milled around the helicopter. They were armed and dressed in fatigues and army boots, some with baseball caps and others with jungle hats.

"I don't think this is a good idea, Boss," Zach said. Simultaneous to the last word, a bullet struck the dirt in front of the Land Rover. Another zipped by Brett's head and he heard the supersonic crack.

"Get us out of here, Zach." Brett rolled down the window, leaned out, and sprayed three short bursts of automatic fire over the hood to keep the soldiers' heads down as Zach backed up the lane. Back on the main dirt road going toward Luiza, Brett turned around and looked over the three passengers.

"Everybody OK?" They nodded. "We'll get back to Luiza and figure out how to get out of here." The late afternoon sun reflected off of the white dirt road, almost blinding them as they drove.

"Sir, excuse me, but I need speak French. My English is no good." Maura switched to French. "I don't know who you are, but thank you for picking us up. I have been through these kinds of political changes. Things will be bad for the next several nights. Gangs and militias will fight for control. Everyone will get drunk celebrating the death of N'dalu. There will be rapes and robberies, old debts will be settled in blood, and anyone caught in town will suffer. I suggest that we find a place to camp for the night and not go into town until daylight tomorrow."

"She is right, you know. When General Ilunga was murdered back in 2007, the rioting was huge," Angelica said.

Brett just nodded. "What do you think, Zach?"

"Makes sense to me, Boss. Especially since we have N'dalu's wife with us."

"Alright. We'll get a little closer to town, then pull over somewhere so that we can make camp. Give me that sat phone, will you?" Brett dialed Whitehorse.

*****

Bixby Wilson cursed the television set in his room. All the channels were in French except CNN International. I am sick of watching the news. This room is like a prison cell. Man, I need something to eat, he thought. Now that N'dalu's dead, I don't have to stay in my room anymore. No one will be looking for me. Besides I've been stuck in this room for days. I need to go for a walk.

Dressing quickly, he stepped out of his room just as the dusk gave way to night. The cool breeze felt good against his face and kept most of the mosquitoes away. He pulled out his wallet and located his debit card. Now I need to find an ATM. Zach said that there was one around here. Then I'll look for a restaurant. I want some good French food. His mouth watered at the thought of a good steak with a couple of bottles of wine.

The eyes of the locals locked onto Bixby as he walked out of the courtyard and turned toward the central square. But he did not notice.

A black youth fell in behind him, keeping back about a hundred paces. Another teenager shadowed him on the other side of the street. The broken sidewalk along with the manholes missing their covers threatened Bixby's ankles, and he smiled, dodging the obstacles. Wow, it is good to be out of my room, he thought. My feet are all healed up. Almost no pain.

The square came into view, and Bixby never noticed that there were no people out. He was enjoying the walk and the fresh air, reveling in the feeling of his heart beating nicely in his breast. Another fifty meters and he saw the ATM, the sign proclaiming services in three languages. Putting in his card, he punched the amount for the maximum amount of francs, not sure how much it equaled in dollars. I'm sure that it'll be enough for dinner, he thought.

Whirring noises signaled that the machine was about to spit out his money, and Bixby held his hand down near the slot. Out of the corner of his eye he saw the teen come up. The long knife slipped between Bixby's ribs and punctured his heart. He crumpled to the ground, dead. The youth put his hand to the slot just as the machine pushed out the bills.

*****

Michael Stauffer leaned against the rail and watched the brown water part off the bow of the river boat. The big, fast vessel sent a wave all the way to the far shore of the wide Congo River. He was all packed. In two hours they would get on a bus to go the twenty miles around the rapids, and then change to another boat for the trip into

Kinshasa. Desiree sidled up beside him, standing very close.

"Are you happy?" he asked.

"Yes, very. I checked our bank account and the money hit this morning."

"Already? Great. Say, have you thought about my offer?" he said.

"Yes, I have. But I have some questions."

"OK."

"Why are you interested in me? Is it because you think I would be good, or because you think that I would be good in bed?"

Michael looked her up and down, and he wanted to take her in his arms and kiss her. This is very unprofessional, he thought, sleeping with someone I work with. But last night when she had come to his room to check on her payment, their mutual need erupted.

"I already know that you are good in bed, my love." They laughed. "But really, you have proven yourself in a very tough business. There will always be work for someone like you. You are educated, you speak French, English, and some African dialects, you are beautiful, and courageous." They stared into each other's eyes.

"I have work lined up all over Africa. We can be a great team."

"Well, I've already told my mother that I'll be working with you. My sister is going to use the money to open a club in Belgium. Mother will manage the restaurant and bar and Christina will run the girls."

"Then we can send them off to Brussels when we get to Kinshasa. I have another assignment in Mauritania. A group of businessmen wants a certain general to join his ancestors." She nodded and they hugged.

*****

An hour after dawn, the Land Rover rolled into Luiza, and Brett was sickened by the carnage on the street. Smoke still smoldered from several fires, broken glass sparkled in the morning sun, and bodies and body parts littered the road. They rolled up into the hotel courtyard and found the doors open and their rooms ransacked. Bixby was nowhere to be found. The owner sat on his front steps crying. Brett went over to him and respectfully waited for the old man to acknowledge his presence.

When he looked up, Brett asked, "Have you seen my American friend from Room Seven?"

The old man just shook his head.

"He's dead, boss," Zach said. "There's no way an unarmed white man is going to make it through this."

"Let's go look for him."

"We'll miss the plane. Whitehorse said eight o'clock sharp. And that if we weren't there, the plane will take off again without us."

"OK. But we'll keep an eye out for him while we drive out."

The airport sat on the north edge of town. Whitehorse knew of a missionary pilot who owed the Agency for saving his wife from a kidnapping several years ago. When Brett called late last night, Whitehorse called in the favor and arranged for the single engine Cessna Caravan to pick them up in Luiza in the morning.

As they drove through the square, Brett spotted Bixby's crumpled body near the ATM. He pointed, and Zach pulled to the curb. They opened the back, rolled his body inside and headed for the airfield.

"We need to park close by, but not on the ramp. Or else, others will know that an airplane is coming and may try to rob it," Brett said. So Zach pulled over to the side of the road and waited until 0757.

At 0759, they parked out close to the end of the runway and saw the big Cessna pop up over a hill and make a short approach to Runway 08. The plane landed then rolled to the end, never shutting down the engine. The pilot feathered the propeller to cut the wind across the door.

Zach and Brett wrestled Bixby's body into the plane, and then helped the women. When the door shut, the pilot turned into the wind and took off. Brett looked down and noticed the people running down the road toward the airfield, some with machetes.

"Will Africa ever change?" Brett asked Zach above the noise.

"Never."